River Rising

RIVER

RISING

ATHOL DICKSON

BETHANYHOUSE
MINNEAPOLIS, MINNESOTA

Published by Bethany House Publishers
11400 Hampshire Avenue South
Bloomington, Minnesota 55438

Bethany House Publishers is a division of
Baker Publishing Group, Grand Rapids, Michigan.

Printed in the United States of America

———————

Library of Congress Cataloging-in-Publication Data
Dickson, Athol, 1955-
  River rising / Athol Dickson.
    p. cm.
  Summary: "Hale Poser arrives in Louisiana in 1927 to find racial prejudices
missing from the small town of Pilotville. In pursuit of a missing child, however,
he uncovers a dark secret"—Provided by publisher.
  ISBN 0-7642-0162-X (alk. paper)
  1. Missing children—Fiction. 2. Racism—Fiction. 3. City and town life—
Fiction. 4. Louisiana—Fiction I. Title. PS3554.I3264R58   2006
  813'.54—dc22   2005028049

For Stan Potocki
and Vincent Gaddis.
You inspire me.

River Rising

$\mathbb{T}$he colored fellow came early in the morning, poling a pirogue through mist so heavy on the river you could not see a stone's throw out. Jean Tibbits watched him from his chair on the wharf, noting the unruly brim of his black felt fedora, his white shirt buttoned to the top, and his black wool suit, shiny from wear. As the newcomer came closer, Tibbits realized his trousers were rolled up over his calves, something you did not often see on a man wearing a suit. At his neck a pair of brown leather shoes dangled from tied-together laces. The laces were white and did not match the shoes. The colored fellow stood at the back of the flat-bottomed boat, guiding it alongside the wharf in silence except for the musical ripple of the river against the hull and the soft bump when the lichen-streaked boat kissed a piling.

Jean Tibbits spoke to him without raising his voice or rising from his chair. "Hey, mon. What you do there?"

"Sir." The Negro touched the floppy brim of his hat. "I come looking for work."

"Well, you got to tie up somewheres else," said Tibbits. "This here de commercial dock." As owner of the ramshackle fleet of rusting trawlers tied to pilings up and down the wharf, and as Pilotville's official harbor master, Jean Tibbits was entitled to provide direction in such matters.

"Yes sir." The colored fellow pushed off, gently slipping his pole into the water to guide the pirogue away upon the current. Tibbits heard him humming something softly. Although he was soon almost out of sight in the mist, the sound of his humming carried across the water, as low sounds often do. The tune was foreign yet familiar, maybe something Tibbits had heard a long time back, an old melody from far away somewhere. It had an eerie, disturbing effect upon him, reinforced by the fact that the river mist now completely obscured the pirogue at the colored fellow's feet, making it look like his dark and crooked form was out there walking on the water.

"Hey!" shouted Tibbits. "You can pull up yonder, you."

The colored man called softly, "Thank you, sir," and pushed toward the muddy bar Tibbits had indicated near the wharf.

"What kinda work you lookin' to do?" hollered Tibbits across the little cove.

"Whatever needs doing." The pirogue nosed up to the bar.

"Try de infirmary. They always lookin' for a hand, they is."

"Yes sir. Thank you kindly." He was out of the boat now and tying it to a nearby mangrove branch. "Will my pirogue be all right here?"

"It a nickel a week."

"I don't have a nickel."

"What you got?"

Still barefoot, the stranger stepped gingerly through the mud. "I could get you some persimmons."

"Not unless you got 'em in your pocket. Ain't no persimmons 'round here, no."

"Believe I could find you some."

"Not 'round here."

"Hold on, sir," said the colored fellow. Walking directly toward the dense cluster of mangroves a little farther down along the riverbank, he turned sideways and slipped into the thicket out of sight. Tibbits shook his head and tilted his chair back against the roughhewn siding of his office shack. Everyone knew there were no persimmons near town. They had been picked clean long ago.

A moment later the colored fellow reappeared, hat in his hands. As he approached along the riverbank, Tibbits noticed his slight limp for the first time. Next to Tibbits's chair stood an upended oil drum. The colored fellow came up the wharf and turned his hat upside down above the drum, and ripe yellow fruit rained upon the metal, beating out a hollow sound.

"How many days will those buy me?" he asked.

Staring at the fruit, Tibbits said, "Ain't no persimmons 'round here."

"Is that enough to leave my pirogue for a week or so?"

Jean Tibbits tried to look the colored fellow in the eye, but the stranger kept his gaze down, as Negroes generally did until they got to know him better. "You jus' found them over in de bushes?"

"Yes sir."

"I be dogged." Tibbits selected a piece of fruit and examined it closely. "I love persimmons."

"Yes sir."

Staring hard now at the stranger's dark face, still trying to get him to look up, Tibbits asked, "I know you?"

But life in Louisiana had taught the colored fellow well.

Examining his own bare feet, the stranger merely shook his head and mumbled, "No sir."

Tibbits felt a fleeting twinge of disappointment as he bit down. Juice trickled through the gray stubble on his chin, ignored. "Don't worry 'bout dat boat," he mumbled around the persimmon in his mouth. "It be just fine yonder."

At that, the strange Negro finally looked up, and Jean Tibbits found himself staring man to man into a remarkable pair of sky-blue eyes.

The stranger followed the wharf inland and soon found that the wooden walkway did not end at the shore but continued into the swamp. Cypress, mangrove, and tupelo trees loitered in the inky black water on either side, crowding the edges of the boards. The spindly structure beneath his feet shivered with each step, its pilings sending tiny ripples out across the water. Thus warned of his approach, bullfrogs sprang into the mire below from floating tree trunks or low-slung palmetto fronds. A hundred paces later the boardwalk angled to the right, offering a glimpse of Pilotville beyond the swaying Spanish moss. Passing into the tiny village, he observed small wooden houses standing in a clearing, and beyond the clearing, back by the river, the corrugated iron roof of the Acme Shrimp and Oyster packing plant above the cypress tops. He saw no roads or sidewalks, just more raised wooden walkways fanning out between the buildings. He came to a small store. High on the front wall were the words *Delacroix's Dry Goods* in peeling black paint with a thin red stripe beneath. Three white men in stained overalls and filthy felt hats lounged before the building, speaking French. One of them passed a slender piece of sharpened wood rapidly back and forth through a fishnet, tying a rip. The Cajuns paused in their conversation to squint at him.

Eyes down, the stranger nodded and smiled and was mildly surprised when they offered friendly greetings.

He began to hum again as he walked, passing more small structures of rough-cut planking, aged and green with mildew and slowly decomposing below rusting metal roofs. All of these shanties—mostly dwelling places—teetered precariously on stilts, six to eight feet above the swamp. A few leaned at crazy angles, empty interiors too lopsided for living, slender pole foundations pressed down unevenly into the mud below. One old shanty had foundered all the way over on its side and lay half sunken beside the boardwalk, with black swamp water lapping at the window openings.

Moving on, he approached a small church. Unlike most of the other buildings, it was neatly whitewashed. Glossy black trim traced the outlines of the doors and windows. The same black paint announced the name of the church from a rectangular board affixed to the siding: PILOTVILLE COMMUNITY CHURCH. Pausing to peer into the open front doors, he saw a woman sweeping the floor. The tiny sanctuary accommodated maybe twenty folding wooden chairs on each side of a central aisle. A single stained-glass window high on the far wall glowed red and yellow, a rare bit of store-bought finery for such a primitive place. The colored glass allowed very little light to pass into the building. The woman stopped sweeping to look up at him. He saw her pale blond hair tied up in a rag, but could not make out her features in the darkness of the interior. "Can I help you?" she asked. Quickly lowering his eyes, he touched the brim of his black fedora and said, "No thank you, ma'am." He moved on, striding away from the white woman purposely, as if he knew where he was going. The limp barely slowed him down. He breathed the scent of grilled fish on the river breeze. A solitary dog barked away off somewhere. He glanced back.

The woman had come to the door of the church to stare at him. Indeed, the entire village seemed to pause and watch his progress. A small group of children formed in his wake, hanging back and whispering to each other with giggles and quickly covered mouths. Some were browned by the sun, others by nature. None wore shoes, and only the older girls wore shirts, but all wore thin veneers of mud smeared in one place or another. Still humming the ancient tune, he reached into his pocket and removed a long string of black licorice. The children's eyes went wide. He tore a small piece and popped it in his mouth. Then, favoring his hip, he bent and placed the rest on the walkway. Chewing slowly now in time to his own humming, he set out once more. Behind him, the children pounced upon the licorice.

Turning a corner, the stranger came upon a second church, about the same size as the first. It too bore a proud new coat of whitewash. In fact, the two buildings appeared almost identical. But this one had a chain and padlock on the front doors, and neatly painted letters on a wooden plaque that read AFRICAN ASSEMBLY OF GOD. Standing on his toes, he peeked through an open window along the side. There was no glass. He could not make out any details of the dark interior. He backed away, still humming the same tune, and looked up at the roof, then down at the pilings. Nodding his head, he said, "Yes sir," under his breath. He walked on.

At the inland edge of the village, where the air hung heavy with pollen and mosquitoes beyond the reach of cooling river breezes, he found the Pilotville Negro Infirmary. It was almost as big as the Acme packing plant, yet of all the buildings he had encountered thus far, only this one did not benefit from the flood protection afforded by a foundation of tall piers. It stood on a small rise a few inches above the swamp's usual water level, unconnected to the network of boardwalks and accessible only by a narrow path of broken oyster shells. It alone was made of bricks, a strange choice of materials for its isolated location, which surely must have cost a great deal. He paused at the top of the narrow steps descending from the boardwalk. Gazing at the rambling three-story structure, he slapped at a mosquito on the back of his neck. "Mercy me," he said, noticing a brown high-water stain encircling the building several feet above the earth. The stain went right across the bottom half of the closed front doors. He saw no sign of occupation except for a pair of tapioca-colored curtains hanging limply in an open window. Insect screens and flat iron bars guarded the outside of the window.

Sitting at the top of the steps, he did his best to wipe the dried mud from his feet. He rolled his trouser cuffs all the way down to his ankles and slapped at the fabric in a vain attempt to smooth the wrinkles. He removed the brown leather shoes from around his neck and untied the knotted white laces. Pulling the shoes on over his bare feet, he looked up at the infirmary again.

"Lord," he said. "Have mercy."

"We pay forty-five cents a day," said Nurse Dorothy Truett. "Plus a bed when one is free. Let you eat what board is left after the patients are fed. But you got to get your meals someplace else every now and then. Food is scarce and the patients come first, of course."

"Why, surely," said the man, following Nurse Dorothy Truett down the hall. He started whistling softly through his teeth in time to the beat of her polished shoes upon the wooden floor. Some old gospel music maybe, something familiar, although she couldn't quite place the tune. It irritated Dorothy Truett for some reason. She walked a little faster to break his rhythm, pulling ahead. He stopped whistling. Good. But now she heard him draw a deep breath through his nose. She knew what he was doing. She wore her hair straightened and slicked back with an oil that smelled of roses. Some men seemed to like it, although she certainly did not wear it for that reason. Now here was this fellow breathing in her scent like a bee seeking blossoms. Dorothy Truett frowned. She had no time for such foolishness at her work place. And him supposed to be a minister.

She stopped and looked him in the eye. "I'm sorry we have no budget for a chaplain."

"That's all right."

His eyes had startled her at first. Blue like a robin's eggs they were, an obvious legacy of mixed parentage somewhere down the line. Of course, this was Louisiana, where such things were not uncommon. Still, it took a little getting used to. "You sure you want this job?" she asked.

"Yes, ma'am."

"If it isn't too forward to ask, why would someone give up being chaplain at a New Orleans orphanage and come down here to scrub floors?"

"I serve the Lord wherever he chooses, ma'am."

Something was wrong, but she couldn't tell what. Not yet. So she held his eye for a moment, showing him she was nobody's fool, then she shrugged and continued down the hall. "You'll sleep in different beds from time to time . . . wherever there's one empty. We don't have a separate room for you."

"All right," said the so-called reverend, peering in a doorway as they passed. He slowed and stopped. She did not have to look into the room to know what he saw there. Four beds, three of which were occupied. In the closest, a young woman sleeping on her back, belly greatly distended, eyes flitting around beneath smooth eyelids as if watching a moving object, a passable-looking woman, with full lips and flawless coffee-colored skin. Dorothy Truett came to the man's side in time to see Rosa Lamont frown slightly, then work her mouth, speaking silently to someone in her dream.

Standing at his shoulder, looking with him at the sleeping woman, Dorothy Truett whispered, "You'll be responsible for keeping the floors clean. I mean everything, not just the floors, of course. Walls, basins, bedpans, windows, and so forth. Everything. We only have three nurses here counting me, and we don't clean. We have enough to do without cleaning."

"All right." He mumbled it absentmindedly, not really paying attention to her.

She felt a rush of impatience. "I want to show you the janitor's closet, Reverend."

Still looking into the room, he nodded. "Yes, ma'am." He did not move.

"It's this way," she said.

"Is that woman all right?"

"Mrs. Lamont should be fine. This will be her fourth child."

He shook his head. "Something's wrong."

"What do you mean?"

"Something's wrong with her baby."

It took her a moment to understand what he meant. After all, how could he possibly know? And yet of all the things to say. . . .

"Dr. Jackson says it's placenta previa," said Dorothy Truett, an eerie feeling rising inside. "Her baby is lying too low. We'll have to take it by cesarean."

"Cesarean?"

"The doctor will have to cut it out when the time comes."

The man took a step closer to the open door. "Have mercy," he whispered.

Watching him more closely now, she asked, "How did you know?"

He continued to stare at the sleeping woman. "Hmm?"

"How did you know about her condition?"

She saw him shake his head slightly, as if rousing himself from a far-off place. Turning to her, he said, "I just had a feeling."

As Dorothy Truett searched his face her irritation went away, replaced by something warm and comfortable. Suddenly she felt as if she could trust this man with anything. Anything at all. It was a sensation she did not recall having before, about anyone. It was very strange. "You said you've never worked in a hospital, correct?"

"That's right."

"Don't worry. Rosa will be all right." Why did she want to reassure him?

"Yes, ma'am," he said. "I believe she'll be just fine."

And how could he know *that*? Oh, enough of this foolishness. He was just a roustabout looking for a job, and she was being a silly romantic. Extending her hand toward the far end of the hall, Nurse Truett said, "Shall we . . . Reverend Poser?"

"Yes, ma'am," he said. "And, ma'am? If I'm to be a janitor, it doesn't seem right for you to call me 'reverend.' Just plain old 'Hale' is fine."

See? Here less than an hour, and already trying to get familiar. "I don't believe we know each other well enough for first names," she said.

He smiled, and in spite of her best instincts, the warmth she had felt before returned. "How would 'Mr. Poser' suit you?"

"That will do," said Nurse Dorothy Truett as she led him toward the janitor's closet, leaving Rosa Lamont to frown in her sleep.

2

The floors needed doing twice that week. Pilotville Negro Infirmary's new janitor scrubbed the lavatories three times each day. On Wednesday Hale Poser did the laundry: rough cotton sheets, towels, patients' robes and pajamas if they owned any, and everyone's soiled underthings in any case. All of these he washed by hand with lye soap at a concrete trough outside the kitchen, after filling the cistern with well water drawn from the bowels of the earth. Once the hand pump was primed, three hundred and eighty-seven strokes were required to fill the cistern. This he did every day except for Tuesday, when the gutters filled the cistern during a good hard rain. Friday was his day to fix what needed fixing. Fallen branches were cleared from the roof, raccoons chased from the attic, kerosene lamps filled, a dry-rotted floorboard replaced, and holes in a window screen patched with a spider web stitching of steel wire. Hale Poser vowed that sooner or later he would get around to painting the high-water stains circling three feet up along the walls on the ground floor. On Saturday he hauled garbage to a large iron box out behind the infirmary, where it was burned. There were twenty-seven patients at the

Pilotville Negro Infirmary that first week, plus three nurses, the doctor, the cook, and the Reverend Hale Poser. They produced a lot of garbage to be burned. On Sunday he rose before the sun, wiped his face and armpits with a cotton towel at the inside sink of the men's lavatory, put on his white shirt and black suit and went to church, where he was an oddity.

Brother Julius Gray marched smartly up to the front doors of the African Assembly of God. To his surprise, a stranger stood in the darkness there, softly whistling a tune. Brother Julius thought it might be an old gospel song, but if so, he could not remember the name of it. Nodding cautiously at the stranger, he inserted a key in the padlock on the front doors. "Mornin', brother," he said.

"Hello." The stranger touched the brim of his hat.

Brother Julius tried not to stare, but visitors were uncommon, since Pilotville could only be reached by water, and Sister Dorothy Truett had already told him all about this fellow. Some big-city preacher, apparently left a good job up there in New Orleans. Brother Julius did not understand that. He longed to work full time as a river pilot or a pastor, but the realities of small-town life forced him to labor weekdays as a deckhand on one of Mr. Tibbits's boats, and preach weekends for free. Pilotville clung desperately to the river, the southernmost of all settled places on the Mississippi, last stop before the Gulf of Mexico, a meager collection of hermits, reformed outlaws, fishermen, and the pilots who gave the place its name. The river pilots guided ocean-going ships north, between Pilotville and New Orleans. The bar pilots shepherded them south, to and from the treacherous delta waters at the mouth of the river with their constantly drifting shoals. The two groups had formed a common association before the turn of the century and established the village of Pilotville soon thereafter, deeming this a natural spot to hand off control of vessels to each other, near as it was to the Head of Passes, where the Mississippi divided into three major outlets to the Gulf. Few others had cause to visit Pilotville, yet here this fellow was, all decked out in a suit and first one to church on Sunday morning.

Brother Julius swung both doors wide open and stopped them in place with a pair of bricks covered with green felt. He turned to the man. "Here for the service?"

"Yes sir."

Accepting the *sir* as his due, Julius offered his hand. "I am Brother Julius Gray, the pastor here."

"Hale Poser," said the stranger.

As expected, he was the one Sister Truett mentioned after last Wednesday's prayer meeting. "*Reverend* Poser is what I heard," said Brother Julius.

The man smiled. "I'm just a janitor now. Maybe you should call me Hale."

"Well, come along and help me set up for the service. We had a dinner here last Wednesday evenin', and the chairs are out of place."

Julius set the stranger to arranging forty wooden chairs in groups of twenty on each side of the central aisle. When the man finished, Julius directed him to open the shutters, a difficult task for Brother Julius, since he was a short man and the clasps for the shutters were high up on the walls. The window openings were screened but held no glass. This fact annoyed Brother Julius. Here he had another minister come all the way from New Orleans (according to Dorothy Truett), and him with no windowpanes.

Outside, the rising sun had just begun to paint the sky with gold, its heat driving the ghostly morning mist back into the swamp's darker places. The stranger opened all the shutters, then sat in a chair on the back row. Meanwhile, Julius Gray placed a low pine podium at the end of the aisle facing the chairs. With theatrically exaggerated gestures he deposited his Bible onto the podium and posed at the focal point of the room, hands on his hips and short legs wide apart. Opening the Bible, he began reading silently, surreptitiously glancing up from time to time to see if the stranger was paying attention. Brother Julius Gray did not realize his lips moved as he read.

Sunshine crept in through the newly opened windows, flinging itself against the whitewashed framing of the far wall. Someday soon they would start thinking about plastering the walls. After they had proper window glass. Brother Julius heard a cardinal chirp brightly from the cypress tree just outside and felt that old devil, worry, tugging at his insides. Now and then a bird would fly into the sanctuary through the open door, flit around, and perch up among the rafters. Brother Julius closed his eyes and prayed. Dear Lord, please don't send no birds in here today. Not while we got this minister from New Orleans down here among us. Amen. Glancing up again, Brother Julius saw that the man had folded his heavy hands in his lap, bowed his head, and shut his eyes. Brother Julius frowned.

After a little while, the Dempsey twins arrived, wearing modest cotton dresses and white cotton gloves and hats adorned by wood-duck feathers. Brother Julius hurried to the front to greet them. The stranger stood and moved toward the door. Julius Gray said, "Patricia and Rebecca Dempsey, may I present the new infirmary janitor, Mr. Poser?" Not mentioning that the man was a minister. Soon people came too quickly for introductions, and Brother Julius contented himself with standing at the door to shake each hand and take his usual head count, making sure there were no fewer than last week, and with the stranger here, perhaps one more. This gratifying thought was quickly forgotten as Dorothy Truett entered and he saw the stranger smile and nod to her in a familiar way. She did not return the smile, but while he was shaking hands with James Lamont and his children and the last of the usual stragglers, Brother Julius noticed Dorothy stealing glances at this Hale Poser person; him with the black suit on and the clean white shirt buttoned all the way up and the all too ready smile. Brother Julius wished Dorothy did not look so feminine in her Sunday best.

Every seat in the small sanctuary was occupied when the stranger from New Orleans rose to offer his chair to the widow DuPree and joined the usual row of men standing with their backs against the wall on each side of the front doors. Julius Gray felt proud to see so many in attendance. On the other hand, it tended to underscore the small size of the sanctuary. For the first time he considered expanding the building once the windows and the plaster were in place. And come to that, as he watched the men make room for the stranger, he wished they were more presentable. Like the minister from New Orleans, a few of them wore suits—mostly the men who worked at the packing plant—but the fishermen came to church in overalls with denim or khaki shirts, and all of the men smelled of tobacco, a practice Brother Julius abhorred. Coming to the Lord's house in work clothes and stinking of tobacco . . . it wasn't right. He decided then and there to mention these things in today's sermon.

Striding up the aisle to the podium, he said, "Good mornin'!"

Everyone replied together, "Good morning."

He spoke a little louder, very much aware that the resonation of his deep voice could compensate for the shortcoming of his stature. "I said, Good mornin'!"

This time the congregation shouted their greetings to him. Lots of them were smiling now. Brother Julius beamed back. "That's more like it," he said. "Y'all got to make a *joyful* noise before the Lord on a beautiful mornin' like this. Ain't that right?"

"Amen!" shouted several people.

"All right. All right. The Lord is good to us. He provides for our every need, and we gonna talk about that this mornin'. But first, let's offer back a little somethin' to the Lord. Let him know we appreciate a fine mornin' like this one here." He nodded to Patricia Dempsey on the front row. She rose and turned to the congregation. Everyone else rose, too. Without benefit of a musical instrument the woman began to sing in a strong, clear voice. As he did each Sunday at this point in the service, Brother Julius wished they had an organ, but he had to admit Miss Dempsey's voice was a good substitute.

Patricia Dempsey sang, " 'I'm a-goin' to tell you 'bout de comin' of de Saviour.' "

Several of the men along the back wall sang, " 'Fare you well, fare you well.' "

Now some of the women sang along with the woman at the front, " 'I'm a-goin' to tell you 'bout de comin' of de Saviour.' "

This time all the men replied, " 'Fare you well, fare you well.' "

And so it went, first the women, then the men, voices folding in together, finding the weak spots and filling them in, women climbing high and sweet, men hanging down an octave lower, Brother Julius Gray beaming out at his congregation as every voice, encouraged by the other, swelled up, echoed out and traveled off in all directions through the godless swamp around his church.

"There's a better day a-comin'.
Fare you well, fare you well.

Oh preacher, fold your bible.
Fare you well, fare you well.
Prayer maker, pray no more.
Fare you well, fare you well.
For the last soul's converted.
Fare you well, fare you well.
That the time shall be no longer.
Fare you well, fare you well.
For the judgment day is comin'.
Fare you well, fare you well.
In that great gittin' up mornin'.
Fare you well, fare you well. . . ."

On and on they sang, first the women and girls, then the men and boys, everybody now clapping or lifting swaying hands to heaven. Some had stepped into the aisle to dance. Brother Julius noticed the new man clapped and sang but otherwise seemed content to stay in his place beside the wall.

After about an hour Brother Julius waved his hands palms down in rhythm with the voices, smiling and singing but making it clear that the time for song was slowly passing, and he was in control. Voices calmed. Dancers swayed more peacefully, the music slowed, and then his booming voice could be heard above them all. He called them to prayer, and the song was done. Then through the open windows Julius Gray heard other voices singing a hymn in the near distance, the voices more restrained than those of the men and women of his congregation, yet strong and sweet none-theless. Perhaps too sweet, like the apple in the Garden. Brother Julius Gray shouted out his prayer good and loud, lest anyone be tempted to listen to the white folks' distant hymn instead of giving him their complete attention.

Hale Poser and the other men had to remain standing along the back wall, but everyone else took their seats when

Brother Julius began to preach. Now and then someone leapt to their feet to shout support, while other less enthusiastic congregants were content to call "Amen!" at appropriate moments. Many produced small paper fans, which waved languidly in the rising heat as the morning wore on. Brother Julius strode back and forth, dapper in his brown suit and closely cut hair, shouting most of his sermon, his voice surprisingly deep for such a little man. Sometimes he paused or lowered his voice to a whisper for dramatic effect. The Reverend Hale Poser watched this technique with professional interest, but while the sermon had a certain rustic flair, he found it uninspired. His mind began to wander.

He thought of the moment, just a few weeks ago, when he had discovered his file nestled among many others in the attic of an old mansion filled with sleeping children. He thought of the manila paper folder, soft and mildewed from the New Orleans humidity, and the faded pages, barely legible now, bearing a terse, clerically phrased story of a boy of three or thereabouts, brought from out of nowhere, from Plaquemines Parish to be precise, down beyond the end of everything, brought to a peeling twelve-room mansion and left for good. Hale Poser thought of another moment, years ago, when he had returned to that mansion—against all odds a man of the cloth, an educated man—to serve a hundred children who might just as well have been the same one hundred who had lived there when the long-ago boy had been brought up from Plaquemines. He thought of the omnipresent *ping ping ping* of the streetcar bells and the manurial odor of horses and mules wafting in through lofty windows from the red-brick road outside, and the sweet interior sound of a hundred well-scrubbed children reciting John 3:16 in unison from their rows of desks in the old ballroom. As surely as the Reverend Hale Poser had led them, he had been one of them, and he still languished like all of them with a secret desire for the touch of a mother, or a father, or even for the sight of a name on a tombstone together with the cold comfort that the name was also his. He thought of that moment in the attic just a few weeks ago, when he had lifted the file up from the old wooden box, up into an errant ray of sunshine piercing the angled slate above, and he had read the word *Pilotville*, and a sudden thrill slipped past the hard-earned orphan knowledge that such hope only led to misery. With the paper shaking in his hand, he had felt hope destroy a lifetime of defenses, and he had not cared, but allowed it, and in that moment of weak abandon he had known what he would do.

Now up on the little stage, the pastor bent low at the waist, leaning toward the congregation with eyes popped wide, arms flung out as far as they would go, face dripping with sweat. The pastor lowered his voice to a whisper, and only the paper fans moved as everyone waited silently for the eruption sure to follow. In that rare quiet moment, far-away voices drew Hale Poser back from his memories. Outside, through the open window and away off beyond the trees, someone cried, "Amen!" and the swampland echoed with the sound of clapping hands. Rousing himself, Hale Poser stared in that direction, though nothing could be seen through the thick cypress and tupelo branches.

The brother beside him leaned close and whispered, "Wonder what the white folk talkin' 'bout yonder?"

Hale Poser smiled and whispered back, "I'll go find out."

The doors being open to entice a breeze, it was a simple matter for him to step outside, unnoticed by all except Brother Julius and the surprised brother who smelled so strongly of tobacco. Following his ears, the Reverend Hale Poser crossed the little village until he stood on the board-walk outside the Pilotville Community Church. The white preacher's voice rose and fell very much as Brother Julius's did, spanning the distance from a near whisper when Hale Poser could hear nothing, to a full-throated yell when Hale could make out every word. Even though both the white preacher and Brother Julius addressed their congregations in the fire-and-brimstone style, Hale Poser thought it a good sign that neither dwelled on warnings of hellfire and damnation. Instead, even when they shouted, both delivered words of encouragement. But although he agreed with their theology, when Brother Julius's voice roared in the distance—an apparent echo of the white preacher at the Pilotville Community Church—Hale Poser looked that way and frowned, and when the white preacher shouted again, his frown deepened.

A redwing blackbird swooped down from the treetops in hot pursuit of a dragonfly. The glass windows of the Pilotville Community Church had been polished perfectly clean, making their reflection of the surrounding treetops too much like the real thing. The blackbird crashed head on into the invisible barrier and dropped like a stone. In spite of his misshapen hip, Hale Poser knelt quickly to the boardwalk. The bird before him lay with its head twisted back beside its body. A single drop of blood gathered at its beak. Hale lifted the animal, cupping it between his palms like an offering. The bird moved . . . feebly at first, then all in an instant airborne again, soaring to a nearby tupelo where it began to preen its feathers. Shading his eyes, Hale lifted his face to watch. He seemed to have forgotten whatever it was that had made him frown before. He smiled, closing his blue eyes against the sun. He raised both hands and stood that way for a little while, eyes shut, face and palms up toward heaven. Then one arm stretched to the left toward Pilotville Community Church, and the other stretched to the right toward the African Assembly of God. With eyes still shut he clenched his hands into fists as if grabbing a hold and he seemed to tug inward with both arms shaking like something heavy strained against them, and the two deep voices of the preachers blended together, both of them somehow shouting exactly the same words at once from their pulpits in the wilderness, both of them pausing at exactly the same moment while all the people in both churches near and far praised the Lord together, and for as long as Hale Poser stood that way the synchronization continued. But he grew tired and then slowly dropped his arms, and the single rhythm of the sermons wavered and split and fell apart again.

Flaring his nostrils wide, Hale Poser breathed deeply. He looked back up at the blackbird's perch. It had flown elsewhere. Exhaling with a sigh he turned to limp along the boardwalk toward the infirmary, feeling he had transgressed without understanding how, pondering his failure, and completely unaware that Jean Tibbits, Pilotville harbor master and owner of half a dozen shrimp boats, stood beyond the branches of a nearby cypress tree, watching.

3

T he Pilotville Negro Infirmary's new janitor stood out in the hall looking at Rosa Lamont, who twisted in her narrow bed and strained to press her belly with both hands while the nurses struggled against her arms. A scream escaped the woman, and Hale Poser leaned forward just a little, as if pushing against something.

"Mr. Poser!" shouted Nurse Dorothy. "Get in here!"

Hale Poser entered immediately. Eyes wide and bulging, Rosa Lamont screamed, "What the janitor gonna do? I need the doctor! Why don't you bring the doctor? Oh, make it stop, Lord! Make it stop!"

"Take her arms, Mr. Poser," said Nurse Dorothy. "Quickly! She's putting too much pressure on the baby."

Hale Poser stepped to the head of the bed and wrapped large fists around the woman's wrists. She continued to strain but could not resist the janitor as he slowly pulled her clutching hands from her belly, drawing them up toward her shoulders. Her fingers curled like claws with the effort of fighting him. "There, there," he whispered, bending down to put his lips close to her ear. "There, there."

Rosa Lamont screamed and writhed in the janitor's

grasp, kicking off the sheets. Nurse Truett ran out of the room while the other nurse busied herself collecting things on a tray at the foot of the bed. Hale Poser watched as towels, sheets, a rubber hose with a bellows on one end and a nozzle on the other, two large glass syringes, and several shining steel instruments were all laid out in a row. And knives. Lord have mercy, thought the janitor. What will they do with those knives?

The woman suddenly shouted, "Oh, dear Lord! Please don't take my baby!" Then she cursed, but not at God. Still, the most shameful words came from her mouth. "There, there," whispered the janitor, up close to her ear. It seemed to calm her some.

Nurse Dorothy returned, her forehead deeply creased. "I found the doctor," she said. "He's . . . not feeling well."

The other nurse shook her head. "Not again."

The woman on the bed suddenly convulsed, trying to curl in around her stomach. She screamed, one long scream that did not stop until she shouted, "Dear Lord, forgive my cursing! Forgive me and make it stop, and you can have this baby!"

"I don't know what to do," said Nurse Dorothy.

The woman stared at her wildly. "You don't know? How could you not *know!*" The janitor stood holding her wrists like his hands were made of iron, taking care not to hurt her, looking down with strange blue eyes that never left her face and trying to speak comfort to her. "Where is your husband?" he asked.

She did not speak, but bit her lip instead.

"James is out on the Gulf working nets, I expect," said Nurse Dorothy. "This wasn't supposed to happen for a few days."

"You ever deliver a baby?" asked the janitor.

"Of course. But I never did a cesarean."

"Can she wait for the doctor?"

"I don't know."

A deeper voice somewhere over Hale Poser's shoulder. "She won't have to wait." The janitor heard a slight slur in the words, not much, but enough to make him turn and look.

Nurse Dorothy heard it, too. "Doctor, I don't think you should—"

"Shut up! I'll do what I like!"

"But Dr. Jackson—"

"I said shut up, you stupid . . . stupid . . . you . . ."

The doctor suddenly crouched beside a trash can and threw up. Then he was there again, pushing Hale aside, his breath foul with vomit and alcohol, the little veins in his nose throbbing blue and red.

"All of y'all get out while I open her up."

"NO!" screamed Rosa Lamont, pulling her wrists away from the janitor and flailing at the doctor, beating him away as the janitor tried to regain control.

"What's wrong with this silly woman?" slurred the doctor.

Hale Poser said, "Sir, I believe I can calm her down if y'all will leave us alone for a minute."

"Leave you alone? Who do you think you are?"

The janitor looked up, not at the doctor but directly at Nurse Dorothy. The nurse opened her mouth, returning the janitor's stare, then closed it again and nodded and walked toward the doctor.

"Doctor, I need a word with you, sir."

"But I have to operate," belched the man.

"This will just take a minute," she said, taking him by the arm, turning him.

"Dorothy?" called the other nurse.

"You come, too," said Nurse Dorothy.

Alone now with the woman, Hale Poser leaned down close again. "I'm gonna let go of you," he whispered. "All right?"

She wept and nodded. "Just make it stop!"

He released her wrists. Moving down along the bed, he started humming something. "I hear you," she said. "I know that song."

"I know it," said the janitor, and then he hummed some more.

"It sound familiar. I think my momma used to sing that when I was a baby."

"Yes," the janitor spoke, his voice flowing out of the tune he hummed as if the words were part of the hymn. "Mother, may I touch your child?"

Chewing her bloody lip, Rosa Lamont nodded once. The janitor lifted her gown and placed his palms upon her bare belly. He closed his eyes. He stood that way for several minutes, then his hands began to move, gently pressing here and there, stroking her enormous flesh. He was humming again, and thinking, I can feel you in there. I know who you are.

As his palms slid back and forth, the woman's entire body relaxed, her muscles becoming soft and pliable like warm black mud. Suddenly he felt her child move inside as if following his hands around, seeking out his touch. He made to speak to the woman, but she was sound asleep.

In Dr. Jackson's office, Nurse Dorothy Truett stared at the fly-specked ceiling above Papa DeGroot's head as he said, "I understand you are a miracle worker, Reverend Poser." Papa had taken the padded seat behind the desk while Dorothy and the doctor sat on hard wooden visitors' chairs facing him. Reverend Poser stood near the door.

"Miracle worker?" asked the reverend, obviously confused. "Why, no sir. I'm just a janitor."

Curious about the reverend's tone, Dorothy lowered her eyes from the ceiling to look at him. After what she had witnessed last night she no longer felt suspicious of the stranger, or thought of him as a roustabout. Clearly he was someone she could respect as an equal, a true man of God. What he did to Rosa Lamont last night had definitely been miraculous. So why was he surprised when their employer called him a miracle worker? She saw the reverend lower his eyes to the floor right after he answered Papa, looking nervous, as if he felt he should not have raised them up in the first place. Ah . . . maybe she had misunderstood. Maybe he was not shocked so much as frightened. Come to think of it, throughout their conversation so far she had not seen him look up, except just now when he had seemed surprised. Poor man. She wanted to tell him such fear was unnecessary. Things were different here, and their employer, old Papa DeGroot, was the main reason. There were still problems— the fishermen all worked in Jean Tibbits's boats, for example, and bought groceries from Claude Delacroix, depending on one white man for their money and paying it to another—but at least the pay was fair, and the prices were the same for all, and you could complain about things without a beating. In that sense Pilotville was an island of equality in a sea of bigotry, a place where a Negro could look a white man in the eye. Papa insisted upon it, and as the single richest man in the entire parish, Papa got what Papa wanted. Dorothy wished she could tell the reverend this so he would look up from the floor like a man, but she could say nothing here, in front of these two white men, however benevolent they may be. She knew that some things can be lost when spoken aloud.

"A minister turned janitor . . ." Papa shook his head, and Dorothy watched the old man's triple chins shake like jelly. "Nurse Truett tells me you saved Rosa Lamont's life."

"And her baby," said Dorothy.

For some reason her words seemed to annoy Papa. He frowned, and in spite of living on an island of equality, she felt a little anxious.

"Yes, of course," said Papa. "Her baby."

Now the reverend was shaking his down-turned head as if disagreeing with his shoes. "I didn't save that lady's life," he said. "Really, I just said a little prayer, you know, and—"

"She gave birth normally?" asked Papa, interrupting with a question for the doctor, being just a little bit rude in Dorothy's opinion. She knew old Papa was a pagan and did not care for talk of prayers or incantations or any other thing that he considered foolishness. She had learned a long time back to keep quiet about her religion in his presence. Papa looked at Dr. Jackson, waiting for an answer. She turned toward Dr. Jackson, too, being careful to conceal her disgust with the drunken fool and his bloated red and purple nose.

The so-called doctor said, "That baby came easy as you please, Papa. Just like Rosa's others. But I tell you, it wasn't lying right when I last examined her. Something moved the child around."

"Reverend Poser did it," said Dorothy, feeling it was only proper to give him all the credit. "He laid hands on Rosa and saved that baby."

"Oh no," said the reverend beside the door. "It was the Lord did that."

Immediately she felt ashamed, knowing she should have given God the glory, but forgetting. Or not forgetting, exactly, just not putting things right. And being reminded by this stranger in front of a drunk and a pagan. Being reminded with a certain tone she felt was unnecessary.

Dr. Jackson swelled up like a rooster. "I best not find out

you were pushing and pulling on that woman's belly, Reverend. Stick with the Lord's work and don't go trying to practice medicine."

"Yes. The Lord. Naturally," said Papa. "Be that as it may, I wanted to meet you, Reverend Hale." Dorothy watched him shift around with a grunt and pull his golden watch from a pocket in that old white linen suit of his. Using just one hand, ugly with age spots, he flipped the lid open, glanced at the face, and shut it again. His thin gray hair clung to his moist forehead, his cheeks dangled full and flush, and although he was good-hearted and Dorothy hated to think bad thoughts, she had to admit he was ugly, even for a white man. He spoke again in his funny little accent. "I wished to meet the fellow who caused all this excitement at my hospital."

"Your hospital, sir?" The reverend sounded surprised.

"Oh my. Have Nurse Truett and the good doctor not explained the lay of the land? Then of course I must. I am Vincent DeGroot. You may call me Papa. Everyone does. I funded this institution in 1894. Bought the building from the Methodist missionaries, brought the staff down here, and keep it running even now. Do I not, Doctor?"

"You surely do, sir," said the doctor. Dorothy nodded, eager to show appreciation.

"Yes. Thirty-three years. My gift to the community, you see. So, of course, when I call this 'my hospital' I merely reveal a protective instinct, which is natural to the situation." With those last few words the consumption rose up and he began to cough—a prolonged rattling sound. Dorothy wished he would let her take care of it. A week or two of bed rest and steam inhalation and she would have his lungs cleared up; she was certain of that. But Papa was a stubborn man, with no more patience for his own illness than he had for her religion. Wheezing and hacking, he pulled a plain white handkerchief from his suit coat pocket. He spat, shoved the handkerchief back into his pocket, and leaned heavily on an ebony cane tipped with silver to rise from behind the desk. "Dorothy, if you and the reverend will excuse us, Dr. Jackson and I have a few business matters to discuss."

Papa extended his hand toward the reverend. Dorothy Truett was not surprised to see the reverend's eyebrows shoot up, nor was she surprised when the reverend looked at Papa's hand for a long moment before slowly reaching out.

The reverend seemed to take care not to squeeze old Papa's fingers, and she noticed he kept his arm limp as Papa shook hands with him warmly.

See? Things are different here.

Moments later, Dorothy led the miracle worker down the shadowed corridor. She intended to say a thing or two about his rudeness, correcting her in front of a drunk and a pagan. She opened her mouth to begin . . . and found she could not speak. How irritating to play the role of a tongue-tied schoolgirl. Miracle worker or no, she should tell him to behave with more respect. But how do you say such things to a man who has the ear of God Almighty? Besides, a thousand more interesting questions came to mind as she walked next to this miracle worker. What are your prayers like? Do you ask for specific things, or are your requests more general? When God answers, do you actually hear his voice, or is it just a feeling, like I get now and then? Oh, her curiosity was boundless, but Dorothy sensed a hidden danger in such conversation, a potential for indiscretion that she could not risk. Sometimes questions answered more than they asked, and there were secrets she held dear indeed. Better to stay silent. Better to simply watch and learn.

Interrupting her thoughts, the miracle worker asked a

question of his own. "Ma'am? Who is that old man, exactly?"

"Papa DeGroot is the boss, Reverend Poser. Biggest man in Plaquemines Parish, maybe biggest south of New Orleans."

"I'll bet that's why I feel I know him. Must of seen his picture somewhere."

"That could be." She marveled that a man of God would say "I'll bet," when gambling was the devil's work. This, combined with his rudeness, nourished a comfortable hint of doubt. She said, "Papa's family has been important since way back. He's a fine man, Reverend. Done a lot for colored folk hereabouts."

The stranger said, "There's no need to call me 'reverend,'" dealing her suspicions a humble blow. "Where did Mr. DeGroot get his money?"

"Inherited the first of it I imagine, but I don't know where it comes from nowadays."

"He shook my hand."

"Stood up to do it, too."

"Yes."

"You ever shake a white man's hand before, Reverend— Mr. Poser?"

"No, ma'am."

"I guess you don't have to call me 'ma'am.'"

Hale Poser smiled. In spite of herself, she felt the warmth of it from head to toe. He said, "Shaking hands and calling me 'mister.' Do you think he means all that?"

"Oh yes. All the brothers and sisters he comforts here, I can't help but think good thoughts about the man."

A stream of shouted words echoed up the hall. Papa hollering at the doctor. Dorothy paused, looking back, and heard the muffled sound of Dr. Jackson's slightly softer reply. Neither man's words were clear, but it certainly seemed as if Papa DeGroot was taking the doctor to task. Good. Someone must have told Papa that the old drunk was too far gone to operate last night.

Of course, as it turned out, that was a blessing in disguise for Rosa Lamont.

The thought led Dorothy back to her questions. Did this miracle worker know the doctor would be drunk? Did he come to Rosa's bedside knowing the doctor would be unfit to save her? Was he a prophet as well as a healer? Did God share future happenings with him? Did he know what would happen later on today? Tomorrow? Next week? And if he knew what would come to pass tomorrow, did he know what she was thinking now?

Oh, dear.

Dorothy's discomfort with that possibility was compounded when the white men down the hall continued shouting. Although Pilotville was different, it was not wise to bear witness to such things. "Perhaps we should move on," she said, setting out a little faster than before.

Nodding, the man who might be a prophet limped beside her, yet kept up. She felt a sudden wave of embarrassment about the olive-colored water stains along the walls, though they were barely visible in the dark hallway. The infirmary could not afford to burn kerosene during the daytime. Even Papa DeGroot's philanthropy had its limits. Perhaps it was the illusion of privacy provided by the darkness that inspired Dorothy Truett to ask one of her questions in spite of herself.

"Rosa's baby," she said. "You did heal her, didn't you?"

"Of course not, ma'am. Why is everyone saying that?"

"When we left you alone with her, she was in such pain, and then I came back and she was sleeping comfortably!"

"Yes, ma'am."

"What did you do while we were out of her room?"

"I just prayed is all."

"Did you do some kind of procedure?"

"No, ma'am."

She glanced at him from the corner of her eye again. Then, looking forward, she said, "What did you pray?"

"Same as you, I imagine. Asked the Lord to comfort that poor lady."

"Yes, I asked for that. But I . . ." She caught herself before she said the words out loud—about to confess to this strange man, about to tell him a secret she held dear. She did not have that kind of faith. But although he might be a healer and a prophet, her weakness was none of his business, so instead she said, "I know it wasn't me, so it must have been you."

The miracle worker trailed his index finger along the high watermark on the wall. "God is good," he said, as if that was explanation enough. Dorothy Truett felt a confusing rush of anger.

Eight hours after baby Hannah's birth, James Lamont returned from the Gulf of Mexico at the wheel of the shrimp boat *La Vie Joyeuse*, with his first mate and pastor, Julius Gray, beside him in the house. Jean Tibbits shouted the news from the dock as James guided his employer's little trawler into its slip at the cove. Julius gave a holler and slapped him on the back. With his employer and his first mate cheerfully agreeing to tend to the dock lines and transfer the catch, James Lamont set out running all the way to the infirmary, pounding the boardwalk with his bare feet. Everyone hollered congratulations as he dashed by.

His little Hannah truly was beautiful. In a towel-lined wooden box on the table beside Rosa's bed, Hannah squirmed and reached for the ceiling with both hands, pushing up against the mosquito netting draped over her and silently working her mouth as if impatient to tell the whole wide world a story she could not yet possibly know. A colorful label on the end of the box read *Texas Red Grapefruit*. James stood just inside the door of the room, smelling of shrimp and diesel fuel, staring at Hannah and then at his Rosa, then back again at Hannah. He could not decide which of them to hug first.

Beneath her own tent of hazy white mosquito netting, Rosa looked like a veiled bride as she reached up with both hands like Hannah. But Rosa Lamont reached toward her husband, not the ceiling. That made his choice easier. James Lamont rushed to his wife. Both of them spoke at once, lips moving against each other's cheeks. They both paused. Then they spoke together again. They laughed and pushed back, and Rosa wiped her eyes as her man asked if she was really all right, and she said yes.

James Lamont turned toward Hannah's makeshift crib. He lowered his large unshaven face down above the baby. "Hello, Hannah," he said. "Hello, baby girl." With thickly callused hands the fisherman wrapped his baby in her thin white blanket and brought her up against his chest. She curled there in the fold of his arms with drool trailing down her chin. James crossed to the window and stood swaying slowly side to side, searching Hannah's face in the fading sunlight, memorizing the moment. He noticed how unusually thick and long her hair was, and admired the little pink bow that someone had clipped there. Lifting his own face, he gazed at the clouds gathering up beyond the trees and whispered words of gratitude. Tears welled in his eyes. He had a miracle baby. And he still had his precious Rosa.

The iron bars across the window were not enough to satisfy James Lamont. But he could not sleep at the infirmary that night. He had to help Rosa's mother mind the other children. And before that, he had to return to his employer's trawler to tend to the catch. Oh, how he longed to remain with Rosa and Hannah! Oh, how leaving them tore his heart!

He replaced Hannah in her makeshift crib, stroked her full hair and adjusted the position of her tiny bow. He withdrew a coil of hemp twine from his pocket. "Give me your hand," he said to Rosa. She held it up to him. James Lamont wrapped a loop of twine around her wrist. He unwound the coil and then tied another tiny loop around baby Hannah's wrist, ever so tenderly. "There," he said. "Now y'all can sleep."

"Stay," said Rosa, lying there, tied to her baby.

"We been all through this, honey," said James, touching her cheek. "Ain't nothin' gonna happen. It's crazy to be afraid of foolish talk."

She lifted her arm, indicating the twine around her wrist. "You tryin' to tell me you ain't afraid?"

"Just careful." Rising up, he turned toward the door. "Be back in the mornin' long about five. Y'all try to sleep now. Ain't nothin' gonna happen, I promise."

Ignoring him, Rosa Lamont resolved to stay awake all night. She did her best, but the birth had worn her out. Hannah's cries awoke her with a start, and she rose to nurse her child at midnight, and again sometime after three. It was very dark. Rosa awoke again when someone stopped by the room to check on them in the early morning hours. Despite her exhaustion she was fitful in her sleep, mindful of her baby in the little wooden crate on the table by her bed.

James returned at five that morning. He came to Rosa first and kissed her on the cheek. She smiled as she opened her eyes. Then, turning to Hannah's crib, James Lamont lifted the netting and looked inside. There lay the other end of the twine, but Hannah and her thin white blanket and her little pink bow were gone.

4

Hale Poser joined James Lamont, the nurses, and a few of the ambulatory patients as they combed the infirmary halls and storage rooms, looking underneath every bed and in every drawer and cabinet, even looking through the attic, but the child was nowhere to be found. Rosa Lamont screamed unceasingly from her bed as the search moved ever wider. When the sun reached its zenith they went outside. The nurses fanned out through the village while James Lamont and Hale and a few others waded into the swamp. It was decided they would move abreast in a single line, each of them keeping sight of the man to his left and right. The one closest to the infirmary would circle it very slowly, while the others spun around him like a spoke on a wheel. Hale Poser was farthest out along the line, which meant he had to move fast to keep up. The walking was difficult, since his hip was bad and the black water stood up to his thighs in places and unseen things below seemed to clutch at his feet and ankles with every step, yet he had to do it because there was not enough room between the trees to use a boat. Hale Poser's lips moved constantly, whispering words of prayer as he trudged through the mire. At first, some of the others called baby Hannah's name, then James Lamont in a fit of rage shouted, "Shut up, you fools! Can't no baby understand y'all!" No one begrudged the man his anger, just as no one begrudged Rosa Lamont her screams.

Throughout the day a few more men and women joined the search of the swamp. Others passed through the village again, checking every possible hiding place. Long about three in the afternoon Brother Julius's unmistakable bass voice roared in the distance, "Come in! Come in!" Hale trudged in toward the infirmary. There he found fifteen or twenty adults and a few of the older children milling around on the shell path in front of the building, with Jean Tibbits the sole white person among them. The harbor master was soaked from the waist down like everyone else.

Brother Julius Gray stood with James Lamont on the covered front porch. Hale Poser thought the preacher looked even smaller somehow, dressed as he was in his fishing clothes instead of his suit. "People!" called Brother Julius. "People, come close." Everyone stopped their quiet conversations and moved to stand before him. Brother Julius reached up and awkwardly put his arm around James Lamont's shoulders. The short preacher seemed to hang from the tall fisherman's side. He said, "James wants me to tell y'all how much he appreciates your help." James Lamont stared defiantly at the small crowd, his eyes red and wild. Hale Poser bent and rolled his wet trousers up to his knees and removed three swollen leeches from his right calf. Blood from their bites trickled down and further stained the filthy white laces on his brown leather shoes. On the porch, Brother Julius continued, "And I want to talk about how to proceed from here. Now, I believe—"

"Could we pray before we talk?" interrupted Hale Poser.

Julius Gray stared down at him a moment, then said,

"We have a lot of work to do, brother. There's a time and a place for—"

"He right," interrupted James Lamont. "We should pray."

Julius Gray took a deep breath, still staring at Hale Poser. "Yes. Of course, Brother Lamont." Bowing his head, he lifted his deep voice to heaven, speaking of the blessings all present had received and the gratefulness they felt and how sorry they were for all their sins, and asking for forgiveness, and finally getting around to baby Hannah and how much they hoped the Lord would see fit to deliver her from evil. Amen. Looking up, he said, "Now if I may move on, we need to get better organized. I understand some of y'all been wandering 'round without direction. If we had more help that might be all right, but with just us, we need to divide up the land so to speak, with everyone responsible for one area."

Someone said, "Why don't we get more people?"

"I have directed everyone in our congregation to come," said the preacher, "but most are out working oysters and whatnot. Y'all are the only ones in town right now."

Looking around at all the black faces, Hale Poser said, "What about the white folks?"

Ignoring him, Brother Julius said, "What we got to do, we got to get more organized. Now, I have a plan—"

Hale Poser interrupted. "Why don't we get the white folks to help?"

Brother Julius sighed. "Mr. Poser, I don't think—"

"Yes," said James Lamont. "Do that."

Brother Julius Gray removed his arm from around James Lamont's shoulder. "Seems to me this is something we can do ourselves," he said. "I have a plan on how to go about it."

"The more folks we got lookin', the better," James said.

"I want to ask them to come help."

"All right," said Brother Julius. "I will speak to Reverend Vogt."

"Naw," said someone in the crowd. "I'll do it." Hale turned toward the voice. It was Jean Tibbits, who was already climbing the steps to the boardwalk.

Lifting his chin, Brother Julius said, "Thank you, Mr. Tibbits, but it will be best if I am the one to speak to Reverend Vogt."

At the top of the steps now, Tibbits paused to look down on Brother Julius. With calm deliberation he turned and spat a stream of tobacco juice into the black water on the far side of the boardwalk. "Have it you way, preacher."

When the sun had slipped beyond the treetops, they pulled the kerosene lanterns down from their usual places high on poles along the boardwalk and continued the search. Ned Pierce brought his bluetick hounds, which bayed constantly away off in the distance. Most people would not walk the swamp after dark, but Hale Poser and James Lamont and a few others waded on, holding lanterns high, ignoring the rippling sounds of nearby swimming creatures, and hoping . . . always hoping. About two dozen whites had responded to Tibbits's call, Dr. Jackson and Reverend Vogt among them. The doctor reeked of alcohol and swayed slightly where he stood, which explained his absence when the child first disappeared, but he was here now. Reverend Vogt and his people were assigned a section of swamp to the west of the infirmary. Hale Poser was in the next group to the east. There were no whites among Hale's companions, and no blacks with Reverend Vogt. Jean Tibbits was off somewhere searching by himself.

Throughout the night the men around Hale Poser's group called softly to each other. "Check behind that log yonder" or "Got a fresh broken branch here" or "Come look thisaway." Now and then the sweat on someone's face would flash in the sudden illumination of a flaring match as they lit a hand-rolled cigarette. Bright kerosene lanterns bobbed in the distance, casting gigantic shadows as the white group waded away off between the looming cypress and tupelos. Blacks and whites alike beat the water about themselves with short sticks to frighten away water moccasins, which were no respecter of color. Deep-throated bullfrogs sang from hidden places, their bass voices a soothing undertone for the bright chirps of the tree frogs and the pulsing calls of katydids and crickets. Rosa Lamont's distant wails added urgency to the surging concert. The searchers were driven by her screams, but always in the back of everyone's mind was the thought that whoever had taken little Hannah had probably slipped away on the river in a canoe or pirogue, thus leaving no sign of their passing. As the night waned and the morning sky began to glow between the moss-draped branches overhead, hope died in every heart except Hale Poser's and James Lamont's. It was only for the sake of James and Rosa that the others carried on after the sun was up again, when it had been more than a full day since Hannah's disappearance, and there was no other reason for the searching anymore.

Later on that second day, Hale Poser stood ankle deep, surrounded by a floating carpet of duckweed, its tiny green flakes ringing his trousers in circles one above the other, each circle indicating a different depth of water he had waded through. Everyone else assumed the kidnappers had left the swamp with little Hannah, but Hale believed they were still out there somewhere, so he kept on. Looking down at his trousers he thought of the water stains around the first floor of the infirmary. He visualized the water up that high, flowing through the halls. Then for some reason he thought about the baby Moses, floating in a basket. He almost felt as if Moses were a memory instead of an old story. He could almost see what that baby saw as he drifted on the water. He shook his head to rid it of such foolishness. His thoughts often rambled now. He was too exhausted to control them anymore. Hale Poser had searched without stopping for thirty-six hours. He had plucked twenty-three leeches from his body. He had not eaten since the night before little Hannah was lost. He had returned to the infirmary only twice for water. His bad leg trembled violently where he stood as he tried to summon the will to move on.

"Lord," he said. "Look down here."

He took a step, and immediately fell hard upon his hand and knees. Rolling over he assumed a seated position in the water. "Mercy," he whispered, wiping his face.

Hale decided it would be wise to rest awhile. A small tupelo stood nearby. He crawled to it on all fours, avoiding a cluster of knobby cypress knees rising from the water. Once there, he leaned back against the trunk. The tree's outward flare was a perfect match to the curvature of his aching spine. He slept. He dreamed of crying babies and stinking swamps and very bad men and children afloat and a choir of angels singing ancient songs from another continent.

Hours later a beam of sunshine slipped a fraction to the right, reaching Hale Poser's eyes. They opened. He sat motionless, looking at the quagmire before him, thinking about what brought him here. He had come to find his mother, or his father, or at least a tombstone with their name—his own name, whatever that might be—and here he was, looking for a stranger's child instead. He whispered a prayer for baby Hannah, and for James and Rosa. He listened, but heard no voice or sound of human movement. He did not even hear Ned Pierce's bluetick hounds. He decided the others had probably quit or else moved very far away. Someone might have quit on him, away back before his memories took hold, might of sent him to that twelve-room mansion with the red-brick road out front, but he would never quit. No sir. Slowly, grunting with the effort, Hale Poser rose to his feet. His leg no longer trembled but he moved stiffly nonetheless, with his hip tilted just a little. At first he focused on his motions, careful not to fall upon the unforgiving cypress knees. Watching his feet he took one step, then another. Finally he felt confident enough to look up.

On a low-slung branch before him hung a small pink ribbon.

Hale cocked his head. He waded closer. Kneeling with difficulty, he lifted the ribbon off the small branch where it had snagged. He put it in his pocket and rose and turned toward Pilotville.

Hale Poser's discovery renewed everyone's hope and provided a direction for their search. Those who had given up on the swamp returned to look again. But no other clues were found that day. Most stopped looking on the third day, and by the afternoon of the fourth only Hale Poser and James Lamont continued searching. They moved painfully and slowly. The night before, Brother Julius had tried to convince James that his place was with his wife, but to no avail. Now even Hale was beginning to think they should stop.

"Mr. Lamont," he said, bending under a branch. "Maybe there's a better way to do this."

"What's that?"

"I don't know, but it doesn't seem like we're doing any good."

"You go on home anytime you want."

"No," said Hale. "Not yet."

"Why you still here? Why you doing this?"

Hale Poser did not reply.

The men wandered aimlessly through the swamp, covering ground that others had already searched. Hale hummed a tune while James Lamont merely grunted with the effort of lifting his feet from the sucking mud and placing them one in front of the other. Although he was haggard and weak from all the hard days and sleepless nights, somehow James Lamont stayed ahead of Hale, always pushing farther, always searching beyond one more fallen log or mangrove stand. Hale no longer looked left or right for the child. Instead, he mostly watched James Lamont's back. From time to time Hale thought he saw the man's shoulders heave up and down, as if he were sobbing. Once he called, "Mr. Lamont, are you all right?"

When James Lamont faced him to reply, his eyes were dry. "Where is God?" he demanded. "Tell me where he at!"

"Why . . . right here," said Hale.

James Lamont clenched his hands into giant fists; then he unclenched them and went back to wading without another word.

Near dark on that fourth day they finally turned back toward the village. For the first time Hale took the lead, pausing sometimes when James Lamont fell back in his exhaustion or in his reluctance to give up, or when the father stopped to listen as he often did with his head cocked slightly to the left and his eyes shut tight. They were still some distance from the infirmary when the frogs and insects began their evening chorus. With a scream James Lamont pressed his hands to his ears. Thinking a snake might have bitten him, Hale hurried back. In spite of his bad hip he lifted his knees high to clear the water. He called, "What's wrong, Mr. Lamont? What's wrong?" But

James Lamont simply pressed harder against his ears as if trying to block out all sound. Stopping before the man and listening now, Hale suddenly understood. He had never before noticed how some wild creatures sound just like crying babies.

Hale Poser waited patiently for James Lamont to lower his hands from his ears, but after several minutes he grasped the big man's wrists and pulled them down himself. "Mr. Lamont," he said, still holding on, "it's too soon to give up."

Shaking his head violently, James Lamont said, "She lost!"

"With the Lord there's always hope."

"Don't talk to me 'bout no Lord. He let them take my little Hannah."

"You don't know that. We might still find her and bring her back."

"The others never came back," cried the grieving man. "Why should she?"

"Others?" Hale Poser gripped the man's wrists more tightly. "Lord, have mercy. What others?"

5

I seen you outside church last Sunday," said Jean Tibbits, sitting below the shrimp boat's gantry. "I seen you make de preachers talk together, you."

The colored fellow stood on the wharf beside the trawler, holding a nickel. "I'm not sure I understand you, sir."

At first Jean thought he meant because of the accent. He was almost the only Cajun in town, and some people had a little trouble understanding the way he spoke. But he looked at the colored fellow closer and saw that wasn't it.

The nets swayed on the gantry overhead as Jean lowered himself belly down onto the filthy boat deck and stuck one arm through a small hatch into the darkness below. Feeling around blindly for the seacock, he spoke without looking up. "You hold you hands out and all of a sudden they saying de same thing." Remembering the way it had happened made Jean feel strange again, curious and nervous both, the same feeling he had the other day. When he thought about how this stranger found those persimmons, and how he seemed to drift in through the fog from out of nowhere. . . .

The colored fellow said, "Saying the same thing? Are you sure?"

Jean found the seacock handle at last and gave it a good tug. Nope. It was sure enough stuck. He muttered a curse and rose back onto his knees. Squinting up at the colored fellow, he said, "You don't remember, you?"

"I remember saying a prayer. . . ."

Why was this man being so cagey? Was he hiding something? Jean grunted and returned his attention to the seacock, leaning his head and shoulders down into the hatch, wishing the stranger would move along.

Above him the man said, "Sir? I brought a nickel for next week."

"Hate to charge dockage for that old pirogue. Prob'ly sink like a stone next time you go out." Jean's voice sounded hollow, bouncing around down in the bilge. With a hard tug he finally managed to turn the seacock's handle.

"It's the only boat I have," said the stranger. "How about I leave this nickel on top of the piling here?"

"All right." Feeling the stranger's eyes on his back, Jean pushed himself up out of the hatch in time to see the man set the coin on the piling. He asked, "How come you standin' outside de white church, anyway?"

The colored fellow smiled, and all of a sudden Jean felt a little better about everything. "I liked the preaching," said the colored fellow. "Why were you there?"

"Just passing a time."

"You don't go to church on Sundays?"

Jean Tibbits laughed. Everyone knew he had no use for church. Silas Vogt was all right for a preacher, he reckoned, since the preacher was also a river pilot and Jean respected all pilots, but old Vogt didn't have anything to say that was worth sitting for two hours on a hard pew.

Smiling at Jean's laughter, the stranger said, "Mind if I ask why not?"

For some reason Jean felt like he ought to give a serious

answer. "What kind of God lay his son down in a feed trough? All that mess in there? All that filth and slobber? I don't think no father do that on purpose, no." He thought a moment, then added, "All that preachin' and prayin' don't make nobody act no better nohow. Shouldn't got to explain that to a colored fella passin' time outside a white church."

"What about the other church?"

Confused, Jean Tibbits said, "You mean, me go there?"

"Yes sir."

"Coloreds round here like Sunday to themselves. Same as white folk, yes."

The stranger winced, and Jean hated to see him frown— there was something about that smile of his—but what he had said was true. You could take a fellow and sit him down for a month of Sundays in either Pilotville church, singing and listening to all that preaching, and as far as Jean could see it didn't make a bit of difference in how he acted. He had been cheated by as many Christian folk as not, and he knew many an honest man who'd rather go fishing than to church. Still, he wished the colored fellow wouldn't frown that way. Suddenly uncomfortable again, Jean dropped through the hatch and squatted belowdecks by the seacock. Wrestling with a clamp that held the leaking hose to the sea-cock, he heard the colored fellow say, "Sir? Don't you have someone around here to help out?"

"'Course I do. James Lamont run this boat for me. But I don't need him fixin' no seacock when his baby just gone missin'." What a terrible thing. Made a man just about crazy thinking about it. Sometimes he pondered what he'd do if he ever got his hands on whoever took James and Rosa's kid. . . . And then an interesting thought came to mind. He hollered up, "I hear you de last to stop lookin' for that baby. Why that, you?"

"I feel I ought to do something."

"How come? Ain't your fault . . . is it?" Sneaking in the question.

"It's just . . . I can't seem to let it go."

Jean considered that. Like most everyone else he had thought the troubles were long over with, but this colored fellow comes along, acting strange, and then it all starts back up again. Was that a coincidence?

Maybe.

Renewing his attack upon the leaking hose, Tibbits called up through the hatch, "You gonna stand 'round, maybe hand me down that wrench up yonder, you. De big one." He felt the boat rock when the stranger stepped down from the dock. Soon a big black hand came through the hatch, clutching a rusting wrench.

As Jean took the tool, the stranger above him said, "I heard something yesterday."

The hose gave way beneath the pressure of the wrench, and suddenly a fountain of river water shot into the bilge. Jean shoved his palm over the hole to staunch the flow and shouted, "Find a rag. Hurry, you!"

The stranger soon passed down an oily rag. Jean crammed it into the opening on the seacock. The flood was now a trickle. Above him the colored fellow said, "Everything all right?"

"Yeah, mon."

The stranger said, "Mr. Lamont told me there were some other babies missing around here."

Jean cursed quietly. Why would James go bringing that up to a stranger? He chose his next words carefully. "Not lately, no."

"But there have been others?"

Jean said nothing as he strained against the other end of the hose, hoping the stranger would go away. After a while the stranger called down, "Sir? You all right?"

"They a big bolt with a washer and a nut on it up there somewhere. Hand it down, you."

"Yes sir."

He heard the stranger's footsteps on the deck above as he went to fetch the bolt. Suddenly a sea gull laughed like a crazy woman. "Who else lost a baby, Mr. Tibbits?" called the colored fellow.

All right. Tell him something. But keep it simple. "Don't nobody *lose* one far as I know, me. But Della Mae Guidry get hers stolen, sure enough."

Against her better judgment Dorothy Truett agreed to take him to see Della Mae's final resting-place. She would never have done it, except he seemed to be some sort of prophet or miracle worker, and she felt such a strong desire for him to like her, and maybe acknowledge her good work for the poor at the infirmary. Now here they were, wasting time beside a six-by-three-foot red brick box at the back of the Pilotville Negro Infirmary cemetery. As a nurse, it bothered Dorothy that the infirmary had its own cemetery. She felt it implied a lack of confidence in her professional abilities. But in this climate it did not do to postpone interment of the dead any longer than absolutely necessary, and she had to admit there was a certain economy in having a graveyard close by a place where many people came to die.

Della Mae Guidry's crypt stood with about two dozen others atop a small mound of shells a hundred yards behind the infirmary. Wood ferns sprang from the crumbling mortar, and a lush blanket of lichen and moss concealed most of the bricks, but Dorothy could still make out Della Mae's name crudely etched in a skim coat of cement on the top. What a waste. Back when Papa DeGroot paid for the crypt she remembered him saying it wasn't right to bury her down in the mud, no matter what kind of life she had lived. Papa was such a saintly man. But Dorothy had believed then, and still believed, that so much expense for such a person was a shameful extravagance. In another five or ten years this little crypt would be completely reclaimed by the swamp. Besides, the dead did not care whether they rotted slowly in a crypt or quickly in the swamp.

Thinking of that, Dorothy crossed her arms and shivered in the heat. "Della Mae was a skinny little thing," she said, just to make conversation. "Probably a lot of extra room in there."

The reverend bent to pull a fern from the mortar. It did not come easily. "How did she die?"

"Broke into the pharmacy one night and swallowed everything she could get her hands on." Stupid woman. Dorothy had no patience for suicides.

"Why would she do that?"

"Didn't Mr. Tibbits tell you about her baby?"

"Yes."

"Well, then."

The reverend yanked on another fern, cleaning up the grave. Why didn't he just leave it alone? Dorothy would just as soon see it sink into the swamp. He asked, "How did that happen? The baby, I mean."

"Who knows? She came into town one night, screaming loud enough to wake the dead." Suddenly aware of her choice of words, Dorothy Truett glanced at the crypt and felt another shiver coming on. "Said someone broke into her place while she was sleeping and carried the child away. Said she didn't wake up until they were out the door."

"They? More than one of them?"

"Figure of speech. Della Mae never saw who it was."

Wiping soil from his hands, the reverend said, "Mr.

Lamont told me there have been a lot of kidnappings around here."

Dorothy sighed. "We ought to get back. Papa is supposed to visit today."

"All right."

Dorothy felt the mussel shells crunch under her leather soles as they crossed the small cemetery, weaving their way between the other crypts. Behind her, the reverend asked, "Do you know how many other babies have been taken?"

I will not discuss it, she thought, marching down the path, swinging her arms like a soldier.

Limping behind her the reverend called, "Have there been others?"

Ignore him, she thought. Maybe he'll leave it be.

"How many, Nurse Truett?"

"We've got to get back to the infirmary. I can't be gone when Papa comes, and you have to get some laundry done."

"Why don't you want to talk about this?"

"There's nothing to be gained."

"How do you know that?"

She no longer cared if he liked her, or acknowledged her good work for the poor at the infirmary, or even if he worked miracles. This conversation had to stop. "Mr. Poser," she said, "I appreciate what you did at Rosa Lamont's delivery, and I think it's fine you've tried so hard to find her baby, but that doesn't mean you can neglect your duties. The patients at the infirmary need us now. Concentrate on them."

"Are you afraid of something?"

"Don't be ridiculous."

"Then why won't you tell me if there have been other missing babies?"

"Old stories, Mr. Poser. It's a waste of time to put stock in them."

"How old are the stories, exactly?" Using both hands, Dorothy swatted at drifting cobwebs as she marched along the overgrown path. When she did not answer, he asked again, "How old?"

"Oh, for crying out loud. There's no stopping you, is there?"

"No, ma'am. Most likely not."

"I don't believe the stories, Mr. Poser. I grew up in Plaquemines, but I'm not ignorant. I studied nursing at Tuskegee, you know."

"How long have these stories been told down here?"

"All I know is I heard foolishness about missing children before I left for school, and they were still talking about it after I got back. Nothing but fairy tales. My momma used to tell them when I was little to make me behave."

The reverend stopped dead in his tracks. "That long ago?"

She felt the blood rush to her face. Spinning on her heel to face him she said, "I beg your pardon!"

"I didn't mean it that way."

He thinks I'm old, thought Dorothy. I am not old! And I do *not* want to continue this conversation! Fighting to control herself, she said, "Well? Are you coming or not?"

He did not move an inch. "What about Della Mae's husband? Is he still around?"

"Husband? That's a laugh." Answering him in spite of herself.

"She wasn't married?"

"She was a prostitute." Dorothy took pleasure in using the word. She might not be a miracle worker like him; she might be nothing but a spinster nurse at a third-rate clinic, but at least she had never stooped to anything like *that*. "The father could have been anyone with half a dollar."

Dorothy waited, expecting the reverend to join in her

outrage. Instead he said, "Poor thing."

"Poor *thing*? You make it sound like she was some kind of victim! Della Mae knew what she was doing."

"We all make mistakes."

"No decent person would make that one!"

"I wish that was true," he said, his voice trailing off like he was deep in thought.

She waited, but he did not continue. Finally she said, "What, Reverend Poser? What are you trying to say?"

"Hmm? Oh. I was just thinking about something that happened last Sunday at church. Sorry."

At church? What did that have to do with anything? Dorothy watched the reverend closely, wondering what on earth he was thinking. Suddenly it occurred to her that he might be the dangerous kind of prophet: the kind that calls down fire from heaven.

He shook his head as if to clear his thoughts, then asked, "How would I get to Della Mae's place, exactly?"

"She lived in a shack away out in the swamp. I have no idea how to find it, and no idea why anyone would go there."

"Maybe whoever took her baby left something behind."

"Mr. Poser, Della Mae lost her baby years ago. There's nothing left to see."

"Her house is gone?"

"Far as I know it's still out there somewhere. But you won't find anything useful. Now, I'm going to the infirmary, with you or without you."

Dorothy Truett set out again at a brisk pace. With his limp Hale Poser could not keep up, so she arrived at the infirmary first, just as Rosa and James Lamont emerged from the infirmary's main doors.

James stood to Rosa's left. In one hand he held a small cotton bag, probably filled with Rosa's nightclothes and toiletries. In the other hand he clutched his wife's elbow, although it did not appear to Dorothy that the woman needed physical assistance. Dorothy was mortified to see Papa DeGroot standing at Rosa's right side, holding her other elbow in a token effort at support while he himself trusted in his ebony cane. He's doing my job, thought Dorothy. I should have been here, instead of wasting time with that crazy man. As she rushed forward to help, the Lamonts and Papa paused on the infirmary's small front porch. "Ah, Nurse Truett," called the old white man looking up toward the boardwalk. "Just the thing, meeting you here. Could you help Mrs. Lamont up those steps?"

"Of course, Papa," she said, hurrying down the path with the reverend right behind.

Rosa Lamont said, "There's no need to make a fuss over me."

"Not at all," said Papa DeGroot. "You have had a difficult time of it, my dear. We are only too glad to do what we can. Isn't that right, Nurse Truett?"

"Of course," repeated Dorothy, taking his place at Rosa's side.

James Lamont looked at the reverend. "I thank you for what you done," he said. "Looking for our baby for so long and all."

Dorothy saw the reverend smile, but Papa spoke before he could respond. "Yes indeed, Reverend Poser. Jim has been telling us about the admirable way you stayed by him while he searched the swamp, right to the end."

Rosa Lamont sobbed loudly, suddenly shaking in Dorothy's arms.

"Come now," said Papa DeGroot to the crying woman. "I did not mean the *end*, of course. Just the termination of that phase of the search, as it were." Rosa nodded her understanding, even as she wept. "Please, please," said

Papa, removing a handkerchief from the side pocket of his white suit coat. "The sheriff will find your child. I am certain of it."

"Sir," said the reverend hopefully. "Is the sheriff looking now?"

The man is going to stir up all kinds of trouble with his questions, thought Dorothy. She was fully aware that no officer of the law had been present during their earlier search of the swamp around the infirmary, and fully aware that the law outside Pilotville did not share Papa's unusually benevolent attitude toward Negroes.

"Most definitely he is looking, Reverend Poser," said Papa DeGroot, unfolding the handkerchief and giving it to Rosa Lamont to wipe her tears. "I instructed him to do so myself."

"I gonna keep lookin' too, Rev'rend," said James Lamont. "You made me see there always hope."

"See?" said Dorothy. "Just keep at it. That makes more sense than traipsin' out to Della Mae's place."

The old man said, "Della Mae Guidry? Why would you go there?"

"I don't know where else to look."

DeGroot nodded. "Precisely why Sheriff Shiller is the man for this job. You and James had best leave the search to him."

James resolutely shook his head as Hale Poser said, "I want to help."

"Admirable, admirable. But you might do more harm than good. There has obviously been foul play. What if your efforts alert those responsible? You could frighten them in some way, perhaps cause them to take drastic action against the child." Again, Rosa wailed loudly and turned to bury her face in James Lamont's chest. Papa DeGroot laid a comforting hand upon her shoulder and said, "There, there, my dear. Don't worry. I'm sure Reverend Poser does not wish to take that risk. Isn't that correct, Mr. Poser?"

"No sir," said the reverend. "I wouldn't want to do that."

But Dorothy Truett was not sure this fool of a miracle worker always told the truth.

6

║ **S**urprise put a stop to the usual pre-
service socializing when the front doors opened and James
and Rosa entered the African Assembly of God. Hale Poser
watched with everyone else as the Lamonts led their children
to a row near the front, shuffling along like old people, arms
around each other's slumped shoulders. Even the Lamont little ones seemed pressed down by a heavy load. Hale Poser's
lips began to move the instant he saw them enter, silently
praying them all the way to their seats. When Brother Julius
Gray called one of the twins to the front to start the singing,
she chose a mournful song known all too well to everyone, a
song first sung not so long ago by ancestors bent in bondage
under the watchful eyes of pale overseers. Every word a double entendre, the congregation sang of freedom from the
chains of sin. They tried to raise their voices to the rafters as
usual, but no one's heart was in it. Then Hale Poser heard
another hymn in the distance . . . an altogether different kind
of song. He heard white hands clapping and white voices
shouting, the sound of people on the edge of heaven, clam-
oring to get in. While these people here sang low and mournful, the sound of jubilation from the white church across town

was an unsettling reversal of the norm, as if the world now spun in the opposite direction. It was a hard thing to hear while the African Assembly of God sagged beneath its burden, but still Hale Poser was drawn to the distant joyful noise like a sparrow to its nest.

Just as he had the Sunday before, Reverend Poser slipped out the open door and limped along the boardwalk toward the other church. With each step the mourning behind him faded and the celebration swelled ahead. Listening carefully, he walked until the volume of the two verged upon a perfect balance. He stopped. He backed up a few paces, still listening. He stood with his head cocked and eyes closed. In that exact place, the volume of the hymns was identical. He was certain that it mattered. He did not know why it mattered, or for whom, but in his heart dwelled a pure conviction that these people must come together or all was lost, a conviction based on something so deeply buried he was unsure if it was memory or revelation. Hale Poser smiled wide toward the sky and lifted both arms as he had the week before, reaching toward each church as though he were an orchestral conductor drawing out a faultless symphony, with one section low and rich with earthy passion for the Lord and the other high and clear and filled with light, until from where he stood the two songs seemed almost made for each other, halves of a matched set, ready to blend into a richness far beyond the ability of either one alone. And as he reached wider, wider, praying to the master of the universe for just one moment of absolute perfection, stretching his arms out, grasping for it . . . a different voice arose nearby and brought the perfect possibilities crashing down like broken glass.

"You gonna do it again?" asked Wallace Pogue.

The Negro dropped his arms and turned around. Wallace stepped from behind a cypress branch overhanging the boardwalk, pushed the brim of his straw hat up a little, and took a drag on his Lucky Strike.

"Sir?" said the stranger.

Wallace savored the smoke a moment, then blew it upward. "Tibbits told me what you did last Sunday. You gonna do that again? 'Cause I sure would like to watch."

"I was just enjoying the singing."

"Yeah?"

The stranger smiled.

Feeling a little off-balance, like he usually did around colored people, Wallace said, "I ain't much of a singer myself. Usually wait out here till the preachin' starts."

"You going to church this morning?" asked the stranger, indicating the building away off between the trees.

"Sure. Got to keep the Sabbath holy." Wallace took a final drag on his cigarette, savoring the smoke as it hit his lungs, letting it out slowly, and then flicking the butt off into the swamp. "Name's Wallace Pogue."

"My name is Hale Poser."

"'Course it is." Wallace nodded. He knew all about this guy. Or at least everything everybody else knew. "Go ahead and do that thing if you're gonna. I need to hurry back before my wife gets aggravated."

"It doesn't work that way, sir."

Wallace tried to keep the skepticism out of his voice as he said, "Lord's timing, huh?"

"Yes sir. Exactly."

"You really heal Rosa Lamont's baby?"

"People don't heal people."

"Glad to hear you say it."

The stranger continued to smile. "Only the Lord heals."

"Oh, no doubt of that. None whatsoever. But you know, I hear these things, make me worry you might be here to take advantage. Fleece some widows. That kinda thing."

"Sir?"

"Was a holy man up to Tidewater a couple of years ago," said Wallace, remembering. "Came from somewhere back east with his own tent and all. Got a few folks all worked up, healin' left and right. Those he healed were also from somewhere else, but nobody minded that. Didn't cause a bit of hesitation when the collection basket came around, which is all right with me. 'The workman is worthy of his meat,' you know."

"You know your Bible."

"Thing is, this fella up to Tidewater, he set to visitin' a couple of the older colored ladies. Eatin' their cookin', keepin' them company out on the porch and so forth. Time he left town, that rascal had talked those old women outta every penny."

"I'm sorry," said the stranger.

"No need, no need. We caught him and got most of the money back," said Wallace, feeling proud of what he did for the colored ladies. "Gave him a fair trial and sent him to Angola for thirty years."

"You did that?"

"Why sure." Wallace smiled, ready to spring it on him. "I'm the law 'round here."

"I see."

Wallace watched him for a second or two, searching for the uneasiness they usually showed when they found out who he was. "Well, I sure enough hope you do see. For your sake, I truly do."

The stranger started to say something but stopped after forming just one syllable. Wallace continued to watch him, deliberately putting on the skeptical expression of a lawman who has seen too much. By now the singing had ceased at the churches and the preaching had commenced. The thing was, this Poser fellow wasn't showing any of the usual signs. His hands were still, his remarkable blue eyes steady, his breathing normal. In fact, it seemed to Wallace that the guy was actually enjoying his company. Maybe even wanted to keep talking. Ever since he heard about the so-called healing, Wallace had assumed this stranger was some kind of confidence man he would have to arrest or run out of town sooner or later. But now that he'd met the guy, with his threadbare old wool suit and those white shoelaces standing out like sore thumbs, Wallace felt a twinge of doubt. Confidence men usually made an effort to look successful.

The stranger said, "Don't you need to go to church?"

"No hurry. I can see you got somethin' on your mind."

"Well, yes. I was wondering . . . what do you think happened to the baby?"

Deputy Wallace Pogue cocked his head, surprised at the question. "I have no idea."

"Could I help you look for her?"

"Why?"

"It just seems right. Could I?"

"I guess not," said Wallace.

"Please, sir . . . why not?"

Wallace wished he had another cigarette. "It just occurred to me . . . you come here with no relations and no work lined up, and you hire on over to the infirmary, and you do something to help Rosa Lamont's delivery, and then all of a sudden the baby goes missing."

For the first time the guy seemed a little nervous. "I had nothing to do with that."

Wallace gave him the look again. "Uh-huh."

"Have you found any signs of the child? Anything I could tell the Lamonts, to give them a little hope?"

Putting it right out in the open that way, the guy was either very smart, very stupid, or innocent. Whichever it was, Wallace felt a sudden wave of depression as he thought about the answer to the question. "I don't know a thing."

"Then who should I ask?"

"I'm the only lawman south of the parish seat."

The stranger's brow furrowed. "I was told the sheriff was searching for their baby."

Wallace sighed. "The sheriff said y'all coloreds did as good a job of lookin' as we could. No use spending time going over old ground."

"But Papa told me—" The guy stopped in midsentence, his face turned hard, figuring it out.

Wallace looked away. "Listen," he said, "you got to understand I can't spend full time on everything that happens. It's a big parish and I'm spread mighty thin."

Nodding, the stranger held his peace.

It's not my fault, thought Wallace. Putting on his official voice, he said, "You best remember 'bout that fella up to Tidewater, all right?"

The stranger nodded again, obviously not at all concerned. Wallace stared at him hard for a moment, trying to give him the look again but getting it back instead. Feeling ridiculous he turned toward the church. Somehow he knew the guy was standing there watching his back as he walked away. Ever since Jean Tibbits told him what he saw this stranger do last Sunday, Wallace had planned to keep an eye on him, to see if the man would try something again, maybe try to lay the groundwork for a religious scam of some kind. But now it felt as if the stranger had turned things around somehow, as if Wallace were the one working a scam. It irked him something fierce to have to sit by and do nothing about James Lamont's baby, but the sheriff had given him no other option. Wallace had a job to protect, and a wife to think about. For some reason he felt like he ought to explain that to the stranger, as if he owed the man an explanation.

Reaching the covered entry of the church, Deputy Wallace Pogue stopped and stood in the shade facing the doors, thinking. He had been a lawman most of his life. He knew how to read a man, and he was pretty sure this guy was on the up-and-up. In fact, there was something about him . . . something Wallace couldn't quite identify, but something . . .

He turned around and walked back to where, sure enough, the guy was still standing, watching him.

"James Lamont give you anything for healin' his baby?"

"Sir, I already told you I didn't heal that child."

"The Lord did."

"Yes sir."

"The Lamonts give you somethin' for the Lord? A little tithe, maybe? Love offering? Somethin' along those lines?"

The stranger frowned. "Why would they do that?"

Wallace made sure his eyes never left the guy's face, searching for a lie. "Answer yes or no."

"No sir. Of course not."

After studying the stranger's face a moment longer, Wallace nodded. "You ain't no kind of flimflam man at all, are you?"

The guy simply shook his head.

"Don't know why, but I believe you," said Wallace. "Can you read?"

"Passably."

Wallace scratched his chin, thinking about it. Crazy idea, really. The sheriff would skin him alive if he found out. But he couldn't just sit around and do nothing. James and Rosa might be colored, but they were good people. No, he couldn't just do nothing.

"Come on," said Wallace, taking off toward the church

again, feeling good about himself for the first time all week. This time the stranger trailed behind. Wallace walked right by the church's front doors. His wife, Jenny, wouldn't like him missing the service, but this was something he had to do right now, before he lost his nerve.

Hale Poser followed the deputy along the boardwalk toward the center of the village, where they stopped before a small white house. On the wall above the front door, painted in black, were the words *Plaquemines Parish Sheriff's Office—Pilotville Station.*

"Come on in," said the deputy.

Hale hung back. "I haven't done anything wrong, sir."

"It's not like that. Come on."

Hale Poser followed. Inside he stood in a narrow front room furnished as an office. At the center of the back wall was a thick wooden door with a small opening crisscrossed by iron bars. "There's two cells in back," said the deputy, nodding toward the closed door. "This here's where I do the paper work and all." Crossing to sit behind an oak desk that nearly spanned the little room, the thin man dropped his straw hat on a filing cabinet, removed a set of keys from his pocket and used one to open a lower drawer. Reaching in, he withdrew a clothbound ledger, obviously very old. He placed it gently on the desktop. "Have a seat," he said.

Hale raised his eyebrows.

"It's all right. Take a seat over there." The deputy waved toward an empty wooden chair directly across the desk. Hesitantly, Hale Poser sat. The thin man said, "You understand, the sheriff don't allow civilians to read our case notes. That goes double for coloreds, I guess."

"Yes?"

"So there's no way I could show you what's in this book here, even if I wanted to."

"I see."

The deputy opened the book's cover, spun it around so it faced Hale, pushed back his chair and stood. "Do you?"

Looking at the book, Hale Poser said, "Yes sir . . . I believe I do."

"All right, then. I got one or two things to tend to out back. Why don't you just wait here while I'm gone for, say, ten minutes? Suppose that'll be long enough for me to do what I got to do?"

Hale Poser was unaccustomed to duplicity. It took a moment before he understood and said, "I'm a little slow at . . . waiting."

"All right. I'll make it twenty."

Alone in the room, Hale Poser pulled the book close. It smelled of old attics. He used his finger to trace the words. His lips moved as he sounded them out, one after the other. Across the top of each page were two names— one an officer of the law and the other a victim of a crime. Beside the names were written the types of crimes, single words such as *assault* or *burglary*. In the upper right corner were two dates—the date of the offense and the date the case had been closed. Noticing the date on the first page was February 13, 1875, Hale flipped to the back, seeking more modern records. The last few pages were blank, but he worked his way forward until he came to the final entry in the book, September 17, 1927. Just the other day. The names were *Pogue* and *Lamont,* and the crime was listed as *kidnapping.* Beneath that was a brief description of the facts, which matched what Hale knew. It was written in a surprisingly neat hand, as if Deputy Pogue wanted to be absolutely certain there could be no future misunderstandings. The account read:

James Lamont, origin unknown, 27, fisherman, Negro, arrived at the Pilotville Negro Infirmary approximately 5:00 AM to discover that his daughter Hannah Lamont, a newborn minor child, was missing from her crib. Although Rosa Lamont, Houma native, 24, mother of the missing person, Negro, slept in the same room as the missing person, she was unaware of the child's absence until awakened and so advised by James Lamont. No witnesses. Subsequent civilian search did not result in discovery of the missing person's whereabouts.

Hale frowned. This was nothing new. Why had the deputy gone to all this trouble? Pushing back in his chair he began to rise. He paused, frowned again, and settled back down. Pulling the book closer, he licked his thumb and turned a page back toward the front. The date was almost three months earlier than the Lamont kidnapping, and the crime was *drunk and disorderly*. He turned another page, and another, and another. He found what he sought. The names were *Pogue* and *Guidry*, the date just over ten years past, the crime listed as *missing person, possible kidnapping*. The case notes were very simple and very similar. As Hale had been told by Nurse Truett, Della Mae Guidry, a known prostitute, claimed she had been awakened by something in the middle of the night only to find her newborn baby girl missing. Other than that, she could offer nothing. No sounds, sights, or smells. No clues whatsoever.

Hale sighed deeply. He licked his thumb again. Flipping randomly back and forth through the pages he saw a motley list of crimes ranging from petty theft to one capital murder, which took place in 1915 when two drunken men at Delacroix's Dry Goods fought over a woman. Knives were drawn, and when it was over, a fisherman named Snead lay dead below the boardwalk. Hale shuddered. Touching the book as if it burned him, he turned more pages and read the strange story of a young boy found in a pirogue abandoned among the mangroves along the Mississippi south of town. No family had come forward to claim the child, so it was assumed the parents had drowned upstream. The boy had been sent up north to an orphanage in New Orleans. Hale recognized the address, knew it well, could visualize the peeling twelve-room mansion on that red-brick road. His hands began to tremble. No family had come forward. No mother. No father. Not even a name upon a tombstone. Hoping to find more, Hale Poser turned the pages. There were several other tragic cases. Even in so small and isolated a place as Pilotville, original sin tainted everyone. But he saw nothing that was not also found in every other city, town, and village in the world, nothing particular to himself, nothing he could use to find himself . . . until he read the first entry for the year 1911.

The names were *George* and *Helms*. Mr. George had apparently been Wallace Pogue's predecessor in office. This time the crime was simply listed as *missing person*. The case notes were eerily familiar. The Helms family had been sound asleep in their modest home on the outskirts of Pilotville when the sound of the screen door closing awakened Mrs. Helms. Believing the door was flapping in the wind, she rose to secure it. Along the way she passed by her newborn daughter's crib. It was empty. An alarm was raised and an extensive search undertaken, but the child was never found.

Hale Poser turned the next page, his hand shaking like a man reaching into a snake pit.

7

Deputy Wallace Pogue returned to his little office to find the colored fellow slumped in his chair, cheeks awash in tears. Unsurprised, Wallace offered him a handkerchief before sitting behind the desk.

"So many," whispered the stranger, wiping his eyes.

"Yes," said Wallace.

"Eleven?"

"Twelve. You must of missed one."

"All the way back to 1883 . . ."

Wallace nodded.

"But . . . why doesn't someone *do* something?"

"I tried. Looked hard for Della Mae's baby. Never found nothin'. And it wasn't until last year that I noticed the others. Who bothers to read old cases?"

"What did you do when you found out?"

"Sent a report up to the sheriff in Pointe a la Hache, of course. At first he didn't believe me, but I mean, here it is." Wallace tapped the book, feeling the old anger rising again. "So I pushed him a tad. Told him I'd lead the investigation myself. But he denies the pattern. Says it's too old and the events are too far apart. I mean, by then it had been more than nine years since Della Mae's baby got took. But that was the longest time between them so far. Before that they was never spaced more than seven or eight years apart, which is still a long time, all right. I got to admit it's hard to believe anyone who has these kinds of urges would wait that long."

"Urges? What kind of . . . oh, dear Lord have mercy! You think they're *doing* things to these children?"

"What else could it be?"

The poor fellow covered his face with a moan and slowly bent forward at the waist until his head was almost on his knees. "Hey now," said Wallace as the fellow started rocking slowly to and fro. Remembering how he had felt the day he first realized what was happening, Wallace rose and came around from behind the desk and stood awkwardly at the stranger's side. He extended one hand as if to touch the Negro's shoulder, then drew it back. "I didn't sleep for two days," he said.

"It's so . . . so . . ."

"I know."

Minutes passed with the stranger trying to collect himself and Wallace standing beside him. Finally, the stranger said, "I have to ask you something."

Here it comes, thought Wallace. He balled his hands into fists and turned to stare at the window. He said, "You want to know why I'm not out there looking for the Lamont baby."

"Yes sir."

"Last year," said Wallace, "after the sheriff told me to back off, I knew there wouldn't be no help from up his way. So I started nosin' around on my own."

"What did you find?"

"Nothing. But I must of stirred things up a bit for someone. One night they took my wife. Her name's Jenny. They jumped her while she was walking home from Wednesday evening services, not two hundred feet from here. Threw a tow sack or something over her head and knocked the sense clean out of her."

"Mercy."

"I 'bout went crazy that night looking for her. Woke up the whole town. We all did what you do—searched the buildings first, then the swamp. Even some of you folks came out to help. Couldn't find her nowhere. Then 'bout nine in the morning Jenny come walking in here on her own. Had a doozy of a goose egg on the back of her head, but nothing worse. Couldn't say where she'd been. Couldn't say who done it. All she had to show was the goose egg and a little note, pinned to her dress. It said, *Stop looking.*"

The stranger shuddered. "Why are you telling me these things?"

Unclenching his fists, Wallace said, "These people 'round here—the ones grew up 'round here—they let this go on without doing a thing. But I want to stop it. Thing is . . . Jenny, she's all I got. So I been waiting. Just waiting." Turning from the window, Wallace searched the stranger's downcast face. "Did you really do what Jean Tibbits said?"

A sudden peace seemed to settle on the stranger, replacing his grief. "Something happened. I was praying and wishing, and . . . something happened."

"How 'bout the baby? James and Rosa's baby. You really save it?"

"No sir. I can't save anything."

I wish I had more faith, thought Wallace Pogue. I wish I believed this would work. But there's nothing else, so I might as well ask. Taking a deep breath, he said, "It's gonna take a miracle to find that child, and we don't get too many of them 'round here, so I was hoping you could do . . . something."

"What can I do?"

Wallace frowned, uncomfortable with saying it right out loud. "Couldn't you work some kind of miracle?"

A bark of laughter erupted from the stranger, who quickly cut it short by covering his mouth with a hand. "I'm sorry," he said. "It's just . . . Sir, you have the wrong idea about me. I'm no miracle worker. I'm just a regular person, trying to get by." Wallace Pogue's new hope died, and he let out an involuntary sigh. Looking serious now, the stranger said, "We could pray about it," turning it around on Wallace somehow, making it his responsibility again.

Wallace said, "I don't . . . uh, I don't know."

"Why not? You're a Christian, aren't you?"

The question erased Wallace's disappointment, replacing it with something less noble. "Of course I am," he said, speaking too loudly, hiding his uneasiness with a little bluster.

"Well then, let's ask the Lord for help."

"You mean right now?"

"Why wait?"

This didn't feel right at all. "Maybe later," said Wallace. "Right now I got to get back to church."

Normally, Brother Julius Gray worked weekdays on one of Mr. Tibbits's trawlers, *La Vie Joyeuse*, which James Lamont captained. Unfortunately, James had taken the trawler down the river to search for his daughter. He had asked Julius to go, but there was the church to run, and a living to make, and besides, everybody knew it was pointless to keep looking for that child. Mr. Tibbits didn't have the heart to say as much to James, so he let the man take *La Vie Joyeuse* even though that left Julius here ashore with nothing to do but mend nets, which didn't pay enough to mention. So here he was, trying to make a few pennies running a shuttle in and out of a dragnet outside Delacroix's as Captain Sam

Waterhouse moved a red checker to the far row and said, "Crown me."

A great lover of the game, Julius Gray had seen that coming for the last five moves. Now he smiled as Captain Waterhouse's opponent, the Reverend Silas Vogt, gingerly placed one checker on top of another with fingers resembling two well-cooked Polish sausages. Vogt's obesity was a constant source of amazement to Julius Gray and the other fishermen and river pilots who gathered regularly on the boardwalk in front of Delacroix's Dry Goods store. He was not only the pastor of Pilotville Community Church; like Julius Gray he was also a waterman during the week, a bar pilot to be precise, charged with bringing massive vessels in from the Gulf through the treacherously shifting shoals of the river's mouth. This required that he meet and board his charges outside the bars, out in the Gulf, standing on the rolling deck of the small pilot boat that carried him out, nimbly leaping across three or four feet of water to grab a rope ladder or a cargo net and climb the freighter's side. Once while coming in with James on *La Vie Joyeuse,* Julius had watched through James's antique telescope while Reverend Vogt did this. It took grace, speed, strength, and luck to board a ship from a small boat tossed upon the open ocean, and Julius Gray had expected the rotund Vogt to lose his grip and fall to his death into the chomping maw between the sides of ship and boat. It was a fate he would not wish on anyone, not even a white man.

Now Captain Sam Waterhouse chuckled as Silas Vogt moved a checker. A river pilot and somewhat overweight himself, Waterhouse said, "Gotcha now, Silas."

"Game ain't over yet," grumbled the fat man.

"Might as well be."

"Put another dollar on it if you're so sure."

Waterhouse laughed out loud. "My, yes. Any amount at all."

"All right, make it ten."

Brother Julius Gray sucked in his breath. Ten dollars brought the total wager to fifteen, over a month's pay for a first mate on one of Jean Tibbits's little shrimp boats. And Silas Vogt a preacher. Typical. White preachers were all hypocrites as far as Julius Gray was concerned, teaching their people to honor the Lord on Sundays and keep the niggers down the rest of the week.

"Silas, you surprise me, seeing as you're a man of the cloth," said Captain Waterhouse, thinking along the same lines as Julius.

Reverend Vogt grunted. "That don't stop a man from making a wager. Especially if it's a sure thing."

Waterhouse laughed again, and the two white men hunkered down to play in earnest as other white pilots watched through the rising smoke of their cigarettes. Julius stood some distance away, running the shuttle back and forth through the hemp net and stealing glances over the pilots' shoulders at the checkerboard sketched in chalk on an upended pickle barrel. Julius Gray envied them their free time. He knew Waterhouse would not guide a vessel that day, since his name was low on the duty board posted just outside Delacroix's front door. That explained his copious consumption of warm Old Union beer, available in the dry goods store for a nickel a bottle. Julius also knew Reverend Vogt was not a drinking man, which gave him a slight advantage, even though Waterhouse already had a checker crowned. But no matter how much money he had, Julius would never have bet fifteen dollars. My, that would be fine: to be rich enough to bet fifteen dollars.

It was the white men's third game in a row, a tie breaker, and serious business no matter what amount was wagered.

Thinking about it that way, Julius Gray decided to abandon his nets to observe. Such entertainment was his main connection with Pilotville's only store, since old man Delacroix insisted on dealing in cash money unless you had something he could right turn around and sell to someone else. Brother Julius figured there was no sense in trading such things to Delacroix, when they could be sold or exchanged directly to eliminate the middleman. Like most of the residents of Pilotville, what food Julius needed came mostly from the swamp, the river, or the Gulf. Clothes and household sundries were bartered for with his neighbors or obtained from the captain of the *El Rito* who did business on the side when his packet cruiser docked at Tibbits's cove. Some staples were essential, of course, and securing them could not always be postponed until the *El Rito* came to town. For this reason, salt, flour, and ammunition were Julius Gray's main purchases from Delacroix, followed closely by kerosene and matches. With wealth beyond imagination by Julius's standards, the bar pilots and river pilots bought factory-rolled cigarettes, bottles of beer, boxes of Cracker Jacks, and other frivolous items no fisherman could afford. In a town populated by masters of self-sufficiency like Brother Julius Gray, the bar and river pilots were old man Delacroix's financial salvation.

The pilots frequently spent their off-hours sitting on chairs and benches in front of the store, playing checkers or dominoes and gossiping with each other or with the fishermen who chose that location to mend their smaller nets, near as it was to Tibbits's docks. Like Julius Gray, most of the fishermen who worked for Jean Tibbits were Negroes, but the conversation between them and the white pilots was usually a model of democratic equality. Religion, politics, sex— no topic was considered taboo. While their discussions were often forthright and sometimes even heated, Julius had to admit he'd never heard a pilot retreat to the defense of racial superiority when pressed to the limit of debate by a colored fisherman. Still, there were boundaries to Pilotville's unusual spirit of equality. More than anything, Julius Gray resented the fact that Negro fishermen were never offered employment as pilots. Though this was rarely discussed, when the subject did arise, the white pilots generally blamed the shipping companies, claiming none of them would allow a Negro at the helm. They said the companies did not believe people of color were capable of the intellectual rigors required. It wasn't true, of course. So, when he wasn't fantasizing about getting paid for preaching, Julius Gray dreamed of taking the helm of each mighty freighter he saw steaming slowly up or down the river. To command so much raw power, to shoulder such responsibility, to enjoy that kind of respect in his community was life's greatest possible achievement. Compared to piloting great iron ships, steering a shrimp trawler was boring and unrewarding drudgery. The only other thing that came close: standing behind a pulpit with the word of the Lord full in your mouth and all the people looking up at you with adoration in their eyes.

Some of the white pilots said it was a shame the shipping companies would not accept a Negro, for everyone agreed that Julius Gray and the other fishermen had an intimate understanding of the waters of the Mississippi delta, rivaling that of even the most experienced pilot. For their part, most of the Negro fishermen were willing to allow that the white pilots sometimes worked miracles on the Mississippi. Julius had heard some say this grudging respect between men who faced the treacherous river as a common enemy explained the racial harmony that seemed to exist in Pilotville. Others said the town's unusual isolation forced them to treat each other right, knowing there would be no easy escape for any-

one if things got ugly. A few of the most naive in Brother
Julius's congregation said it was because the Lord had seen
fit to make things different here. But Julius Gray had once
seen a small African freighter cruise by with a colored man
at the helm while the white pilot stood smoking a cigar at
the port side railing, far away from the wheelhouse. From
that moment he had known there existed shipping companies that allowed Negro captains after all, so the pilots'
explanations were all lies. There was really no difference in
the way white people thought about colored people in
Pilotville, except for the fact that anywhere else in the South
the whites would not have bothered to explain. So Julius
had thought about that Negro captain for a while and
watched the way things worked in town, finally deciding that
the racial harmony of this place depended upon the simple
fact that Papa DeGroot would not tolerate open racism. And
no white man in Plaquemines Parish was willing to go up
against Papa DeGroot, not even the pilots. Realizing this,
Julius had ceased to trust any white person's word. He firmly
believed they were all evil. All of them except Papa DeGroot
and maybe Jean Tibbits. For them Julius Gray made an
exception.

Now the newest resident of their little town limped up
the boardwalk and paused to watch the game of checkers,
interrupting Julius's bitter thoughts. The janitor moved in
close for a better view and, to Julius's great surprise, rested
a hand on the shoulder of a white pilot sitting before him.
Intent upon the checkerboard, the pilot did not turn or
shrug off the janitor's hand. Julius frowned as they
remained that way, the colored man standing just behind
the white one, hand resting on the seated man's shoulder in
a pose of easy camaraderie as if they were the best of friends.
This was not true, of course. There was no way this janitor
had made a friend of Theodore Beauregard, so maybe the

white man assumed the hand on his shoulder belonged to another pilot. No matter the explanation, the janitor's shameless toadying was offensive. Julius Gray had not forgotten this man's interruptions as he organized the search party on the infirmary steps, insisting they pray before talking strategy, and suggesting they get the whites involved. This alleged reverend made him look bad before his own people. And Brother Julius Gray had not forgotten the expression of longing on Dorothy Truett's face in church the other day when the janitor did not know that she was looking. No, Julius Gray had forgotten none of that.

In spite of his better instincts, Julius wished that Captain Waterhouse would notice the janitor's familiar display. Waterhouse was too stupid to fear Papa DeGroot, and he was the most blatant bigot in Pilotville. He would make an issue of such forward behavior, humiliating the stranger at the very least. But Vogt had been moving a checker along the edge of the board until it was a single square away from being crowned. This made the game even running and added still more intensity to the play, distracting Waterhouse from all else. The captain's posture changed. Forgetting his beer, he hunched forward to concentrate, much as Vogt had been doing all along. With this change in position, the contestants on either side of the upended barrel became almost mirror images except for the different girths of their bellies. Like all the other spectators, the new infirmary janitor seemed frozen in place as the play went on, his hand still resting on Theodore Beauregard's shoulder. Maybe what Julius Gray had heard about this stranger's miracles was true. What the man was doing right now—what he was getting away with—seemed to confirm the wildest rumors. Or maybe the man was just crazy.

Driven by curiosity, Julius edged closer and whispered,

"What you doing, man?" The janitor turned and smiled. In so doing, he lifted his hand.

"Looking for a guide," the janitor replied.

"Can't you boys let a fella think?" said Reverend Vogt. The fat man moved a checker, and Waterhouse whooped loudly, making an immediate countermove as if expecting Vogt's action all along. Waterhouse's checker jumped two of Vogt's.

"Give up, Silas," crowed Waterhouse, lifting his bottle of beer.

Dejected, Silas Vogt sat back, the hickory slats of his chair creaking under his substantial weight. "Oh, all right," he said, fishing for his wallet. "I wouldn't of given you that opening except Reverend Gray here distracted me."

Choking back an indignant denial, Julius Gray returned his attention to the nets, passing the shuttle through the strands around a ragged hole with the speed and precision of a weaver.

"Go on," said Waterhouse. "Blame it on Julie if it makes you feel better, but everyone knows I can lick you anytime." For some reason, Waterhouse and a few others liked to call him "Julie," a woman's name. Theodore Beauregard had started it months ago. Beauregard had a habit of calling other men by nicknames that made them sound like girls or little boys, and a way of daring you to make an issue of it without actually saying anything outright. He just smiled in that handsome, ice-cold way of his, and you knew if you objected there would be the devil to pay. Of course, handsome and well dressed as he was, Theodore Beauregard still wasn't nothing but a cracker, so Julius expected such behavior. But lately even some of the colored men had joined in, and for the life of him Julius did not know why his brothers would show such disrespect.

Vogt handed the money to Waterhouse. "Julius, why'd

you go and confound me thataway?"

"I was just asking this fellow what he was doing here," said Julius, still weaving.

The fat white man looked the stranger over as if noticing him for the first time. "And what did he say?"

"Something 'bout looking for a guide."

"Well?" said Vogt, still staring at the janitor. "Explain yourself, if you please. I got a right to know, seein' as you just cost me fifteen dollars."

The stranger smiled. "Yes sir. I'm looking for someone to take me to Della Mae Guidry's place."

"Who in tarnation is Della Mae Guidry?"

Captain Waterhouse said, "Silas, this is gonna shock a holy man like you, but Della Mae was a sportin' gal. Wasn't she, fellas?" Several men made laughing noises of assent.

Reverend Vogt sat straighter in his chair and tilted his head to look up at the janitor. "If you're going to sink to such a level, at least keep it to yourself."

Men of both colors chuckled.

"Relax, Silas," said Waterhouse. "Della Mae's been dead for years. Besides, you're the one asked this boy to explain himself."

"Why would anyone want to visit a dead whore's place?" asked Vogt.

The janitor said, "I heard she had her baby stolen."

Instantly the jovial atmosphere in front of Delacroix's Dry Goods store evaporated. The men all looked away or studied their hands. Even Captain Waterhouse lost interest in the conversation, busying himself with setting up the checkerboard for another game. Only Theodore Beauregard remained relaxed, leaning back in his straight-backed chair and tilting the brim of his hat even lower over his eyes. But Captain Vogt did not seem to notice the change of mood. "What do you mean?"

The janitor told Della Mae's story pretty much as Julius Gray remembered it. Listening, Vogt's eyes never left the janitor's face. They seemed to shrink back until almost lost between the flab of his cheeks and his heavy lids. When the janitor finished talking, Vogt said, "Sounds like what happened to James Lamont. That why you want to go out there?"

"Yes," said the stranger.

Vogt shook his head. "What a terrible thing. James is a mighty fine captain."

Since there was obviously no connection between James Lamont's maritime skills and the tragedy of his daughter's kidnapping, Julius was angered by this hypocritical praise for his friend's seamanship. Tossing us a bone, he thought. Won't do nothin' serious 'bout what happened, but talking nice like that'll make it right.

Acting on impulse, Julius Gray said, "I'll take you out to Della Mae's."

The janitor looked at him. "I don't have much money."

"Don't worry 'bout that. I'll do it for James and Rosa."

"Thank you."

"Best not go," said Theodore Beauregard, still lounging back against the wall of Delacroix's store.

"Excuse me?" said Julius.

The handsome white man did not bother to repeat himself. Instead, he inclined his face enough to lay his eyes upon Julius and said, "You heard me."

Julius Gray felt afraid, and hard upon the fear he felt a rush of anger. Turning his back on the handsome white man, he spoke deliberately to the janitor, watching his English and making his voice deep and powerful. "We will go in my pirogue. I have seen yours. It will sink the next time you take it out."

"Hope not," said the janitor, smiling.

Julius Gray placed his shuttle on a bench, and the two of them set out for Tibbits's cove. Captain Vogt rose to follow, moving fast for a fat man. "Hey, Julius," he called, catching up.

Julius turned. "Reverend."

Breathing heavily, Vogt came close and said, "I was over there the other day you know, searching for the little girl."

You didn't come until Jean Tibbits went and got you, thought Julius. But he smiled to hide his thoughts and said, "I saw you, Reverend. Imagine James did, too."

"Tell him I just wish there was something more I could do." The fat man looked away into the surrounding swamp. After a moment, he spoke again. "I have a little girl, you know. You tell James my family and I will be praying for his baby, all right? Be sure to tell him that."

The janitor spoke up. "Why not tell him yourself?"

"Well, I can't. He's off looking for his child, ain't he?"

"He'll probably be back in time for church next Sunday. You could come and see him there."

Julius Gray froze. Where had that come from? Was this fool seriously inviting Silas Vogt to their church? Was he crazy? First laying hands on a white man and now this. Maybe he was beyond crazy. But Silas Vogt's reply was civil. "That would be mighty difficult, seein' as how I got a sermon to preach across town."

"You're the preacher at that other church?"

"I am." Looking the janitor up and down, Reverend Vogt continued, "Speakin' of that, ol' Tibbits told us a whopper the other day. Said he saw you standing outside my church during services, stretching your arms out like you was Moses by the waters. Tibbits swore he heard me and Julius start saying the exact same words at the exact same time." The large man leaned a little closer to the janitor. "That true?"

"I don't know."

"You saying Jean Tibbits lied?"

"No sir."

"So what were you doin' with your arms stretched out thataway?"

The janitor searched the boards at his feet. Look up, man, thought Julius Gray. Don't let him run over you.

"I suppose I was asking the Lord to get us all together," said the stranger.

"Get who all together? What you talking about, boy?"

The janitor continued to stare down at his feet, but his words belied his humble posture. "I was praying for us all to sing and praise the Lord together."

"In one church you mean? They do that where you're from? Coloreds and white folk in church together?"

"No sir. But I think we should, don't you?"

Now he's gone too far, thought Julius Gray as the vein at his temple began to throb and Reverend Vogt searched the stranger's face, apparently looking for signs of disrespect. Then, to Julius's surprise, the white preacher gave a serious answer. "No, I don't believe that would work out."

"Why not?" asked the janitor. "We're all brothers, aren't we?"

"It's the music, for one thing. The preaching, too. You people get so excited, you know, and we like things a little more calm."

"Might do us all good to try something new."

Julius rubbed his temple as the throbbing increased and the white preacher said, "We visit back and forth sometimes, don't we, Julius? I remember y'all coming over to sing for us one Christmas. Besides, there's nothing wrong with the way we run our churches. We have our ways and y'all have yours. The good Lord didn't make us all the same."

Now the janitor looked up, straight into Silas Vogt's eyes,

and said, "You know the Psalms? 'Sing to the Lord a new song?' It would do you good to worship with us."

The white man's tiny eyes seemed to slip further back into the folds of his face. "I don't know why I'm standing here listening to this. You make it sound like I've done something wrong, and here I am trying to treat you fellas right."

"I'm sorry, sir. I just—"

"Things have always been this way," interrupted Reverend Vogt. "And talking about it won't make any difference, will it, Julius?"

"That's a fact," said Julius Gray, confused to find himself taking a white man's side against a man of color. "Won't make no difference at all."

The janitor sighed and turned to limp away toward Tibbits's dock without another word. Staring after him, Reverend Silas Vogt worked his mouth as if planning to say something else, but then, seeming to think better of it, turned and huffed back the other way toward Delacroix's Dry Goods store. Julius stood in the space between them, trying to decide which one to follow. Finally he set out after the stranger.

After a five-minute walk without a word exchanged between them, they descended a dilapidated set of steps. The final step was broader than the others and acted as a dock of sorts for three pirogues tied in the shallow water at the bottom. Tiny flecks of duckweed traced spidery green patterns on the ebony surface and gathered around the pilings beneath the boardwalk. The janitor stood aside to wait for Julius to step into one of the pirogues, but Julius remained one step above him, looking down. "Why you after Vogt to come to my church?"

"It seems important, somehow. Or at least it seems like the right thing to do."

"You think so?"

The janitor cocked his head. "You don't?"

"We don't want them coming 'round on Sunday mornings."

The janitor sighed again.

Disgusted, Julius Gray spat into the water. "I can't believe I got to bother saying this. All week long we got to deal with those crackers. Calling us 'boy' and . . . 'nigger.'" Julius had been about to say "Julie," which for him was somehow worse. He continued, "There's just so many places we can get some peace."

"They wouldn't call us that at church."

"Man, what kind of Negro are you? They'd be thinking it!"

The janitor sat down heavily on the bottom step and rubbed his face with a callused hand. Then he waved toward the pirogues. "Can we just get out to the house?"

"You have intentions with Miss Truett?"

The janitor said, "What?" pretending to be confused, pretending he didn't know what Julius meant.

"You heard me."

"Nurse Truett? No. No intentions. But I don't see what that—"

"What you want at Della Mae's?"

"I . . . I just have a feeling about it. Something I can't explain."

Julius Gray shook his head. "Man, you are nothing but trouble." With that, he started back up the stairs, leaving the janitor alone at the bottom.

8

Hale Poser poled his ancient pirogue south along the river's edge. Just ten feet farther out the current was strong enough to fling him all the way to the Gulf of Mexico. He took care to hug the shoreline, taking advantage of the little back eddies that confused the massive Mississippi, breaking it into manageable sections of slower ebb and flow. Frequently he had to crouch down as the boat floated beneath overhanging willows and lazy tendrils of Spanish moss. His eyes remained upward in search of water moccasins among the limbs. Now and then he paused to wedge his pole between a cypress knee and the side of the pirogue in order to hold the boat in place while he scooped water overboard with hands cupped together. Each time he did this, he thought about the final words Jean Tibbits spoke after giving him vague directions to Della Mae Guidry's house. "You crazy, you," Tibbits had said. "That old pirogue gonna take you to de bottom, sure."

He almost missed the mouth of the small bayou Tibbits had described. A stand of cypress huddled close together made it look like solid shoreline. Finding a spot between two trunks just wide enough for the pirogue, Hale nosed in. The swirling force of the river's current went against the bayou's flow at first, assisting his progress. Then about a hundred feet past the mouth, all signs of the river's incursion disappeared and the water calmed. A thin white film of something like mucus coated the surface. Hale's pole left holes in this substance as he went along. Bars of light sliced down through the overhanging canopy, illuminating the drifting pollen. It put Hale Poser in mind of glowing stained glass and clouds of incense in the St. Louis Cathedral, up New Orleans way. He spoke aloud, thanking his creator for the beauty all around. At the sound of his voice, an otter splashed into the bayou a few yards up ahead. Ten seconds later it surfaced and fixed him with a fierce stare. Hale laughed at the way its whiskers seemed to tremble with indignation. Undaunted by the creature's challenge, he kept poling.

An hour passed in that gentle place.

Another.

Tibbits had said this bayou would lead directly to the old Guidry camp. Hale should have seen it by now. Back by the river, low embankments had contained the sides of the stream, but here the waters spread out farther on each side, with the banks lower and not easy to make out beyond the rows of conical cypress trunks. With so many trees standing in the water, it became more and more difficult to determine where the main channel lay. Did it run between those tupelos yonder, or did it cut off to the left? Everything around him looked the same, yet nothing was repeated. Hale took his best guess and continued.

He often spoke aloud to his creator. Words of thanks. Requests for help. Prayers for baby Hannah and her parents. Or simply comments on life as it happened: "Oh, look at that, Father. What a curious shape for a tree." Ignoring his own curious shape, the way his hip cocked out. Sometimes Hale Poser paused as if listening. At these times, he often nodded in agreement, or, frowning, shook his head the other way. Sometimes he said, "Yes. Yes." Once he said, "No. I see what you mean. No, not at all."

As Hale Poser traveled deep into the swamp, a kingfisher flew down fast and perched on the pirogue's bow. A few minutes later, when Hale could not decide which fork to take, he observed his feathered passenger peering to the left. He took it as a sign and went that way. Another time a nutria escorted him for almost ten minutes, swimming alongside not three feet away. Three bright yellow butterflies lighted on his shoulders and remained there, opening and closing their wings. Hale sang hymns to entertain his companions, then took to humming an ancient melody with long-forgotten words. He felt comfortable here for some reason, as if he were heading home. He had such a fine time that the setting sun went unnoticed until the slanting light disappeared altogether and he could no longer see the overhanging branches in time to stoop beneath them. When a passing limb knocked him on the forehead, he stopped and wedged the pirogue up among a cluster of cypress knees to be sure it would not sink after he finished bailing. He lay down in the bottom of the pirogue. After the water there had soaked through his shirt and trousers it was no longer uncomfortable, and in the morning when the coo of a mourning dove finally coaxed Hale Poser back to consciousness, he smiled before rising and spoke aloud to God, offering thanks for yet another day.

His only unfulfilled desire was for something to drink. He had seen many half-eaten waterfowl and nutria floating on the water's surface, discarded by satiated alligators, and knew it was unwise to drink stagnant water choked with rotting vegetation and decomposing flesh.

At midday he abandoned all hope of finding Della Mae

Guidry's place and began searching for the Mississippi once again, to go back to Pilotville. The constant poling was no trouble for a man with such thickly callused hands and work-hardened arms, though his hip ached unmercifully from the hours on his feet without a chance to shift positions. Up came the pole. Forward he stretched, dipping it down ahead. Then backward pressure with both hands as the pirogue slid along by. Up came the pole again, and so forth, on and on throughout the day. He listened for the charging sound of diesel engines or the slower huff and puff of a steam engine. He listened for the slap of paddle wheels on the water and prayed to hear a packet steamer blow its whistle. He watched the still waters, trying to detect a current to guide him toward the river. But the passing hours offered no clues whatsoever to guide him home.

By dusk that second day all signs of the bayou had been lost, and his leaking pirogue lay adrift within the massive swamp. The pain in Hale's hip no longer allowed him to stand. Instead, he sat on the single bench near the rear of the pirogue, his off-center weight driving the bow up out of the water. He tried to pole the little boat along from that position, but his efforts were slow and laborious, and even if he could have flitted across the surface with the energy of a water bug, the question remained: which way to go?

Everywhere he saw the same isolated stands of cypress, tupelos, and willows rising from the waters. Cattle egrets and great blue herons loitered one-legged on half-sunken logs, eyes intent upon the shallows, waiting for their dinner. Here a muskrat, there a nutria, paddling with fixed resolve across the open places toward their dens. Unseen bass, crappie, alligator gar, and catfish plucked unfortunate insects from the surface, their minor conquests etching the water with a thousand interlocking circles. Hale saw things differently now. It had taken just a day and a half for these creatures to transform from friends to passive onlookers at best. Some might even be enemies. Mosquitoes, for example, which had been strangely absent, began to find uncovered places on his body. Even the thin cotton fabric of his shirt was no protection from their merciless attacks, soaked as it was in sweat and stretched tight across his back. He removed his hat from time to time and used it to swat around behind like a horsetail shooing flies, but this brought only temporary relief. And still he had no idea which way to go. Still he kept moving.

That second night was unlike the first. The mosquitoes made sleep impossible. Animal calls in the near distance disturbed him, where before they had been a comfort. He lay face up in the pirogue, slapping at his body and praying hard for rain to slake his thirst. But the morning of the third day dawned clear and bright, with no hope for drinking water from that quarter. His lips began to crack. It was difficult to swallow. While none of this could stop Hale Poser from thanking his maker for another day, instead of rising right away to resume poling he lay where he was and had a practical talk with the Lord. He wondered aloud if the Spanish moss stuffed into the cracks around the bottom of his pirogue could strain the impurities from the water leaking in, perhaps enough to let him take a drink without doing too much harm. Voices in his mind assured him otherwise one moment, then had him convinced the next, and he realized this was not God answering but merely a debate between common sense and wishful thinking. A waste of time. Impatient with himself, he rose and gripped the pole and started out again. At least the night spent on his back had given his hip the rest it needed. Hale Poser stood on his own two feet again.

It did not last. By the time the sun had moved almost overhead he was down on his bottom again in the back of the boat. His hip had failed him early, leaving him with no choice but to simply sit and drift as the day wore on and the third night fell. He slapped mosquitoes in the darkness and thought of the water well behind the Pilotville Negro Infirmary. He found a penny in his pocket and put it in his mouth to suck it, having heard that desert Indians did this with pebbles to generate saliva. It did not seem to help.

Then the sun rose, and oh, the water! How beautiful it looked! He marveled at himself for ever thinking it was filthy. Why see, that patch there had nary a speck of duckweed and none of that ugly mucus whatsoever! He reckoned it would feel cool going down. Sweet, too. If only he could get over there without stirring up the bottom. Leaning over the side, he dipped his hand into the water and paddled, but the pirogue pushed debris ahead and ruined everything. If he could just get moving, another patch of fresh water would appear presently, he was sure of that. He stood unsteadily and pressed the pole down and down and down again. He tried to speak his morning prayers out loud as usual, but his swollen tongue and lips conspired against him.

By noon of the fourth day Hale Poser became convinced the water round about was a patchwork of good and evil, a metaphor for heaven and original sin. Here was a filthy spot where only fools would drink, but there, just out of reach, a little pool where a spring or some clean source came up from underneath. It had to be, with the surface so smooth and clear. So there were places a man could drink and be just fine, if only he could get to them without bringing the filthy stuff along beside his boat.

Hale released the pole and sat down. Forgotten, the pole slowly settled in the quagmire back behind as he reached out to paddle with his hands. It would not disturb the surface near as much, would not defile that clear, clean patch he saw ahead. He found the spot and leaned over the side, almost swamping the little boat as his lips touched the black water and his throat worked, taking it down and down as he drank and drank and drank, until, satisfied, he sat back in the shallow water at the bottom of his boat and gave thanks, for he was certain this was of God. Water from the rock of ages, cleft for me, let me hide myself in thee ... in the ... in the water and the wine ... the wine is my blood, given ... for you. . . . Hale Poser's belly erupted. He flung himself to the side of the pirogue, but it was too late. The filth shot out across his chest, his legs, everything. Something cold and merciless gripped his entrails with superhuman strength, squeezing and twisting as if to tear them from his body. Oh, Father! Save me! His belly muscles contorted, flipping him to and fro like a fish upon the shore. Noises rose within him that he did not recognize. Oh, Father! Take me! He did not care to go on living, not if living brought such agony.

The torture gradually eased, leaving Hale Poser adrift in his pirogue, unmoving, uncaring, and, eventually, unconscious. He drifted overnight until the pirogue found a slowly moving current. It pushed him westward through the swamp, always westward. The sun rose. He opened his eyes for a while, motionless in the bottom of the slowly sinking, slowly drifting pirogue, watching with a faraway smile upon his cracked lips as tree limbs passed overhead. Unconsciousness returned. Night fell. He awoke once more in the darkness. Nearby animals fled for their lives at his groans and raspy cries of terror. Digging fingernails into the sides of the pirogue with the force of whatever nightmare gripped him, Hale Poser's wild rocking nearly sank the boat, though this sudden burst of energy was too much for him to sustain. He lost consciousness again.

He dreamed he was a child floating in a basket, with four fine horses pulling and a suit of silk upon his back, smooth and cool. He opened his eyes to watch the treetops, looking up as they passed by, seeing the blue sky away beyond the branches and the white clouds here and there. He heard the chickadees and titmice calling, the cardinal's bright chirps. How he loved the woods! He was so blessed to be here, riding along and looking up. He dreamed he was a rich man, a pharaoh's son. It was a familiar dream, which often came in times of trouble, the dream of a boy found in a pirogue and sent to a peeling twelve-room mansion before the dawn of memory. He dreamed, and dreamed, and dreamed some more.

Darkness flung its baneful cloak across him. Was he lying in the grave? Oh! This cannot be! I am here, and not in Paradise! Father, forgive me! I know not what I did! But the creatures whispered cruelly, "This is all there is," taunting him, slinging accusations at him. He lay in a coffin looking up, and all he saw was darkness, darkness . . . night. Grasping left and right he felt the roughened wood of his confinement. His fingernails dug in, but he could not bleed in death. He cried, but was too dry for tears. He spoke, but could not move his swollen tongue. My God, my God, why have you forsaken me? He slept, and dreamed some more.

Resurrection! Glory! He was risen once again. Golden light fell into the shelter of the temple. Look how the beams are so like branches, the walls like standing trunks. How the black marble of this floor shimmers like the rising sun on water. Oh, what a marvel! Paradise! How wonderful to find it so familiar. In the distance, Hale Poser heard angels singing an ancient and familiar song, like something from another continent. Their voices gave him strength to rise up, body sanctified, flesh immortal, strength to set out across the marble floor of heaven. He stood up from his coffin and took a step. The floor sank down and flowed beneath him, around him, over him. Then he rose again, baptized. Arriving at the edge he fell upon the holy mount. He found he had to move on hands and knees. He had not expected it to be difficult to walk in Paradise. How could anything be difficult here? It was disturbing. But perhaps he was supposed to crawl into Paradise like a baby. *"Whosoever shall not receive the kingdom of God as a little child shall in no wise enter therein."* Praising God, he pushed onward just that way: like a little child, crawling upward toward the angels, bound to enter.

The sacred mount lay strangely flat and regular, about twenty feet above the water. It ran in a perfectly straight line away off into the cypress stands on both the left and right. Underbrush and small trees crowded the slope, offering handholds for Hale to drag himself up. Black soil and bits of leaves caked his waterlogged clothing as he crawled ever higher toward the source of heavenly voices. Once, as he neared the top, he lost his grip and slid back down, chin bouncing along the ground. He lay unmoving for a moment, then shook his head and resumed his climb. Slowly, slowly he ascended, gripping one root, one vine, one branch at a time, pulling hard, digging old leather shoes into the good earth, his entire body trembling as he inched ever closer to Paradise, voices filling his ears, muscles shaking, and the effort taking all the final bits and pieces from his deepest places until his manic pale blue eyes peered at last over the top and he saw what lay beyond.

9

A mile of fields laid out in rows, brown and straight and littered with pure white. Hale Poser had seen such fields before. During the years before his ordination he had sometimes bowed his back in them from dawn to dusk. They were anything but Paradise, but in a part of his mind—the strongest part not yet defeated—he knew the fields were salvation of a different kind, for among them worked dozens of Negroes, bent double, dragging tow bags, picking fast, voices rising up together in gentle harmony. The undefeated part of Hale Poser's mind suggested he should stand and wave for help, but that was quite impossible. He continued crawling. Inch by inch he descended. Then, when he was five feet down the other side, he saw a white man riding a brown horse along the edge of the field below. The man did not seem to notice him, high up and far away as he was. Instead, the man's attention was fixed on a worker who had stopped picking and now sat between two rows, examining his bare foot as if he had twisted his ankle or cut himself somehow. The white man rode his horse into the field between the rows to help. Hale deeply felt the cruel irony of the situation: that a man with a mere turned ankle or minor cut would get assistance right before his eyes while he lay dying of thirst and exposure. If only he could somehow muster the strength to reach the fields below.

As these thoughts passed through Hale Poser's mind the man on the horse arrived beside the seated man. The rider uncoiled a bullwhip and began to lash the picker mercilessly.

Hale watched in disbelief, certain the other pickers would rush to the poor man's rescue, but instead they bent to their labor all the harder, no longer singing, moving on up the rows, arms in constant motion, picking and passing the bolls back to their tow sacks as their co-worker got to his feet somehow beneath the blows and stooped to lift his sack and began to pick again. Confusion washed over Hale until at last he reached the obvious conclusion: this was a prison work farm, and these were inmates doing time. Hale had heard how harshly the guards used prisoners on chain gangs, and for a moment he was afraid to continue downward. But reason prevailed. After all, he was no criminal, and the white men on their horses had no reason to abuse him. He inched farther down the hill.

As he crawled, the pitiful workers below resumed their singing. Such lovely voices, thought Hale. Such a testimony to the human spirit that they could sing so beautifully under these circumstances. The interweaving of the men's bass voices with the pleasant high notes of the women and children, how wonderful they were! How—

Hale froze.

Women and children? They would not labor alongside men in a prison's fields. But there were women's voices down below, and people so small they must be children, all of them bent double in the rows, and two white men riding round on horses, whipping those who lagged behind while the lovely, mournful voices sang old slave songs. . . .

In that moment Hale Poser understood at last what lay beneath him, and in the instant of that understanding, the frail capacity for rational thought that had somehow survived his ordeal in the swamp fled before a terror forged in a distant land, refined by centuries of torment and buried deep within his bones—a malevolent inheritance from unknown ancestors who undoubtedly bore the burden of the very evil he beheld. Whimpering, Hale tried to turn back up the hill, to reach the top and regain the sweet succor of the swamp. But in his weakness he began to slide. Grasping at roots and branches did no good; his hands were far too feeble. His slide became a tumble. Hale rolled and flipped end over end, making too much noise and raising dust.

At the bottom he lay motionless, staring at the cloudless sky, certain something must be broken. Of course his hip tortured him in familiar ways, but now there were many new pains. And he knew his wild descent had been observed. He turned his head and sure enough a white demon was slowly riding toward him, and behind the fiend a tidal wave of darkness came crashing down, and he closed his eyes against the onslaught and knew nothing.

10

The handsome white man reined in beside the Negro's prostrate form and sat unmoving in the saddle, frowning down from the shade beneath his broad-brimmed hat.

Well now, thought Theodore Beauregard. How about that? All these years, been a few try to get out, but this here's the first one to come in.

The far-off whine of an engine vaguely entered his awareness. Although he did not look up from the Negro on the ground, the distant sound annoyed him almost as much as the arrival of the interloper. Ought to kill this nigger, he thought. Won't be nothing but trouble. Stir them up with talk of what's outside, make them harder to handle.

The handsome man removed a coiled bullwhip from around the saddle horn and let the end uncurl. Slowly, tenderly, he drew it over the interloper's face, back and forth, tracing his features, watching him closely. The Negro did not respond.

Don't he look familiar? I think I seen him over in Pilotville. Yes, I'm sure I did. At Delacroix's, at the checker game the other day. This here's that new boy, who works at the infirmary. Well, best not kill him, then. Least not yet. Beauregard cocked his head, staring down. Wonder if he's playing possum?

The rider flicked his wrist effortlessly, and the whip became a writhing thing, whistling through the air, carving flesh, then returning to dangle limply by the horse's hoofs. Blood from the newcomer's cheek mixed with the fertile soil, but still he did not move. The rider turned and called, "High! Qana! Y'all get over here!" Two of the closest pickers slipped their tow sacks off of their shoulders and straightened themselves, pressing palms against backs as they stood upright. This slight delay filled Beauregard with anger. "Y'all quit loll'gaggin' and come move this nigger!" shouted the rider, flicking his bullwhip once. At the single crack of the whip, the workers hurried out of the field, still partly bent at the waist.

"Where you want him, boss?" asked Qana, the more muscled picker, bending to grasp the inert form at the wrists.

The whine of the distant engine increased a little, and a yellow biplane appeared high up and off to the south. Theodore Beauregard turned toward the sky. Before last month, he had not seen a single aeroplane since he got back from the Great War—almost ten years ago now. He never understood how a man could go so far up in the air in a machine made of nothing but wood and cloth, especially with so many Krauts taking potshots from the trenches. Now, if this one here ever came close enough, he might take a few potshots himself. And it might come close enough. Kept passing by, almost every week. Oil company surveyors, getting closer every day. But if he shot it down, they'd just come looking to find it, and that'd be even worse. Something else had to be done, he supposed, although he hated to see it end after all these years.

Suddenly he snapped his head back down toward the ground. The pickers, who had also been gazing skyward, just as quickly dropped their eyes. "What you looking at?" he snarled.

"Nothin', boss," mumbled High, the tall and skinny one.

"What?"

"Wasn't lookin' at nothin', boss."

Watching them from the hidden shadows of his hat brim, Beauregard uncoiled his whip again, dangling it beside his horse, swinging it gently like a pendulum. The field hands eyed it cautiously. Then, lifting his face back toward the yellow biplane, Theodore Beauregard touched his heels to the horse's flanks and moved away slowly, saying, "Tote that nigger over to your place, Qana. And get some iron on him."

Something tickled his nose. Hale Poser opened his eyes, and a giggling child sprang away, clutching a blue jay's feather. "Marah!" called the little one. "He awake!" Hale Poser saw everything from a strange perspective, lying as he was on the dirt. Everything was above him. Everything was beyond him. A tiny spider slowly descended on a single silver thread as if to take the feather's place upon his nose. Woodsmoke filled the air. Slivers of sunlight slipped through gaps in palmetto thatching. At his shoulder rose a low wall of crudely planed boards bound together by twisted strands of hemp. It was a shack of some sort; he could see that now. Oddly, these crude details seemed as familiar as the inside of a peeling twelve-room mansion with plaster walls and pine floors and gray slates on the roof.

An old woman now entered his field of vision, looming close, staring down with a frowning face and blocking his view of the thatched roof above. He saw her eyes slowly change as she looked into his, saw idle interest become a more intense examination. He tried to speak, but it was more than impossible; it was agony. "Bring that water," she said, breaking their eye contact with apparent regret in order to turn toward the child at her elbow. From a place beyond caring, Hale watched as the woman dipped a rag into a hollow gourd and touched it to his lips. He could not move to thank her. Drops of water traced a path across his furrowed lips, then lay upon his tongue, then crept around it, and finally found his throat. He tried to swallow, a feeble act that barely closed his throat. He felt he might gag as the water rolled too far, but willed himself to take the water down instead. The old woman smiled and removed the rag. "We gonna go slow," she said. "That be best."

Hale managed one small nod before sleeping again.

The next time Hale Poser awoke, the light was gone. He could not be sure where he was, or what was memory and what a dream. He lay on his back, listening to the sounds of someone snoring quite nearby, and katydids in the distance, and a barn owl's mournful call. He turned his head to the side but saw nothing in the darkness. He heard movement, very close. Something touched his shoulder. He heard a word; it sounded like "Moses." Looking upward again, he thought there was a deeper darkness there, hovering just above.

"You awake?"

It was the old woman again, the same voice. Hale tried to answer, mumbling as best he could, making as much noise as possible so she would know he was feeling a little better. "Shh," she whispered. "You'll wake him up." Hale was somehow sure she meant the man whose snoring filled his ears. He sensed the woman moving away, then coming back again. He felt the blessed coolness of the moist rag upon his lips. He moaned and sought it eagerly, lifting his head a little. "Shh. Shh," she whispered. "Lie still and it'll come." He relaxed, surrendering to her ministrations. Again and again she wiped the rag against his blood-caked lips. Again and again the water reached his throat, and with each swallow, the one that followed came easier, until the old woman was fairly wringing out the rag above his mouth.

Finally, she stopped. "That's enough," she whispered. "Sleep now. I'll be back directly."

Hale did as he was told.

He came to consciousness again the next day or the day after that. He suspected more time had passed than it seemed, but how long was unimportant. A slender shaft of sunlight tumbled through a crack between the rough-cut boards to lie hot upon his lower body. Hale wiggled his toes, pleased that the motion caused no pain, then displeased that his shoes were gone. He lay exactly where he was before, alongside the crudely fashioned wall of the low-slung shack, only now he felt it might be possible to move. Looking into the shadows, he saw no one watching. Perhaps the time was right.

Reaching deep into himself, he found the strength to roll onto his side. Hot pain shot through his ribs, threatening to steal his breath away. After a while it subsided, at least enough to let him think. He pressed against the dirt and slowly pushed his upper body up. A wave of dizziness rolled in. He fought against it until finally he was leaning up against the wall, almost sitting straight.

Every inch of him felt pain. He touched his face and found a blood-encrusted slash across his cheek. He found scrapes beneath his whiskered chin, cuts on both arms, splinters under cracked fingernails. Each discovery aroused a different foggy memory so bizarre he began to wonder if even this experience, this damage inventory, might be yet another dream.

Suddenly, through the sun-drenched opening at his feet came the singing once again, and it made him think of angels. Only then did he recall the pickers in the fields. If they were truly the source of this heavenly music, if those impossible fields were really somehow out there in the middle of the swamp, then the nightmares he had dreamed might be true as well. He prayed for other explanations. Then, in spite of his weakness, Hale knew he must go and see. It was only as he made to stand that he heard the chain and felt the iron bands around his ankles.

Staring at the shackles, Hale Poser trembled with a horror far beyond the reasonable fear that inspires self-preservation. His was a horror of independent shape and presence, a horror with a life of its own, born in the history of his forefathers and passed down like an ugly birthmark. He cast around the dirt floor of the dark shack, feeling with his hands for a knife or a chisel or even a stone—anything he could use to break the irons. Finding none, he clawed feebly at the bands with his fingers, trying to slip the shackles over his feet. All too soon this meager hope vanished, for of course the bands were too strong. Exhausted, he fell back upon the hard-packed dirt and began to pray in earnest.

As if in answer, a shadow fell across his face. He opened his eyes to see the old woman's silhouette as she knelt beside him.

"Can you take these off?" he asked.

She turned away. Unprepared for her sudden movement, Hale was left staring into the sun. He threw up a hand to shield his eyes, temporarily blinded. He heard her moving things around. He heard her mumbling softly to herself. Then she was at his side again.

"Eat," she said, holding something close to his lips. Reaching up, he took it and lifted it to his nose. There was no scent. But his eyesight was returning, and now he saw it was a hard piece of bread. He bit off a large chunk and swallowed without chewing. He choked, almost coughing it up.

"Slow," said the woman.

Nodding, he took another bite, chewing this time, and then another, and then the bread was gone. "May I have some more?" he asked.

She paused. At first he thought she would refuse, but then she brought a second piece, no larger than the first, and he took it and ate. When that was finished, Hale asked for another.

"That all," she said, rising.

"I'm sure I could eat more."

"Got no more," she said, leaving the shack as quickly as she came.

Hale called out through the empty door. "Can you take these things off my ankles?" Distant singing was the only reply. He lay still, listening to the voices. Some of the songs he knew. Most he had not heard before, yet they were familiar. Like the shackles, they touched something old and ominous within him. He prayed about his fear until the sky beyond the tiny opening glowed rosy red, then violet, then deepest purple and finally all was black. The singing stopped, but after a few minutes of silence he heard voices drawing near. Many voices. Not singing, but talking . . . and some laughter, too! His heart beat fast with hope.

Someone filled the low doorway, not the woman but a giant of a man who had to turn sideways to slip his shoulders through.

"Please, can you take these shackles off?" asked Hale.

The man did not answer, or pause, or even look his way. Instead he went into the shadows at the other side of the little room. Hale heard soft movements, then a curse, followed by something flying through the air and slamming into the wall near his head. The thing rolled away into a dark corner.

"Marah!" shouted the man. "Get in here!"

The old woman—Marah?—appeared at the door as if she had been waiting just outside. She said, "What the matter?"

"Don't you 'what the matter' me!" he shouted. "Where it at?"

"Where what at?"

The man charged her. Marah was fast for her age, but not fast enough in such a tiny space. He crossed it in a single stride, reaching out like lightning and seizing her ropy hair in his massive fist. Pulling her cocked head close, he bent and put his thick lips beside her ear. "You give it to him?"

"He need it more than you."

Roaring, he flung the woman against the wall. Hale heard the breath rush out of her when she hit, and his shoulder felt the rough boards shake as she slid down. She huddled against the wall, sucking at the air like a fish on the dock. The big man said, "I don't care what *he* need!" He approached her with hands balled into fists. As he passed, Hale reached out weakly and gripped his ankle. Looking up he pleaded, "Forgive her." The man stopped, stared down and kicked Hale once in the ribs. As Hale screamed and doubled up, the man strode cursing from the shack.

After a while the old woman spoke. "You all right?"

"I think so. You?"

She rose to her feet. "That weren't nothin'."

"Who is that man?"

"He Qana."

"Qana? What kind of name is that?" She said nothing, so Hale asked, "What's your name?"

"Marah," she said.

Gingerly probing his rib cage, Hale asked, "Will he be back?"

"This his place."

"Who is he to you? Your son?"

She looked at him with her head tilted to the side, troubled eyes lingering on his face. Then she was gone.

Some time later Hale awoke without realizing he had slept. His bladder ached. He had to get outside before he lost control. Rolling to his side, he pushed himself up to hands and knees and crawled out through the door. The chain between his ankles made little noise, dragging as it did over the dirt. Outside the hut a hard-packed area had been left clear of crops, but just beyond lay a sea of cotton, dappled in the moonlight and extending into darkness as far as he could see in all directions. Hale crawled across the open area and passed between two plants into the first row where he lowered his trousers and did his business on all fours. When he was done he crawled back through the cotton, ignoring the scratches of the burrs. He paused in the middle of the open area to rest and look around.

The full moon shed a cold white light upon the shack where he had spent the last three days, or maybe longer. He saw now that the shack was one of many, all of them standing side by side in a single row facing the giant field, their paltry interiors defined by rough-sawn vertical plank walls and covered with palmetto frond roofs. Hand-hewn branches had been wedged into the dirt to prop up some of the walls. Other shacks, such as the one where Hale had been, stood straighter. All had clearly been here for a long time. The soil at the foot of their front doors had been packed down several inches from countless footsteps. Most had log seats or upended stumps just in front of the walls facing the field. The tops of this makeshift furniture and the board walls behind them were shiny and smooth from the many bottoms, backs, and shoulders that had rubbed against them through the years. Each shack had a cooking place in front; small circles of hand-formed clay, reinforced with twigs to make raised enclosures. Most of these were filled with glowing embers. Iron tripods stood over one or two, with black pots suspended from short chains. Hand tools hung from pegs on the side of each shack. Hoes, mainly, although Hale saw some shovels and a number of sickles. Taken all together, it could have been a sharecropper's shantytown much like others Hale had seen, except this was the poorest by far, with no sign of an automobile, or electric light, or butter churn, or checkerboard, or dog, or cat, or any other thing to indicate the people living here had a life beyond the fields.

Even from outside, Hale could hear the large man snoring loudly in the shack. The rolling hum of katydids formed an undertone to the snoring, punctuated now and then by a sharp animal call from far away. Back beyond the row of shacks rose the hill that Hale remembered from his delirium, twenty feet or more above the place on which he stood. It ran straight and level left and right, disappearing into the darkness as if it might continue to infinity like the cotton rows behind him. He now understood it to be a levee, holding the swamp back from the sunken fields.

A baby's cry joined the snores and animal calls. It came from his right, from one of the other shacks. Forgetting his shackles Hale Poser made to rise up. He reached his knees before his weakness and his bonds betrayed him. Back on all fours he crawled across the open area and found a hoe propped against a shack. By leaning heavily on the hoe for support, he struggled to his feet. He then used the hoe as a crutch, shuffling off with the childlike steps allowed him by the shackles, following a beaten path in front of the shacks, the chains clinking louder now that they swung an inch or two above the dust. The baby's cries drew him irresistibly. He paused to listen in front of each shack's opening, then tottered on until he found the one he sought. Without hesitating, he entered.

The full moon shone a beam of light behind him, else he might have missed them in the darkness. Cross-legged in the dust sat Marah, the old woman who had tended to his thirst and hunger. She looked up at him, eyes wide and sparkling in the moonlight. In her arms lay a baby wrapped in a thin white hospital blanket, with a short piece of twine around her wrist.

     The meager glow of approaching dawn found Hale Poser still awake beside the old woman and the baby. He had tried to ask questions, but Marah had silenced him with terrified eyes and meaningful gestures at the other women sleeping in the shack. Now that the stars had begun to surrender to the sun, she motioned for him to go. Something in her attitude convinced him to comply without hesitation. Leaning against the hoe, he rose with tremendous effort. He stood a moment, looking down upon them, one perhaps seventy years of age and the other perhaps two weeks. Then he stooped beneath the door and left.

     Turning to his right he tottered off toward the shack where he had risen from his sleep several hours before. There was nothing else to do, and no place else to go. The iron bands slid painfully against his bare anklebones with every step. He longed for the high leather tops of his shoes, which would have served to cushion the shackles. He tried to move more carefully. The huts all looked the same in the light of approaching dawn. At first he wondered if he could find the proper one, but just as the baby's cries had guided him before, Qana's snores drew him now. He longed to lie in his little place upon the soil. The usual soreness of his hip was lost within a riot of aches and pains in every other joint and muscle. His stomach was a bottomless pit with unsteady sides threatening to collapse. His head wobbled on his shoulders, barely erect and nearly overcome by waves of vertigo. The hard-packed floor of the big man's little hut would be heaven compared to this agony of motion.

Just as he arrived at the doorway the snoring inside stopped. Hale froze, somehow certain this was bad. Suddenly Qana filled the opening before him. Without a word, he pushed Hale aside on his way out. Feeble and fettered by the shackles, Hale lost his footing and fell backward, hitting the ground hard. The impact awakened every injury he had suffered in his slide down the levee, nearly overwhelming his consciousness with a roiling cloud of pain. He lay there still when the big man returned from his morning ablutions in the field and sat above him on a smooth-worn log. Bending over, Qana began to tie the laces of the shoes upon his feet—brown leather high-top shoes with white laces. "Where you been, boy?" he asked.

Hale breathed in short bursts through clenched teeth as he fought down the pain. He had no energy for talking.

Grunting, the big man fumbled with the white laces, his fingers too thick for the task, or perhaps he did not know how to tie a knot. The more he tried, the more he tangled the laces. Hale watched until he had his pain under control, then he said, "Would you like me to show you how to do that?"

The big man stared at him, then sat back. "Don't show nothin'. Just do it."

Hale Poser slid around to face the man's feet and began working on the knotty mess. The big man cocked his head and watched him. "I the only one here with shoes."

Hale did not respond.

"Nobody else," continued Qana. "Just me."

Hale freed the right hand set of laces and deftly tied them properly. The giant leaned back against the wall and stared across the fields. "I gonna need you to tie them shoes up every mornin' now, hear?"

"All right," said Hale, down on the ground, finishing with the shoes.

Qana rose quickly, looming over him. "That all you got to say? 'All right'?" He snorted. "You no kinda man at all."

Proud of his humility, Hale responded by wiping the dust from the top of the shoes.

"Get away from me!" growled the big man, kicking at Hale but missing. Scooting back as quickly as his chains and injuries allowed, Hale slid halfway into the opening to the shack. Qana marched off without another glance in his direction. Hale Poser watched him go, then crawled to his spot inside, curled into a ball, and closed his eyes.

Marah did not want to wake him. He was sleeping peacefully, like baby Moses in a basket, and peace was so very rare. She longed to simply stand and look at him, everything she had dreamed about, all these years; everything she had hoped, come true right here at her feet, come to save them all. She could look at him forever. But delay would only make things ugly, so she knelt and touched his shoulder, ignoring the usual spike of pain in her aging knees. When her touch did not wake him, she gave his shoulder a firm shake. He rolled over with a groan and opened his eyes. She said, "Get up. The boss want you outside."

"The boss?"

"Uh-huh. The white man want you."

"Oh." He rubbed his eyes. "Tell him I hurt too much."

Dread wrapped familiar tendrils around her belly. "No, you got to come. You got to hurry."

Finally—after waiting far too long—he nodded. "Help me."

She bowed her shoulder beneath his arm and grasped his wrist in both of her hands. She would not allow herself to think of what might happen if they did not hurry. He was so heavy, but with his trembling help, she managed to get him to his feet and together they shuffled out into the sunshine.

Beauregard, the handsome one, sat on his horse several yards away, whip coiled around the saddle horn and Panama hat tilted low, obscuring his eyes. Beside him sat another white man on another horse. Marah had known the handsome one for years, but the other boss was new. He was slightly shorter, and instead of a nice straw hat with a good wide brim, he wore a gray one that did not even shade his features. His tiny ears, wide nose, fat cheeks, and the roll of flesh on the back of his neck were all sunburned. He looked directly at her with eyes the color of a wet possum, and said, "Bring him over here."

"Yes, boss."

She struggled beneath his weight, barely able to stand, although she knew he was doing the best he could. When they made it to the patch of ground in front of the two bosses, the handsome rider said, "Stop leaning on that old woman, boy."

For just an instant, Marah thought to protest, but the foolish instinct vanished quickly, leaving added fear behind. Marah believed these white men could read her mind, and so she tried to avoid rebellious thoughts when they were near. Desperately hoping they would forgive her moment of weakness, she withdrew a few feet, leaving the new man unsupported. The handsome boss looked away into the distance as he often did when speaking, looking at nothing in particular but just staring off as if to say near anything was more interesting than to look down at a nigger. He said, "The first thing you got to learn is when I speak, I expect to be answered. Understand?"

"Yes," said the new one.

"All right. And the next thing is, when you speak to either one of us, you call us *boss* or *sir*. Every time you open your mouth to us. Understand?"

"Yes . . . sir."

"Good. Of course you probably already figured out the next thing, but I'm a fair man, so I will lay it right out plain in case you're dumber than you look." The other boss smiled. Marah hated his smiles. They had no effect whatsoever on the coldness of his eyes and were therefore much more dreadful than his frowns. The handsome one leaned forward in his saddle for emphasis, but still he did not look directly at the man fighting to stay on his feet before him. "When I tell you to do something, you hop to it without no back talk or delay. Understand?"

"Yes."

The handsome one lifted the whip from the saddle horn, and Marah felt herself flinch. The boss man said, "What was that?"

Call him boss, thought Marah. But she dared not say those words aloud.

Somehow, the new man seemed to understand. Touching the wound upon his cheek, he said, "Yes, boss."

"All right." The man replaced the whip, and as it coiled around the saddle horn Marah felt her heartbeat slow. "You being new here, I'm gonna let that pass. But that was the very last time. Understand?"

"Yes sir."

The handsome one stared at him a moment, then said, "Marah, get this boy a sack and show him to the back eighty."

"Yes, boss," she said, joy arising in her. It was clear that they had finished with him and would let him alone for now. But her joy was short-lived, for as the bosses rode slowly away he called after them, "Boss?"

Both white men kept riding. Neither turned around. She hoped they had not heard him and would continue to the far side of the field. She concentrated hard and sent her thoughts to him. Don't say anything . . . not another word. But the new one ignored her silent pleas, or else he was just a normal man like all the others and could not hear her thoughts, because he called out even louder, "Let the baby go."

The handsome man reined in his horse. Motionless now but facing the other way, he said, "What that, boy?" Marah heard the menace in his words; how could this new man not hear it, too?

As if he had a will to die, he said, "Please. Her parents are so worried. Won't you take the baby home?"

Still facing away, the boss removed the whip from the saddle horn and slowly let it uncoil to the ground. Marah's heart fell with it. She knew all was lost as the boss turned in his saddle and the whip attacked. The first lash cut the new man across his chest, ripping through his shirt and laying a red welt that would take days to heal. The man fell to his knees, and would have fallen further if Marah had not suddenly been there to hold him up. It was completely reckless, but she braved the bosses' wrath by pressing her lips against his ear and whispering, "Say you're sorry! Call them *boss*."

Nodding, he called out, "Sorry, boss!"

The handsome overseer said, "You sure are, boy. You sorry as sorry can be. Ain't that right, Homer?" The one with the hot red face and cold gray eyes laughed.

Marah nudged the new one and said, "Agree with him."

Nodding again, the fallen man said, "Yes, boss."

The overseer cocked his head, looked down. "All right. There's one last thing. I don't want you talking English 'round here."

The new one frowned. "What do you mean . . . boss?"

"Just don't do it. And don't be teaching it to them."

"But I don't . . ." Again the handsome one's hand moved to the whip, and the new man quickly responded, "Yes, boss."

The white man grunted and slowly rode away beside his partner.

They gave Hale Poser a small burlap bag, the kind the children used. He tried his best, but within five minutes he was out cold among the rows. Perhaps the handsome white man or the one named Homer beat him as he lay there. Perhaps they saw he was beyond caring, and such a beating was a waste of time. Either way, Hale Poser awoke in the shack, feeling no more pain than he had before, and no less. Later, Marah brought him a small piece of hard bread, some soup made with okra, and something like collard greens. He got the same again that evening after the others came in from their labor.

The next day he was back in the field. This time he managed to stay on his feet by moving slowly and pausing often. Although the overseers beat two men and one woman as the day wore on, they left Hale alone. Apparently they were not foolish enough to beat a slave to death, at least not by accident. Or perhaps they saw that, even though the afflictions of his recent trials impaired him, Hale Poser did his best to fill the tow sack. If so, they undoubtedly believed his efforts to be fueled by fear, but that was not the reason. Hale had simply remembered the Scripture, "And whatsoever ye do, do it heartily, as to the Lord, and not unto men."

At first he glanced up from time to time, quickly, so as

not to let the riders see. Observing the lay of the land, he saw fields of cotton spreading out half a mile or more in every direction and bounded all around by the long levees. But he lost interest in reconnaissance soon enough. He had forgotten how difficult it was to pick cotton, or maybe he had blocked the memory from his mind. He had forgotten the sharp pricks of the burrs as they fought you for the cotton bolls, the burning of the bull nettles lurking down among the lower branches, and the stinging green spiders that left hard little knots below the surface of your skin. He had forgotten the deep indentation that the tow sack strap carved in your shoulder by midmorning, an aching furrow that soon became a callus, and the way the inside of your wrist would bleed from brushing across the side of your trousers when passing the cotton back a thousand times a day, as well as the merciless weight of the sack you dragged behind. Also the bitter irony that the more you picked the heavier it got, and yet the way to get your pay—or in this case the way to just survive—was to weigh down that sack as fast as possible.

In spite of all this misery, he fought the impulse to escape. Just as some were fishers of men, so some were pickers of them, and Hale Poser knew in his aching bones there was holy work to do here. Fire spread through his muscles, but he resolved to ignore it, to concentrate instead on the way one person started singing softly over there a ways, and another nearby picker took up the song, and one by one new voices joined in as the richness of it slowly spread across the field until all the slaves were singing near and far. Although some were not so good, they all did their best; and the others, oh my goodness, some voices were just so masterful—blending sweet like honey and molasses and rising up like thunder and falling down like rain and flowing as a cooling breeze across the cotton field.

God was strangely absent from the words the slaves sang, but Hale felt sure no saint in heaven bore offerings more magnificent. While anger at his situation wanted to dominate his thoughts, the singing helped to beat it back, as did the sight of young ones scheming to pick adjacent rows so they might stoop low and steal a kiss between the plants. He would have been a dried-up crust of a man to feel anything but joy at witnessing such a tender spark of life in such a place as this. He told himself that he was blessed to watch and listen to the others picking close beside him, such as the young brothers, High and Low, with physiques to match their names and a merry way of talking while they passed along the rows, as if their world were somehow festive instead of what it was; and several even younger, one of whom must surely be Della Mae Guidry's long-lost child. There were the many, many adults, including old man Simon, who told one tall tale after another to pass the time. And Marah, constant Marah, light upon her feet in spite of age, cheerful and ever ready with a ladle of water and an encouraging word.

The young man next to Hale started humming. He used no words, yet Hale recognized the melody. For him it was a song of comfort and of hope, learned in childhood at the orphanage and filled with good associations. His parched throat and cracked lips had healed enough to let him lift his voice a little, so he did his best to take up the young man's song. But immediately the young man fell silent. Ignoring the snub, Hale tried again a bit later. He began softly at first and sang the words to the young man's melody:

"I got wings, you got wings,
All God's children got wings.
When I get to Heaven I'm gonna put on my wings,
I'm gonna fly all over God's Heaven.

Heaven, Heaven,
Everybody talkin' 'bout Heaven ain't goin' there.
Heaven, Heaven,
I'm gonna fly all over God's Heaven."

Hale looked over at the young man. Though still bent
down, he had stopped picking and stared at Hale with his
mouth wide open. Hale started singing a little louder.

"I got a harp, you got a harp,
All God's children got a harp.
When I get to Heaven I'm gonna take up my harp,
I'm gonna play all over God's Heaven.
Heaven, Heaven,
Everybody talkin' 'bout Heaven ain't goin' there—"

"Jimbo!" called a voice from across the field.

Immediately the young man bent lower between the
rows and grabbed a handful of bolls. He furiously stuffed
them into his tow sack and answered without looking up.
"Yes, boss?"

"You pickin' there?"

"Yes, boss!" shouted the young man.

"How 'bout you, new boy? You pickin', too?"

"Yes, boss," called Hale, holding up a handful of bolls as
proof.

The white man rode slowly away.

Bent back down and picking, Hale Poser asked the
young man, "Does that white man own these fields?"

The man said nothing.

"Does he work for the owner?"

Busy among the cotton, he said, "Don't know nothin'
'bout no owner. But the boss answer to the Master, sure
enough."

"Master? Who's the Master?"

He did not answer. The two men picked in silence for a while, then Hale softly sang:

"I got shoes, you got shoes,
All God's children got shoes.
When I get to Heaven I'm gonna put on my shoes,
I'm gonna walk all over God's Heaven.
Heaven, Heaven,
Everybody talkin' 'bout Heaven ain't goin' there—"

"Hey, new boy!" Hale turned toward the voice. This time it was Qana. Even bent over picking he seemed taller than most men standing. Staring at Hale with narrowed eyes, he said, "Shut up 'bout them shoes!"

Hale stopped singing. For about ten minutes he and the young man picked near each other in silence. Then, without looking up, the young man named Jimbo said, "Newboy," and although it brought a bead of blood to his lip, Hale Poser smiled.

12

Hale Poser was among the last to get in from the fields. His chains slowed him to the pace of the oldest men and women, with the young man Jimbo offering him a hoe to lean upon so he could get by. As he reached the slaves' quarters, an argument broke out somewhere back behind the primitive shacks. Recognizing Marah's voice, he increased his pace and found her behind the last hut on the far end, standing face-to-face with Qana. Cradled in her right arm was the Lamont baby, Hannah. In her left hand was a rope. At the end of the rope stood a female goat, its udder heavy with milk. Marah had placed herself between the animal and Qana. She looked tiny in front of the man.

"We got no choice!" growled Qana.

"There got to be another way."

"Tell me, and I'll do it."

Hale Poser moved closer. "What's the matter?"

"Ain't your business," said Qana.

"He want to kill our goat," said Marah.

"What else we got to eat?"

"They's bread and okra."

"I can't stand no more of that."

"This child need her milk."

"I need *my* meat!"

Appealing to Hale, Marah said, "Ain't no milk nowhere else. Ain't been a baby born here for a long time. All the women are dry. He can't kill this goat."

Hale said, "Couldn't we hunt something in the swamp? Or catch some fish?"

Qana snorted with disgust. Marah said, "We don't go over the hill."

"Why not?"

The old woman replied, "Master say so."

"Besides," said Qana, "everybody know ain't nothin' good out there. Now gimme that goat."

Shaking her head, Marah stepped back. Qana balled his fists. Hale moved in between them and said, "Start a fire, Marah. Put some water in the pot."

"What you got in mind?" demanded Qana.

But Hale was already limping toward the levee. His lips moved continuously in prayer as he climbed. He felt a subtle joy. Here was the beginning of the work he had to do, the reason he should stay. He would feed them all with meat now, and the bread of life later.

The chains forced him to take very small steps. More than once they became entangled in the weeds. Without the hoe, he would have fallen. At the top he paused to catch his breath beside a low thornbush. In the fleeting glow of sunset he bowed his head, his lips still moving. When he opened his eyes again he saw many slaves assembled in the gathering darkness down at the base of the levee, looking up at him. Someone called, "Best come down, Newboy, else the boss man gonna whup you bad."

Ignoring them he set out along the top, peering down at the edge of the swamp on the other side for anything they might eat. The moon was almost full and shed sufficient light. He walked a hundred yards without seeing any sign of wildlife in the densely packed cypress and tupelos below. He paused and bowed his head again. He walked another hundred yards, and another. An hour later he had almost circled the entire field, half a mile on each side. As he drew near to where he started, Hale paused to bow his head once more. The moon had disappeared behind the clouds and with it vanished all hope of finding anything worth eating in the swamp. Eyes closed, he whispered, paused, nodded, and whispered again. He smiled and said "Thank you" out loud. Raising his head, he continued on. As Hale drew near to the place where his search had begun, he saw that the crowd of slaves had dispersed. Only Marah remained, far below in the open space facing the fields. She sat cross-legged before a meager fire. A black pot hung over the fire from an iron tripod.

Hale kept walking. His slow progress brought him back full circle to the thornbush where he had begun. He stopped again, just above the spot where Marah waited below. Standing with the swamp at his back, he lifted his eyes toward the ghostly clouds soaring across the night sky. "Please show me now," he whispered.

Immediately came a soft rustling sound. Hale Poser turned to look behind and saw a wild boar slowly climbing the slope from the swamp. With a thick coat of stiff fur and long yellowed tusks curling up to sharp points, the massive animal could have easily defended itself. But it held its head down as it came nearer, pushing fallen leaves and bits of soil aside with its snout, oblivious to Hale's presence.

He shouldered his hoe and waited.

The pot's too small, thought Marah. I got to get us some roasting sticks. And we need a bigger fire. Using one of the three machetes in the camp, she cut thin branches from a bush at the bottom of the levee and set about whittling them into spits. Meanwhile, Newboy took care of the butchering. She watched him furtively, almost certain now he was Moses, come with plagues and miracles as she had always hoped. What other man could go off looking for meat, armed with nothing but a hoe and come back with a wild boar, just like that? Now and then they might stumble upon a gator or an armadillo or some such animal that had wandered over the hill, but she had never seen anybody go out and get such a thing on purpose. Oh, look at all that meat! He had barely been able to roll it down the hill. And now, as he cut off piece after piece, she speared them and set them on the coals, basking in delicious pride.

The luscious scent soon drew everyone to her fire. They crowded in, jostling for position, every eye on the sizzling pork. Being stronger, the younger ones stood closest while the elderly craned their necks for a view from the back. Marah held her head high. When all was ready, the man they called Newboy selected one of the better pieces. Marah assumed he intended to eat it himself, as was his right. Instead he rose and pushed between the young men and offered it to her. When she reached for the meat with trembling hands, Qana leapt forward and seized it. Newboy tried to take it back, but the shackles at his ankles threw him off-balance, and Qana easily shoved him to the ground as he strode toward the fire. Knowing he would kick her out of the way as if she were a dog, Marah scrambled back. The big man ignored her and squatted beside the coals to eat, shoulders hunched and eyes scanning those nearby with naked animosity. Grease ran down his forearms to his elbows and dribbled from his chin as he crammed the fresh meat into his mouth, hardly chewing at all, grunting with satisfaction.

Moses limped to the fire to get another piece of meat.

Marah felt afraid for him but did not dare to speak or move. Turning, he headed back toward her. Qana sprang up and drove a heavy fist into the back of Newboy's head. He dropped where he stood. Qana picked the meat up from the ground, dusted it off and returned to the fireside. Her eyes on Qana, Marah sidled over to kneel beside Newboy. She touched his cheek. His eyes focused on something far away.

Leaning close she said, "You all right?"

He did not respond.

"Moses," she said. "Can you hear me?"

He pushed himself to a seated position and gripped his head in both hands as she supported him with an arm around his shoulder. They sat that way long enough for Qana to eat three more pieces of pork. The huge man showed no sign of satiation, grabbing one hunk of meat from the fire before he had finished swallowing another. Now Newboy's eyes focused on him. Eventually Qana noticed. He deliberately shifted his position to turn his back on the stranger.

"Help me up," said Moses.

She wanted to stop him, but something in his eyes told her that would be impossible. So, filled with fear and wonder, she positioned herself beneath his shoulder. Leaning heavily on her, he rose to his feet. Once upright he gently pushed her away, then walked unsteadily toward the fire. Inches from the seated Qana, he bent and lifted a piece of pork. Turning, he extended it toward her. For his sake, she looked away, making no movement to take the food. Holding her breath, Marah hoped he would let it go, but Newboy took a small step closer, still offering the pork. Qana came roaring to his feet. A second later Moses lay flat on his back beside the fire with Qana looming above him. Qana glanced around, saw the empty iron pot nearby and picked it up. Gripping the pot in both hands, he raised it above Newboy's head. Without thinking, Marah dove across his body, shielding it with her own. She looked up and saw Qana hesitate, flex his muscles to strike again, then hesitate again. Finally he tossed the big iron pot aside as if it were made of straw and walked away.

The crowd parted around the big man, then faced back toward the fire. All eyes were on the remaining meat, yet no one would move closer. Raising herself from Moses's chest, Marah sat within inches of the succulent pork. She, too, hesitated to eat. It was as if Qana had left behind a barricade of fear. Finally, Young Henry—second in strength only to Qana—stepped forward and defiantly seized a piece of meat. Like Qana, he sank his teeth into the flesh as if he were an animal, barely chewing it before swallowing the first bite. Unchallenged by the others, Young Henry reached for a second piece.

You no better than he is, thought Marah.

As if sensing her thoughts, the stranger rolled over to lay his hand upon Young Henry's wrist. Surprised, Young Henry's eyes met his and held for a moment. He saw something powerful there. Marah knew because she had seen it, too. In those sky-blue eyes she had seen the way a man feels for his possessions, the power of indifference. She had seen those blue eyes clouded by the power that lust imposes on a man when he longs for something he cannot possess. And she had seen an innocent power in those eyes, the innocence of a baby drifting away, away, away. Marah had seen every kind of power that matters in those sky-blue eyes— every kind except salvation. But now with the miraculous provision of this food, she knew salvation would surely come. So she felt no surprise when Young Henry pulled his wrist from Newboy's grasp and left the fireside with his piece of pork, blinking as if blinded, leaving the rest of the pig untouched.

Qana's dreadful spell had been broken. Falling on the fire like locusts on a fertile field, the others reduced the boar to bones in minutes. And like locusts, they left as quickly as they came. Perhaps they feared that Qana would return and take vengeance upon anyone remaining when he found the meat was gone. Perhaps it was shame at leaving nothing for the stranger and the old woman. Whatever the reason, Marah soon sat beside the fire with only Newboy for company. Because his beating had weakened him, and because she was old and small, neither of them had been able to get to the meat. It isn't fair, thought Marah. He killed it. I cooked it. But we the only ones going to sleep with empty bellies tonight. Then, over in her shack, the baby started to cry. It reminded her of why Newboy had killed the boar in the first place.

Don't cry little baby, thought Marah, rising to milk the goat. Moses gonna take you to a better place, for sure.

The yellow aeroplane flew over again that next afternoon. Hearing the distant whine of its engine Hale Poser paused briefly between the rows, risking a lashing in order to work the kinks out of his back while looking up. The plane dipped down out of the clouds for less than a minute, and then it was gone into the haze again. Hale watched it almost the entire time, an act of bravery mitigated only by the fact that his tow sack was almost full anyway. He could always tell the overseers he was heading for the wagon to dump the cotton. They would whip him if their scales showed that the sack was light, just as they would whip him if they thought he was watching the aeroplane, but Hale had learned a trick from the old woman, Marah. Every so often he would drop a handful of soil into the bag. The soil was much heavier than cotton, of course, and didn't require as much work to tip the scale. So with his sack almost full of cotton, weighed down by ten or twelve handfuls of dirt, Hale felt it was safe to stop and straighten up. He slipped the shoulder strap off and unbent himself gradually, each fraction of an inch a bittersweet combination of pain and pending relief. Finally, when he was almost vertical, he pressed both palms against the small of his back like a pregnant woman. He flared his nostrils wide and breathed in deep. The scent of rain in the atmosphere had always been one of his favorite things. He lifted his face toward the deep purple clouds gathering like overripe grapes in gigantic clusters, so low he could almost reach up and pick a bunch. The motionless air held a subtle threat, as if the first half of a hurricane had already passed and they were in the momentary safety of the eye, with the second half yet to come. Hale nodded his head. Yes. Bad storm coming.

He made circular rubbing motions against his back muscles, expecting the overseer to holler at him any minute now. Although it had been only two weeks since he stumbled onto this place, already he had stopped wondering how a slave plantation could exist in 1927. He no longer wasted time wondering who the Master was. The plantation was simply here, and that was all you had to know about a miracle.

Back in New Orleans, some folks talked about miracles like they might could understand them if they threw enough words that way. Hale had never given miracles much thought. He just prayed about things—usually not asking for anything in particular but letting the Lord know how he felt—and God answered as he pleased. Until Hale went to Pilotville, it had not even occurred to him to call God's answers miracles. But everyone there seemed to think he was a miracle worker. Rubbing his back, Hale thought about it. Was that true? That night he had asked for a pig, and there it was. He had asked, and it had come, just as he desired. With that realization came an unfamiliar tempta-tion: Hale Poser thought it might be nice to be a powerful man.

If he were truly a miracle worker, he could send baby Hannah to her parents, free these people, and escape from here with his holy work complete, and then punish the slave drivers and those who owned this evil place. He wondered who they were and how they had managed to keep such a massive secret. If only he had the power to work miracles, he would learn the answers to such questions and make things right. Come to that, there were other things he'd also change. So many things . . .

Someone on the other side of the field started singing. Her voice had a clarity and a force that carried far in the eerily unmoving air. It only took a moment for others on the far side to blend their voices in. The music flowed his way, and when the pickers nearest him finally took it up, Hale longed to join in. But although the tune was familiar, the words they used were different. Even so, the urge to sing along became overpowering, and Hale lifted his voice with the only words he knew.

> "Oh, in times like these, oh, in times like these,
> Yes, in times like these,
> I need the Lord to help me when I'm burdened down,
> Oh, when I'm burdened down . . ."

The others sang nothing of the Lord, but instead they substituted the word *someone*. Hale wondered how they could know such a beautiful song but not its inspiration.

> "When I'm burdened down, yes,
> I need the Lord to help me.
> Come on and help me, Jesus, help me.
> Come on and help me, Jesus. Help me, Lord . . ."

Still singing, Hale slipped the strap of his tow sack over his shoulder and bent to resume his labor between the dry brown rows of cotton. The field all around him was speckled white as if it had snowed hard for a while but stopped in time to leave some of the ground still showing. There was a lot of work to do, a lot of souls to pick, and he was deeply willing. He felt ashamed for having tossed the soil in his tow sack. He wanted to do his best at even this, to the glory of the Lord.

"I need the Lord to help me, all alone.
Well, I'm all alone.
Well, I'm all alone, you know.
I need the Lord to help me.
I need the Lord to help me when I'm by myself . . ."

What he did not have in talent, Hale Poser made up for in volume. He sang with such abandon that he did not realize everyone else had fallen silent until he paused where the song required it and heard only his voice echoing from the levees. Looking around, he saw the others picking with their heads down. Somehow he knew they were ignoring him. Somehow he understood that his participation had stopped the singing.

Marah approached with the water bucket. She paused beside each picker in the rows behind him. Each slave drank from the gourd, drawing the break out as long as they could. Finally she reached Hale, approaching in the row beside him. Dipping the gourd into the wooden bucket, she passed it over the cotton. Like all the others, he took the water while still bent over to avoid the pain of standing straight.

"How come you sing them words?" she asked.

"They're the ones I know."

"This 'Jesus lord' you talkin' 'bout . . . he a white boy or a nigger?"

Hale laughed, a startling sound in the silent field. Three hundred yards away, the overseer turned his handsome face toward them. Marah snatched the gourd from his hand and quickly moved on. Hale called after her, "What's the matter with everyone?"

Marah turned with angry eyes. "He white, ain't he?"

"Who?"

"The *lord*." She stressed the word sarcastically.

"No, he's not white. At least not only white. I guess he's every color that there is."

Hale saw the anger in her eyes change to something else. Was it disappointment?

"Then you best keep him to yourself," she said, walking away.

The storm came through that night. Its wind loosened the lower half of a board from Marah's shack and beat it back against the wall unmercifully. Cowering on her side, she looked out the open doorway and tried to curl around the baby to protect the child from the rain sheeting in at a steep angle. The larger woman who usually slept in the coolest place by the door had moved back against the far wall, crowding everyone else in her attempt to stay dry. There had been some grumbling, but eventually the others fell asleep again. You didn't pick cotton for sixteen hours straight and then waste time fussing when there was a chance to sleep. But Marah had always been frightened of ferocious storms. She lay awake, shaking with fear. How could they all sleep while the world outside was sodden with such violence? She flinched each time the thunder cracked, and when the fields beyond her door exploded with a flash of lightning, she felt certain they were all verging on cremation.

A sudden gust of wind ripped a small section of thatching

from the roof, exposing more of the shack's interior to the elements. This at last was enough to wake the women. Cursing the elements and each other, they scrambled toward the far end of the shack to remain dry. There was no room there for Marah and the baby. Wrapping her blanket around them both, she somehow found the courage to run into the night. Just as she emerged from the shack, a colossal lightning bolt crashed into the field. It seemed to hang there forever, snaking off in every direction, illuminating the rows and everything else with unnatural whiteness and charging the air with a strange power that tugged at the very hairs of Marah's head. She screamed and ran the other way with the baby howling in her arms. In the moments that followed, Marah could see nothing. The lightning bolt had blinded her to everything but a kaleidoscope of color, its afterimage burning red and blue and green in her vision. She stumbled through the mud outside the row of shacks with one arm around the child and the other stretched ahead, feeling for obstructions. Her blanket, hair, and thin cotton shift were all completely soaked. The unrelenting rain pelted her face, trickled icy fingers down her back and blended with her tears. She came to a wall. Guiding herself along it with her free hand, Marah reached the doorway just as another terrifying bolt of lightning scorched the night. She screamed again, and suddenly he was there, wrapping an arm around her shoulders and guiding her inside.

The storm still raged behind her, but here the roof was holding and the planks had not been ripped away. Marah's vision began to clear. His profile slowly emerged through the variegated shroud before her. He leaned close and said, "All right now?"

"Make it stop," she said. "Oh, please, make it stop!"

Moses whispered, "Shhh. You'll wake up Qana."

"I don't care! It has to *stop*!" It did not occur to her to wonder how Qana could be sleeping.

He drew her close, with the baby in between them and his hands upon her shoulders as she sobbed. "Oh, please," she whimpered, "I can't stand when it make me see those colors. I don't want to be blind! You can save me! You made that pig come from out of nowhere. Nobody done nothin' like that before. You can make it go away!"

"Stay here," he said, pushing her deeper into the shack.

"No!" she cried. "Don't leave!"

"I'll be right back."

Tears quivered on her cheeks as she watched him shuffle into the storm with the tiny steps allowed him by his chains. Almost immediately the terrible darkness swallowed him. All she could do was cower inside the doorway and stare out at the black wall of rain. Another lightning bolt danced in exactly the same spot in the field, except this time Marah did not look at the lightning. This time the colors did not come. Instead she kept her eyes on Moses, who stood in the instant of whiteness with arms outstretched and face upturned as the rain stopped and the wind calmed and the storm faded. And in the sudden stillness Marah thought she heard him talking to something horrible, away up yonder in the sky.

13

The rows were a devil's stew of black mud that morning. It stuck to the bottom of the pickers' tow sacks as they dragged along, the added weight digging shoulder straps even deeper into flesh. They had to scrape the caked-on mess away before lifting the sacks up onto the scales, adding time and trouble to the process and irritating the handsome overseer who sat high upon his proud brown gelding. His hand rested closer to his whip than usual, his eyes quick beneath the brim of his hat. Everybody suffered. Everybody cursed the storm, which had stolen their sleep the night before and left them with this added burden in the morning. It was unnecessary proof that they were cursed indeed, for could it not have stormed during the daytime and given rest at night? The ominous clouds hung dark and pregnant and so close they seemed to drag across the levees. Yet it did not rain, and it was hot, terrible hot. Someone started singing "Send Down the Rain," but the overseers looked his way and the slave shut his mouth right quick. They moved across the fields in silence, shoulders down, bottoms up, sweating in the humidity that built throughout the morning until the soil began to smoke with steam. Three water moccasins were found among the rows before midday. Each time a picker called for a hoe and the serpent was decapitated. The triangular heads were turned under the mud with muttered incantations and curses on the overseers in hopes the poison would find its way to them. The serpents' bodies were carefully laid at the end of the row for consumption later on. The devil wasn't the only one who knew how to make a stew.

Hale Poser bent down low with all the others, hands busy among the bolls, mind on higher things. He thought of old Marah after last night's storm had settled, whispering for fear of waking Qana, but whispering frantically nonetheless of blinding colors and deafening roars and imploring his protection as if God had nothing better to do than to sit on high and fling down thunderbolts at ignorant women. Hale Poser pulled the sodden bolls and remembered Marah shaking from head to toe in spite of the miracle he had done to stop the storm and all that he could say about the Lord's majesty and glory, and in the somber grayness of this day he regretted sending her back to her own shack alone, shaking still as she stepped into the darkness with the baby in her arms, casting furtive glances at the pitch-black sky.

At the end of a row he paused to gaze across the field, searching for Marah. He wanted to find some way to pick alongside her, to talk to her until he understood the reason for her fear of God. But Hale did not see her in the field, so he bent down again.

After a while old man Simon filled the silence with a story. At first he spoke in a normal tone of voice, not so loud as to attract the attention of the overseers on the far side of the field. Only those in the first few rows on either side could hear him. All of them but Hale had heard the story a dozen times. Still, no one seemed to mind listening again. Anything to make the time pass faster. As the old man spoke, his voice faded gradually until it became a near whisper, and Hale had

to strain to understand. Then old Simon fell. He gave no
warning but sank down right where he stood. Hale struggled
to rid himself of his clinging shoulder strap and hurried
across the rows between them and dropped to his knees
beside the old man. Simon lay with his cheek pressed into the
mud, breathing heavily. Hale slipped the tow sack strap off of
Simon's shoulder and rolled him onto his back. The old
man's eyes fixed on the clouds disinterestedly.

"Get back there, boy." The overseer approached from
behind, carefully guiding his horse between the rows to
spare the cotton. "Get back to work."

"I think he'll be all right," said Hale Poser, looking back.
"It's just too hard for him, with this mud."

The overseer's whip uncoiled to drape beside his horse
as if it were a living thing. Hale had not seen the white
man's hands move. He rose and stepped over a row of cotton, trying to make it back to his tow sack when the whip
found him, seething across the space between them in an
instant, biting into his shoulder.

"Didn't I just tell you to get back to work?"

"Yes, boss. I'm going, boss!" Hale rushed back to his row.

While pulling on his tow sack strap a dozen yards away,
Hale watched the rider rein in beside old Simon's prostrate
form. "Get up there, boy."

"Sure like to, boss," said Simon, "but I don't reckon I
can."

The rider removed a shiny brass watch from a pocket
and opened it. "I'll give you one minute, boy. Then you got
to get back to work. You ain't too old to work, are you?"

Hale saw fear on Simon's face for the first time. "No,
boss," he said. "I ain't too old."

At first, Simon made no effort to stand as the rider sat
watching his pocket watch. "Get up!" whispered Hale, too
low for anyone to hear. "Get up!" As if inspired by Hale

Poser's admonition, Simon stirred. He rolled over onto his belly. He pushed himself up to hands and knees. He paused again, breathing rapidly.

"Thirty seconds, boy," said the overseer.

"Yes, boss."

Sucking air like a runner trying to catch his wind, Simon reared up until he knelt between the cotton rows. Then, slowly, he pulled one leg forward, gripping it with his hands, getting the sole of his foot flat on the muddy earth, and pushing up until he stood at last, unsteady but on his feet.

The overseer snapped his watch shut. "Now get to pickin', boy."

"Yes, boss," said Simon, bending to lift the strap of his tow sack.

Without a backward look, the overseer rode on across the field.

The day wore on, time grinding away at them like sandpaper on rotten wood. Simon tried to pick but fell far behind the others to his left and right. Hale Poser expected another visit by one of the overseers at any moment. Yet it did not come. Instead, Homer with his cruel gray eyes remained at the field's far end while the handsome one sat in his usual place near the cotton wagon, watching from beneath his hat brim as the slaves brought sack after heavy mud-caked sack to be weighed and dumped. It was impossible to tell how many hours remained before sunset with the clouds so thick above, but finally darkness began to steal in from the swamp, and with it came the promise of blessed relief. When they could no longer see to tell the difference between the bolls and the bull nettles, the overseer called, "Bring it in." It was the call they longed for every evening, the permission to stop their picking until the next sunrise.

Rather than walk down his row toward the side of the field where the cotton wagon was, Hale Poser hobbled across the rows toward Simon. Meeting the old man, he took up his tow sack, barely half full, and slipped it over his other shoulder. He then led the old man to the wagon while dragging both sacks through the mire.

Hale used his fingers to claw away the mud from the bottoms of the tow sacks and placed first Simon's and then his own upon the copper scales. The overseer wrote down the tallies in his black leather book. Hampered by his chains, Hale climbed up onto the wagon to shake the cotton into its bed, then eased back down to hang the empty sacks on the pegs along the wagon's high sides. Simon stood nearby throughout the process, head bowed and arms limp at his sides. The others had disappeared into the darkness toward their shacks long ago. Hale went to Simon. Wrapping an arm around the old man's shoulders, he said, "Come on now." The two of them set out slowly.

After they had taken just two steps, the overseer called, "Hold on there, boy."

Hale felt Simon's shoulders slump still more.

"You still got a hundred fifty pounds to make today," said the overseer.

Hale turned. "Boss, I don't think he can do it."

"Shut your mouth, boy."

"Yes, boss."

Simon shuffled back to the wagon and took a sack down from a peg. Slipping it over his shoulder, he turned toward the fields.

"Boss," said Hale, "can I do it for him?"

"Everybody got to carry his own load 'round here. Ain't that right, boy?"

"Yes, boss," mumbled Simon.

"'Course, I won't be here to check your weight. So tell you what you do . . . see them six rows yonder?"

Simon squinted in the darkness. "Yes, boss."

"I get back in the mornin', you see to it them rows is picked clean. Understand me, boy?"

Hale's heart sank at the thought of it, but Simon simply said, "Yes, boss," and shuffled toward the first row.

It began to rain again.

Simon had no last name, no possessions except his shirt and trousers, no memory of anything but planting and picking in these fields, and no hope. He did not know how many years he had lived in that way. He marked the passing of time throughout his life not in terms of days, or in births or deaths or marriage, but in terms of the extremely rare events that had kept him from the fields. A cyclone in his early years that lifted a mule clean up over the levee and knocked an overseer senseless with a flying shovel. A season when the rains fell for three weeks straight and the cotton rotted on the stems, leaving the slaves with nothing to do but hoe it under. Another when there was no rain, and the swamp had fallen so far the irrigation pumps would not work, and they had watered the fields with wooden buckets, carried from the far side of the levee at the cost of punishing labor. Up and over with empty buckets and then back over and down again with full ones, a thousand times a day. It was the one time in Simon's memory when field slaves had been allowed to climb the levees. Everyone had been terrified. Everyone knew about the horrors waiting for them outside the safety of those looming dikes. From time immemorial, tales had been told of the utter wasteland just beyond the trees, the vast emptiness that would swallow you completely and leave no sign of your passing. The few who had gone over the hill had never returned, and Simon had no illusions about their fate. If a better world lay beyond the levees, as foolish people sometimes whispered, where then was the proof? Why had no one ever returned to tell them so? And why did the overseers single out the old ones

who could no longer work and the stubborn ones who no
longer feared the whip to send beyond the hill? Simon had
known many overseers in his day, and not one of them would
reward the weak or rebellious with a better life. They pun-
ished them instead by sending them outside. They stripped
them naked and drove them out into the nothingness and
gave their clothes to someone else. Many had begged to stay,
but once they had gone, none had found their way back, alive
or otherwise. Nothing good could lie beyond these fields.

Yet Simon sometimes thought about the deceptive
beauty he had seen on the other side during that one dry
season. Quivering with fear, he had dipped his bucket into
the water many times before he found the courage to lift his
eyes and peer between the trees. He remembered seeing
shade out there, and trees that continued on forever, and
wispy clothlike moss clinging to the branches with birds flying back and forth, and something quiet rippling through
the water and green plants floating with white and yellow
blossoms, and sunshine streaming through the shadows the
way he had seen it do inside his shack one day when he was
too sick for picking and they had let him stay there in the
daytime. He remembered how the swamp had seemed
almost comfortable, reminding him of that luxurious day
inside his shack, and how he had felt drawn by a strange,
familiar feeling. He remembered one brief moment when
he had forgotten his horror amidst thoughts of how simple
it would be to drop his bucket and wade away; just walk away
through the water into that cool place between the trees
where the sun didn't seem so hot and the land shifted and
changed as if it were alive instead of fixed in one straight
row after another, and there would be no one to drive him
through the day and no one to fight for a place to lie down
at night. They said that nothing lived out there beyond the

levees, but Simon could have sworn it looked like the perfect place to live.

Now, shaking his head, Simon picked on in the darkness and the rain, feeling for the bolls as best he could. There was no sense in thinking of such things. That moment had been many seasons past, and over in an instant. He had climbed the levee with a bucketful of water and poured it out between the rows and, by the time he had returned outside, all he saw beyond the hill was the emptiness he expected. That was all he saw because that was all there was: the field, the cotton, the endless cycle of planting and picking, and the wall around his world that kept the empty outside world at bay. On good days there were full bellies. On bad days there was hunger or the whip. Anything beyond that was a lie for fools.

Simon reached the end of the first row. He paused to adjust the strap upon his shoulder. After so many seasons, the callus there had become very thick. He gave no thought to this, no thought to the aching muscles in his back, no thought to the new pain in his chest. Life was pain. But for the last few days he had sensed a strange weakness coming on. Coming to get him. He had no doubt it was an enemy. Weakness was the end of life, and life was all he had, pain and all. The weakness seemed to fill him like the water in those buckets long ago, making all the parts of him heavier and more difficult to move. His arms felt like stones, his legs extensions of the earth. Even breath came harder these days. Like the bucket, he had an iron band around his middle.

He had finished just one row and knew he must turn around and go back, picking all the way, but he did not think it possible. Still, he had to try. So he wiped the rain from his eyes and shuffled around the last plant in the row and bent to start along the other side. Working by touch alone in the rain and darkness, his heavy hands searched the first plant for bolls.

They had been picked clean.

He must have made a mistake. Maybe he was turned around; maybe the rows he had to pick were on the other side of where he started. Remaining bent at the waist to avoid the pain of standing straight, Simon hobbled back the way he'd come. Yet the cotton had been stripped from those rows, too. He felt his way in the night, checking the first six rows in both directions, touching the plants from top to bottom all along the way. He found no cotton left at all. He set out toward the wagon across the field, pausing many times to touch the plants, refusing to believe what his callused hands told him, but it was undeniable. Someone had picked every speck of cotton on every row.

Once at the wagon, Simon emptied his tow sack into the bed and hung it on a peg. He then headed for his squalid shack, struggling past row after long straight row of the massive cotton field, thinking about that cool place he once saw away outside the levees and between the trees. He made it to the open area in front of the shacks, where he found Newboy standing, chains around his ankles, ignoring the rain, waiting up for him. As he approached, Newboy came close and wrapped a thin blanket around his shoulders. The blanket felt dry in spite of the rain. With the younger man's help Simon staggered toward his own shack, the place where he had slept among half a dozen other men since before he could remember. The stranger stood aside to let him enter through the narrow door. Once inside, Simon leaned against the wall, too tired and weak to lie down.

"I thank you for what you done," he said.

"Well," said the stranger, "you should also thank the Lord."

In that moment it occurred to Simon that this stranger was the only man who ever came in from over the hill, instead of disappearing out the other way. Why had he not considered that before? He thought of nothing else while the man gripped him gently around the waist, took his weight and settled him down to the hard earthen floor, and from somewhere in the shadows brought him hot okra, skillet bread, and a gourd filled with rainwater. The man waited while he ate and afterward helped him to lie down on his back, covered him with the blanket, and then rose up to leave, his chains clinking all the while.

Ignoring the chains, for they were clearly of no account, Simon said, "Why you stay here, a man like you?"

Newboy paused, looked back. "It's not time to go yet."

So he *would* go! A lightness lifted Simon then, a lightness he had not felt since that moment years before when he saw the cool place out beyond the levees. "Will you take me with you?"

"What makes you think I could?"

Inspired to foolishness by the feeling of lightness, Simon laid a hand upon the stranger's foot, entreating him. Somehow, Simon felt this man's presence in a different way from all the others; he felt more connected to the stranger than to anyone else, even those he had known all his life. The stranger was completely present with him, not just partway there but completely in their moment together, as if all the fear and pain that separated people could simply be ignored, leaving nothing between the two of them but the skin around their bones.

"You can do anything," said Simon, convinced it was true.

Newboy looked down and Simon saw his face change, the openness disappearing behind a proud mask like all the others wore. The lightness Simon felt vanished then, like his youth, for Simon was certain that in asking to go with the stranger he had asked too much. No one with a face as proud as that would bother with an old fool, and when the stranger finally answered, "Yes, you can come with me. Everyone can come," Simon knew it was nothing but a pleasant lie.

14

When the sun came up, it kept on raining. Hale Poser and all the others greeted it with gladness, lounging on the ground inside their shacks, nibbling on hardtack, laughing and joyful at the prospect of a day without labor. But the overseer came anyway, high astride his gelding in an oilskin slicker with the water streaming from his hat's broad brim. He called them out and led them to the cotton wagon. There they took up their sacks and went into the field, all of them looking down to keep the rain out of their eyes, soaked to the skin and muddy to their knees. Everybody knew it was madness. You couldn't pick cotton in the rain. It would rot before it hit the hoppers. You couldn't weigh it. It came apart in your hand when you pulled it from the boll. It stuck to everything. But no one was brave enough or foolish enough to say as much, so they bent meekly down between the rows.

Hale Poser stayed close to Simon. He had prayed for the old man's health throughout the night, and sure enough, this morning Simon moved easier. Hale was proud of forsaking sleep in order to pick the other rows for the old man, feed him, and later pray for him. When the overseer passed

Simon by with a barely perceptible nod, Hale felt personally responsible for the old man's reprieve. But he gave glory to God anyway, as was his habit.

Moving side by side across the field, both of them did their best to pluck the cotton from the bolls. It mostly slipped through their fingers when they pulled, or stuck to their trousers when they tried to pass it back. The rain had beaten some of the lint to the ground in the night. Hale and Simon scooped it up and passed it back as well. Muddy as it was, no one would notice.

After an hour or so, Simon spoke without looking up. "Marah said she saw you stop the storm the other evenin'." Nodding at the old woman picking a few yards ahead of them and four rows over, Simon added, "She don't generally lie."

" 'Course not."

"So you stop the storm?"

"Yes."

It occurred to Hale that he should explain a little more—tell Simon it was God who stopped the storm and not him, exactly—yet as he debated about how to word it, Simon moved a few steps ahead and began picking faster, and once the moment had passed it did not seem an important enough distinction to bother closing the distance. The thing was forgotten twenty minutes later when Hale caught up with the old man at the end of the row. Dragging sacks only halfway full but already weighed down more with water and mud than if they had been dry and overflowing, the two of them walked several rows down, bypassing Marah's row and the rows being picked by High and Low and Qana and several others, and started back toward the other side together. The rain beat straight down all the while, turning the furrows between the cotton plants into little black rivers. The mud squeezed up between Hale's toes and clung to his

heels and to the chain between his ankles. His feet made a
sucking sound every time he hauled them up from the
quagmire. Bent over double, plucking at bolls with both
hands, he watched as a small green frog swam along in front
of him, maintaining the same distance no matter how fast
he worked the row. Someone started singing away off somewhere. Others took up the tune little by little, and eventually
Simon and Hale joined in. The rain beat staccato time on
the cotton leaves. As he had so many times before, Hale
sang the words he knew, which were altogether different
from those sung by the others. They sang of sunshine; he
sang of mercy. They sang of food; he sang of grace. They
sang of a nameless someone; he sang of the Lord God
Almighty. The only things their competing versions agreed
upon were the little words between the big ones, and the
fact that they were all singing about freedom, of a kind.

He caught Marah staring at him from a couple of rows
over. She quickly dropped her eyes. Things had not been
the same with her since the day she asked if God was white,
or maybe since the night he calmed the storm. A distance
had spread out between them, as if she thought he was
above her somehow, high and mighty like a boss. Hale
glanced over at Simon. Unlike Marah, the old man met his
eyes. He did not seem to mind the words Hale sang. In fact,
when Simon fell silent now and then, Hale could have sworn
it was to listen. He smiled and scooped a cluster of waterlogged cotton up from the mud and sang a little louder.

Hale lost himself in the words, praising his creator, feeling his heart rise up and up, forgetting the fire in his back
and shoulders. Hale felt overwhelmed with a wonderful
sense of power. He was a miracle worker, after all; he knew
it for a fact. Filled with joy he sang and sang and sang some
more, dreaming of a glorious God, a mighty God who
roared with thunder and blazed with lightning, a blinding

God who was every color that there is, even if that didn't suit old Marah, and then the overseer was upon him, ramming him with his horse. Hale scrambled in the mud to avoid the great beast's pounding hoofs as the whip lashed out and the handsome man cursed and shouted, "Shut up, boy! Didn't I say *shut up?*" Hale realized then that no one else was singing. More than that, a foreign sound touched his ears, an engine of some kind lumbering in the distance. The other overseer had already ridden to the top of the levee to stare down at the far side with his cold gray eyes, his rifle ready in his hands, with everyone standing silently among the rows in the straight-down pounding rain, holding their breaths without knowing why. Hale began to pray for them all, and then . . .

. . . the fields around him disappeared—the levees, the sky, as well as all the people—until there was nothing but the Voice that bid him close his eyes to see. He thought to ask how that could be, but then remembered he had lost his life to find it, and the least would be the greatest, and so he did as he was told.

The vision he was shown was awful, yet he was not afraid.

Joy and sadness filled him, and in the instant that he wondered how his heart could hold them both at once, he forgot to wonder as the vision was already over and . . .

. . . Hale was in the field again, shaking from head to toe. The joy and sadness faded, the sound of engines faded, and the hard-eyed boss rode down from the levee and spoke briefly with the handsome boss, and they put the slaves to work again as if nothing strange had happened.

But everyone knew different. The overseers moved restlessly up and down between the rows, casting glances at the levee. Three times they ascended to the top to gaze out at the swamp again. Meanwhile Hale Poser struggled with his burdens. The tow sack weighed him down, the mud pulled at his feet, and his wet clothes chafed him terribly. All this took an earthly toll he had not expected, having never picked cotton in the rain before. But to such an important man—to a miracle worker, and now a prophet—these earth-bound torments were merely a distraction from far weightier concerns. Hale Poser dared not look up from his picking for fear his face might shine like that of Moses.

Then, just once, he hoped it did, so everyone would see.

Immediately he chastised himself. As his fingers busied themselves with the bolls he shook his head to clear it and willed himself to beg forgiveness. Pride had no place in this, or in any other thing of God. To wish for recognition . . . he should be ashamed even to think it.

Yet had the Lord not spoken to him, just as he once spoke to Abraham and Moses? What was the point in receiving such a vision if he did not stand before the people and say the words, "I speak for God Almighty"? And as for pride, if speaking for the Lord was not something to be proud of, nothing was. Being singled out this way was an unfamiliar thrill—unfamiliar because he was not accustomed to thinking of himself as an exceptional man. Indeed, he was not accustomed to thinking of himself at all.

And with that realization, suddenly he knew why he had been chosen.

He had not asked to be a miracle worker. It had never crossed his mind. He had not even recognized the miracles he worked until others praised him for them, and he certainly never dreamed the Lord would pick him as a prophet. Like Moses, Hale Poser was perhaps the humblest man on earth. Now came this unexpected power: praying for deliverance one second, rising up to heaven the next, the vision coming awful and glorious and leaving him a prophet on the order of the patriarchs. Most men who heard God's voice had fallen on their faces, yet here he was after such a fearful message, on his feet, picking cotton. So he was not just any prophet. Like Moses of the Bible, he could stand before the Lord.

Oh, how that idea comforted! He allowed himself to dream of the greatness his humility had wrought, and the dream obscured the horror of the vision he had seen—of levees crashing down and a wall of water rushing in, everyone adrift with sightless eyes. He immersed himself in dreaming of his greatness, for only in those dreams could he ignore the echo of the Voice that had revealed the horror, even as it whispered, *"I am more than the red of sunsets. I am more than the green of fields. I am more than the blue of the sky. I am more than the white of lightning. I am more than every color that there is, because I am also less. I am the black of the mud beneath your feet."*

15

In the dark and rain, Marah, Moses, and Simon walked back toward the shacks, following a well-worn muddy path beside the levee. Just ahead of them walked High and Low.

"What was that sound?" whispered Low.

"Some kinda gator, I 'spect," said High.

Moses said, "It was an engine."

Marah had no idea what he meant, and feared to ask.

"Engine?" asked Low, testing the word. "They have big teeth?"

Moses opened his mouth to explain, then closed it again and walked on in silence. Marah figured he was too tired to talk. That was good and bad. Part of Marah wanted Low to ask more questions about the engine, but another part was frightened of the answers. Her Moses had learned many fearful things, and there was already enough fear here inside the levees. No reason to go looking for new monsters on the outside.

After a few more steps, Low said, "You see how it scared the boss?"

"Uh-huh," said High.

"Sounded terrible big." Eyes wide and showing lots of white, Low stared up the hill. "Awful glad for the levee this evenin'."

Feeling a sudden chill, Marah crossed her arms close to her chest. She refused to look up the hill.

When they reached the little cluster of shacks at the edge of the field, everyone fanned out. High, Low, and Simon went to their shack together, and Marah entered hers, which was already filled with women. No one thought of cooking. Where would they find dry wood? Most had small supplies of vegetables and bread that could be eaten cold, but it was a meager meal indeed to follow such a day. Marah lay within the dark interior, feeding goat milk to the baby drop by drop and chewing silently on a piece of yam, too exhausted to dry herself.

Meanwhile the rain held steady, drumming on the palmetto fronds above, streaming down to find its way through the gaps in the walls and trickling in tiny rivulets across the earthen floor. Now and then a distant roll of thunder filled Marah with dread. She cuddled closer with the baby. She knew where the big noise came from. Her father had explained this to her long ago, when she was little. He said something huge and angry hovered away up in the air, trying to see down. Because it could not see through the dark gray clouds, it threw those spears of light. He had warned her not to go outside when the big noise and the light spears came, because the Angry One might hurt her. But now she thought of Moses, the way he had walked right into the storm and raised his face and spoken, and the way the big noise had gone quiet and the light spears had stopped coming. She wondered what it meant that he did not seem to fear the huge and angry thing above the clouds, or anything else for that matter. As Marah lay upon the hard-packed soil and fed the baby and slowly chewed her bit of yam, she pondered this and wondered if her father had been wrong to say the one above the clouds was angry. Maybe the one up there was only lonely and making a blustering fool of itself, like Qana sometimes did.

The distant thunder rumbled again. Or was it thunder? No, that sound was different. Laying the baby in her basket, Marah crawled to the doorway and peeked outside. Sure enough, there stood Moses, out in the storm, in the dark, unafraid. Looking at him, pride bubbled up and over in her. He wasn't afraid of the thunder. He wasn't afraid of anything, standing out there, holding a shovel upside down in one hand and something else in the other—a rock, maybe—something he was beating against the shovel, making a horrible racket.

"What you doing?" she called. Marah wanted to tell him who she was but had decided to hold it back inside against a better day.

"Come out here," he hollered back. Raising his voice even louder, he shouted, "Everyone come out!" As he beat the shovel, other people came to the doors of their shacks. "Come out! Come out!" shouted Moses, and they all did. Soon Marah and the others were standing in the rain, all of them forming a circle around him, Marah standing the closest, and him looking at her, saying, "I have something important to tell you."

"Me too," she said.

Ignoring her, he raised his voice so every slave could hear. "There's something you all need to know." Some of them stood talking to each other, paying him no mind. Marah wished they would be quiet. Then the Angry One above the clouds threw a light spear down, and Moses's wet face shone like silver for an instant, and a roar of thunder silenced one and all. When the only sound remaining was the hard slap of the raindrops hitting home, Moses said,

"This storm will not stop. It's going to keep on raining for days. The swamp outside will rise, and we will work the pumps but it won't be enough. The water will come down over the levees and all of this will be destroyed. But don't worry. I will lead you out before that happens."

If Marah had not just been thinking of the time when he calmed the storm, she would have laughed. Even with that amazing memory fresh in her mind, she had to wonder how—

"How you know all that?" shouted someone from the back. Marah recognized Qana's voice, echoing her thoughts.

He lifted his chin a little, looking proud. "The Lord spoke to me."

"This the lord you singin' 'bout all the time?" Qana stepped from behind the crowd into the open circle at the center. He did not face her Moses but turned back toward the others when he asked, "How come he told you this and not one of us?"

"I don't know."

"Was because this lord talk the white man talk, like you. Ain't that right?"

"What does that mean?"

"You gonna act the fool now? Pretend you don't know nothin'?"

"God has given me a vision."

"Why you?"

"I know him."

"Maybe we do, too," Qana said. "What his name?"

"He has a lot of names. I call him Jesus."

This sounded familiar to Marah, though she could not remember why. She watched as Qana cocked his head. "Jesus ... jesus. Ain't I heard that somewheres? Oh, I remember ... boss man like to shout it when he whip us. 'Jesus christ,' he say. 'How come you niggers is so lazy?'"

Several in the crowd made noises of assent. Yes, that was it. Marah had heard that word once, long ago in her Moses days, and it had seemed a comfort, but ever since she had heard it in a different way, exactly as Qana said, and she had learned to think of *jesus* as an insult. Now Qana turned to face Moses, looming over him in the dark. "You 'spect us to believe what this Jesus tol' you 'bout the rain?"

Moses's eyes went wide. "He would never lie."

"He don't lie? Well, all the white folk lie, so he must be a black fella." Qana smiled wickedly. "That right?"

Marah watched Moses carefully. It was the question she had asked him in the field before, put a different way. She had been thinking about it since then, allowing herself to remember all those things she had worked so hard to forget, and she now remembered just a little more about this Jesus. She had seen him in a picture in that other place so long ago, a picture of a man upon a tree, and she was almost sure he had been white. She had dreamed of nailing all white men to trees, of lining the swamp with them, of plagues of boils and locusts and all the white men's firstborn children, dead, even if she had to lose her own firstborn to make it happen. She had cherished those dreams inside herself, even as she herself had suffered plagues of other kinds. But for reasons Marah did not understand, now she dreamed of something different, perhaps better. And as if he could hear her thoughts like the bosses, Moses looked at her.

He said, "Jesus used to be one of us."

Marah leaned forward, breathless. Even Qana seemed surprised. "If that true, how come he know about the rain?"

"Because he made the rain."

Qana laughed. "Nigger," he said, "you crazy."

"He did!" said Moses. "Jesus made everything. Before there was anything else, he was here. He made the whole world." Moses lifted both his arms, palms up toward the pitch-black sky. "The rain . . . the cotton, the soil and swamp out there, and you and me and everything."

Qana paused, pretending to think about it. "How 'bout the white folk? He make them, too?"

"He made everyone, every color—"

Oh no, thought Marah. Please don't say that *every color* foolishness again. Please don't tell us that.

"—because every color is in him. But he saw how bad things are down here, how we ruined things, so he came down to help us."

"Ol' Every Color come right down?" laughed Qana, strutting in front of his audience, seeing the same foolishness in this story that Marah did. "That must of been a sight. Him all prettied up, like the rainbow."

No, she thought. He ain't no rainbow. He's the white lightning and the blindness that it brings. He's a horrible thing, away up high and angry.

Then Moses looked in Marah's eyes as if the space between them were not there, and she was certain yet again that he could hear her inside words because she saw something changing in his eyes, as if he knew her all at once, and she thought, that's right. I'm her. I'm the one who gave you up for miracles and plagues. And as he looked at her he said, "Jesus came down here so we could see how much he loves us and believe him when he says we can all be free."

"Free?" shouted Qana. "*Free?* It don't look to me like we free!"

"You don't know him yet."

"And *you* do? I seen the boss whip you just like anyone else. You got it *worse* than anyone else! You a fool, boy. Standin' here with them chains around your ankles, talkin' 'bout *free.*"

"In Jesus' world you can be free inside yourself, no matter what they do."

Marah felt a pull at something in her chest, as though the words were drawing her outside herself. That Jesus world sounded fine, and she somehow knew if she could have just one moment of silence, just one minute to think, she would find her way to something more powerful than the thunder and more beautiful than rainbows. But Qana would not stop his questions. He would not stop his strutting back and forth in her Moses's stolen shoes. He would not give her peace. He said, "So this *Jesus* tol' you we all gonna die down here? Water gonna rise an' we got to go before it do?"

"Yes."

"Where we gonna go?"

Moses waved an arm toward the levee. "Out there."

Someone in the crowd laughed, but Marah had the opposite reaction. She knew what was out there; she had seen it with her own eyes. She knew even this life here was better. And she was suddenly afraid.

Qana said, "Everyone know that ain't nothin' but a dyin' place."

"There are towns and people and wonderful things out there!"

Qana took a step closer to the stranger. "They let a nigger be, out there in this Jesus world of yours?"

Moses did not answer at first. When he did, he spoke softly, so she had some trouble hearing. What he said was, "Mostly."

"Mostly? We *mostly* get along here, too. Long as we gets up in the mornin' and gets out to the field, *mostly* everyone gets by."

"It can be so much better than this."

Qana took another step toward Moses. Standing one pace away from him now, looking down at him, Marah feared he would strike Moses. But Qana left his fists at his sides and spoke instead in a booming voice for everyone to hear. "You look me in the eye and tell me all the white folk out there in that Jesus world, they *do* let a nigger be. Tell me all the niggers in your Jesus world got nobody beatin' on them, and everybody just think nice things all day long. Tell me they free on they inside *and* they outside. Swear to that, an' I'll go with you." He looked around at the crowd. "We'll *all* go with you!"

Many people mumbled words of assent, and Marah knew she would gladly forget her past and abandon the present if she could go to such a world. Her imagination whirled with visions of dry roofs, of sitting in one spot all day long, and shoes, and a new place inside herself where fear and anger did not live. Her heart beat fast as Moses opened his mouth to answer, this wise Moses so filled with all that he had learned beyond the levees. . . . But then he closed his mouth and stared down at the mud between his feet and in the end said nothing.

Qana shouted, "Answer me! You say this Jesus gonna make us free out there! Are the niggers out there really free?"

Why don't you answer? wondered Marah, still longing to go with him to that place of rainbows, of every color that there is, even willing to abandon the sweet succor of revenge if she could only get to such a place.

But her Moses seemed to shrink where he stood, mute and down-looking while everybody stared. Then Qana spat into the mud and strode into the darkness. The others followed him in twos and threes until only Marah remained, trying to recapture that sense of being on the verge of something fresh and clean, but the only hope she could recall was a black child in a pirogue and a forest filled with white men hanging on the trees.

16

All was rain, rain and rain. For the next two days it dropped straight down without pause through the motionless air. Beaten off the branches by the deluge, more cotton now lay brown and sodden in the mud than remained within the bolls. Rainwater in the furrows formed unbroken quicksilver rows reflecting pale gray clouds. The bosses had given up on the harvest at last and set the slaves to a new kind of labor. Armed with hoes and shovels, they passed among the rows in two lines, one behind the other. The first line chopped at the cotton stalks with hoes, felling the plants. The second line followed, turning the cotton under with shovels. The water stood up to their ankles in places. Mud clung to the hoes and shovels and had to be scraped off after every thrust into the earth. It was slow work, but no one was in a hurry and no one complained. This was easy compared to picking. They could stand up straight and flex their bodies instead of working bent at the waist all day until they felt their bones would twist them down forever. Also, everybody knew each thrust of the hoe or shovel cost the bosses dearly. It was a pleasurable thought.

Hale Poser was given a shovel and put in the second line. He worked steadily and kept his mouth shut, even when the others sang. Old Simon told an amusing story, making fun of the bosses. When the others laughed loudly, Hale Poser did not smile. Later, when Marah came along with the water bucket, she served the slaves to his right and to his left, but Hale shook his head without a word. Watching her slender back as she moved away, he thought about the brightness that arose in her eyes that night, and the way it had perished with Qana's question. He thought of Pilotville's two nearly identical churches, the way their images had silenced him, just as surely as a gag between the teeth. He had thought of nothing but his silence ever since. He awoke with the shame of it and bedded down with it and walked inside its shadow all day long. He had thought for two days straight without recollecting another moment when a pagan's objection had left him without words. Always before a guiding whisper had filled his mind, refreshing and comfortable, like the cool breeze of an electric fan on a sweltering day. But just as the steady hum of such machines was soon no longer truly heard, the whisper had receded to the background of his life, its recession going unnoticed until Qana had asked his question, and Hale had received no answer. The silence left him reeling.

He had been sent to this impossible place and given a vision to save these people. He could have run, but instead he was faithful and remained in this place, although he was not a part of it. Yet when it mattered most, the whisper had been silent, and he did not know why. He only knew he would not lie, not even to save these people.

Hale Poser slipped his shovel into the mud and turned the cotton under slowly, very slowly. Even Simon, old as he was, worked faster. Why should he hurry? As he had when he first set his hand to work these fields, he remembered

ancient words, written to believing slaves: "Whatsoever ye
do, do it heartily, as to the Lord, and not unto men." How
many times had he quoted those words to rows of wide-eyed
orphans sitting at their desks in the old mansion's ballroom?
Always he had spoken of the character those words instilled,
of the fact that they had not been easy words to write
because the author was himself imprisoned when he wrote
them, and therefore no stranger to the bondage of his read-
ers. But now, with the mud of an unknown master's field
rising to the chains at his ankles, Hale Poser had a new perspective. A prisoner's bonds might fall away one day, but
slavery was forever. You might could serve a prison guard
with all your heart who only robbed you of your time, but to
serve a slave driver who also stole your hope . . . that was a
different thing altogether.

Hale had never thought of those ancient words that way
before, and with that way of thinking, for the first time in
his memory, he doubted Scripture. Why should he work
with all his heart for these evil men, these sadistic bosses?
Why serve them and their kind, who had corrupted all that
was beautiful in life? He would speak no more easy words to
these modern slaves because he knew the hopelessness of
this place was not bounded by the levees. He thought of
every time he had stepped down from a sidewalk to the
filthy gutter while a white man passed him by, of sleeping on
the ground with a pocketful of money because no rooming
house had beds for colored folk, of eating standing up
beside an empty table when the colored seats were full, of
white youngsters calling him "boy" when he was twenty
years their senior, of carrying water to the park in a pickle
jar because drinking fountains were forbidden, of lynchings
for nothing more than speaking to a white woman, of chain
gangs filled with Negroes when white men paid a fine, of
sharecropping land there was no hope of owning, and a

thousand other insults and atrocities out beyond these fields.

He had always hoped to someday find a place of refuge from the unnaturally divided world, a place where love drew everyone together, just as God had promised. He had dared believe such a refuge might be a house of worship, where true believers of every kind clung together rather than stood apart, where love salved the wounds inflicted on the outside and all God's people formed a single family, with Jehovah as their Father and Jesus as their brother. A place where the resentment of the Negro and the white man's guilty conscience might both ease down together on the steady shoulders of the Lord Almighty. Growing up in New Orleans, he had never seen this kind of paradise. Then he had come to Pilotville, searching for his parents, and the first person he encountered was Jean Tibbits, a kindly white man at the docks who would do a colored man's work to offer sympathy, and the next thing he discovered was an infirmary for Negroes built by Papa DeGroot, another kindly white man. He had seen Negroes and whites gathered together around a common checkerboard, trading jokes and good-natured insults and speaking of important things without any regard for color, and he had thought, at last, this is the place. And so he had gone to church with renewed hope, but found only Negroes there, and white folks elsewhere—exactly as it was every other place in this split asunder world—and although men of every color shared work and sport and whisky, incredibly, God's own house remained the final refuge of the Fall.

Hale drove his shovel into the mud, taking his time, glad to destroy the white men's crop, but unwilling to do even that any faster than he must. His own weight pushed him down into the mud, clear down to the iron bands around his ankles. He had never noticed his own gravity before.

There had always been a buoyancy to him, something that was now lost along with the blindness of his faith. Why did God allow these divisions to continue? He had prayed so earnestly back in Pilotville, prayed to draw the saints together. Even then, before he understood he was a prophet, he had known they should be unified. But his faith had been unequal to the task. A few moments when all believers sang together, or when all pastors preached the same sermon, were not enough. If these people, these slaves, were to follow him and live, he needed a much bigger miracle. He needed to create a world out there where they could go.

Was that possible?

In spite of their anger and their ridicule, in spite of the weight of his loneliness, even in spite of these unfamiliar doubts—or perhaps because of them—Hale resolved to work a miracle. As the scowling clouds darkened with the setting sun, he hoped he still had faith enough, and framed his hopes in terms of Marah, the only one who seemed ready to believe. Sometimes in the Bible, miracles depended on the faith of those they touched. He tried to envision it, to see how it would be in order to find courage enough to try.

She would be lying in her shack. She would take a tiny bite of hardtack and chew it slowly, drawing it out, making it last. She would hear something . . . no, she would smell something in the air. Smoke? Yes, woodsmoke. Hale thought of the burning bush, and smiled as he idly pushed his shovel through the mud. Smoke and fire where none should be. That was it. She would assume someone had built a fire inside their doorway with a little dry kindling stored away, deciding a hot meal was worth putting up with tearful eyes and ticklish lungs from the smoke. She would envy whoever had built the fire, because all too soon her small piece of bread would be gone.

Hale paused in his labors and raised his eyes to seek out Marah in the field. There she was, a hundred yards away, chopping slowly with a hoe. He frowned at the sight of her, a child of God, a slave. But surely not much longer. Surely God would not punish her for his own weakness, not when he was ready to prove his faith this way. He thought of her tonight, finished with her meal, smelling smoke. She would decide it was time to milk the goat. James and Rosa Lamont's baby would be crying with an empty belly, and heaven knows the women in Marah's shack would not put up with that. So Marah would rise, take a bowl for milking and pause before the door, staring out into the rain. She would wonder at the strangeness of this rain. It went on and on . . . never faster, never slower, seldom any lightning or thunder, just strong, steady rain coming down so straight it hung beyond her doorway like a curtain. She would wrap her arms across her chest to clutch her elbows for warmth as he had seen her do so many times, and she would step outside. The rain would hit her neck and roll down her back. She would not try to miss the puddles as she walked, for the puddles were everywhere, and getting deeper. She would wade right through, following the beaten path along the front of the shacks, heading for the small pen back behind. She would not look up, since she knew the way so well there was no need, and besides, holding her head down, facing the ground, was the best way to avoid the pounding rain. So when she raised her eyes, she would already be very near the fire that Hale would build.

Now Hale's frown disappeared as he watched her chopping cotton over across the field. He smiled at the thought of Marah seeing the fire roaring and dancing with life as if celebrating something joyful. He thought of what he would look like to her, standing there on the other side, gazing into a pot that hung above the flames. The warm light would bathe his features with a yellow glow. His skin would glisten. He would take care to stand perfectly still as the rain, falling into the flames, crackled and rose again in waves of steam that almost hid him from her sight. Marah might think he was a vision. She might think the fire a vision, too. She would certainly wonder how anyone could build a fire in such a downpour. How would you get the first tiny flame to catch and hold? Where would you get dry wood? She would consider such a thing impossible. Yet there it would be—there he would be, a miracle man— somehow.

And she would wonder, how?

And, believing, she would come closer.

The warmth of the flames would caress her, make her feel almost comfortable again. When she stepped into the circle of firelight, he would pretend she had only then attracted his attention. He would act as if such miracles were nothing much, just to make it all seem easy. He would look up at her across the fire and smile, just exactly as he smiled at her now.

As if in confirmation of Hale's fantasy, Marah turned. There in the field they stared at each other through the rain, Marah with that strange expression he had seen before, as if she wanted to tell him something but did not dare, and Hale thinking that his first words when he spoke to her across the fire would be simple. "Do you want some stew?" Not mentioning the miracle of the fire, as though it were a normal thing. She would kneel and dip a wooden bowl into the pot, and she would bring it up rich with vege- tables and meat and smelling of heaven. She would watch him over the edge of the bowl as he turned from the fire and went to the nearest shack, stuck his head inside and

called, "Hey! Got some stew out here for them that wants
it."

Now, here in this field, thinking of how fine it would be
when everybody understood the kind of man he was, Hale
waved at Marah. She clutched her hoe with both hands and
did not return his wave, but in the shifting of her chin he
could see that she definitely wanted to tell him something.
Well, tonight she would have her chance. The stew that he
would serve would be like manna from heaven, like fishes
and loaves on a hillside. It would have a peculiar, delicate
flavor. She would hold it in her mouth and sigh with pleasure as she watched him moving to the next shack and the
next, poking his head in each one and offering invitations
to come and eat. She would wonder what he was thinking.
She would see the pot was far too small for everyone. It
would hold enough for maybe six or eight at most. But
many more than that would come, clutching bowls made
from gourds or hollowed out from logs. Marah would rise to
give them room, and they would cluster round the pot. In
Hale's imagination, nobody would push or shove. Everyone
would make room for those who came behind. Even Qana
would wait his turn. Hale would stand on the far side of the
fire, and steam would rise and fall in waves, and he would
watch the others dip their gourds and bowls. Sometimes the
steam would almost obscure him. Sometimes it would part
and Marah would see him clearly. The others would not
notice that he did not eat. Only one or two would thank him
as they passed along beside the pot. He, of course, would
not care about their selfishness. He would smile at one and
all with brotherly love and true humility.

Now, across the field, Marah turned back to her chopping. Apparently catching him staring had made her angry,
for she brought the hoe down harder than before. Hale saw
the handsome boss look his way, and so resumed his work,

lethargically flipping half a shovelful of mud over a cotton plant as his imagination whirled with wonders to perform.

Eventually, just as Marah would question the fire blazing in the rain, she would begin to ask herself why the pot had not been emptied. There would be so many people, and some would take two helpings, yet each hand that dipped a bowl into that pot would raise it up again filled to the brim. She would consider explanations. Could he have refilled it in an instant of concealment by the rising steam? Could anyone move that quickly? If so, where did he hide the raw materials? There would be no pile of logs waiting for the flames. And the fire . . . No longer would she marvel that the fire had been started in this rain. She instead would marvel that it kept on burning, because through it all the air would still be filled with falling water, as it was now. She would know a fire could never burn in such a rain. She would know a pot could never feed so many. But in spite of all her knowing, she would believe. Then her belief would fuel the fire and they would all believe, and by believing, escape the impending flood. Oh, it was a fine thing to work miracles. A powerful thing.

In his excitement Hale began to pray, and forgetting himself, he worked at his usual enthusiastic pace, outpacing those to the left and right, almost catching up with Marah's group before the glowering clouds faded at last and the handsome overseer called them in to line up in the dark at the wagon to return their tools and then slog along the path beside the levee, toward another sleepless night of cold food and relentless drips and trickles.

In the shack they shared, Qana ignored him as usual and ate all the bread they had. Hale sat in a dry place, leaned against the rough-sawn planks of the wall at his back, and continued praying, on and on. Sometimes he moved his lips to the words in his head but never gave them voice, for he knew that was something the massive man across the shack would not abide. When Qana started snoring, the time felt right. Still praying, Hale Poser stirred himself and hobbled outside in his chains to build the fire. He found three small logs and placed them crossways in a puddle on the ground. One for the Father. One for the Son. One for the Holy Ghost. He had no idea how the fire would start. He had no idea where to find ingredients for the stew. He proudly left such details to the Lord, knowing the waterlogged wood and empty pot would be enough. Kneeling awkwardly in his chains and in the ceaseless rain he bowed his head beside the sacred logs. He prayed for a miracle greater than a shower of persimmons on a metal drum, or his own arms spread wide between two churches in perfect harmony, or an unborn baby moving suddenly beneath his palms, or a resurrected blackbird flying up from those same hands, or a savage boar drawn in from the wilderness. He prayed for a miracle greater even than the thunder and the lightning in obedience to him, and after he had knelt and prayed that way for many hours, Hale Poser did indeed receive a revelation. He began to understand that he did not stand in a line of prophets extending all the way back to loaves and fishes and the burning bush. Hungry orphan that he was, Hale Poser's legacy had begun with birthrights abandoned beside another pot of stew, for although he prayed with all his might, no miracle occurred.

17

Newboy!'' shouted the handsome one, away up on his gelding. "Get over here!"

If there was still a sun above the looming clouds it shed no cheer as Hale Poser shuffled across the field, taking care not to step too freely and by so doing wrench the iron bands into the naked flesh at his ankles. Dragging his shovel behind and avoiding the sharply broken cotton stalks poking through the mud, he did not so much as glance at the others he passed along the way. In the week since his failed miracle, he had spoken to no one. He worked lethargically, drank little and ate less, visibly losing weight with each passing day. Some of the older ones whispered fearful things about him, speculating that he was cursed somehow, that this slow collapse into himself would end in his complete disappearance. They warned each other not to stand too close, lest they be caught up in his doom.

Hale Poser neared the monster on the horse. Halting just a few feet away, he said, "Yes, boss?" and waited numbly in the rain, eyes low.

"Follow me, boy."

Boy.

There it was.

Hale lifted his shovel a little, thinking violent things. He knew the others believed he had gone crazy, but they were wrong. Actually it was just the reverse. His thoughts had never been so clear. They consumed him, demanding everything. He had been thinking about violence, examining it with curiosity and reaching the conclusion it was something one should practice if one could, to get it right. He did not recall ever harming a man deliberately. He had always feared the Lord. But now the divine whisper had been silenced, and in the remaining void he recognized a righteous provocation for unfamiliar dreams of violence, of taking away the boss man's whip and rifle and imposing proper justice, of burying him in the mud of his own fields and so fertilizing the cotton with him. Strangely, these dreams were stirred by intellect, not by passion, and that fact made them all the more proper. Though he supposed he might feel something again one day, for now this numbness, this sense of distance, was all consuming. It lent a validity to his thoughts that he did not wish to lose.

So he coldly considered ripping his own shoes from Qana's feet and driving that insensible animal out of the shack into the unceasing rain. He thought of returning to Pilotville on a Sunday morning and driving out the hypocrites and burning their churches to the waterline. In Hale Poser's mind, these acts had somehow blended into one. But although he had lost the miracles, and with that loss had gone his fear of God and thus his fear of Christians with their white churches and their black ones, and although he had never really feared the overseers upon their horses (who at least were honest in their sin), Hale knew fearlessness was not enough. Just as he had not become a minister overnight, it would take time to learn how to do violence correctly. But with patience the learning would come, for here were expert teachers.

"Leave that shovel," said the white man, smiling just a little.

Hale said, "Yes, boss," and, dropping the shovel to the ground, set out behind the handsome man's horse. As he followed in the driving rain, the animal lifted its tail to defecate. Hale did not bother to walk around the mess, but shuffled barefoot right on through. What did it matter? Soil was soil when the whole earth opposed him.

The slave driver led him across the huge fields to the far end, away out beyond the cotton they had picked, toward a place where Hale had never been. They passed row upon row of limp plants lying ruined in the mud. Each and every one of them would be turned under by a slave. So many rows. So many thrusts of the shovel. Still, it was better than picking.

Without pausing at the levee on the far side, the white man drove his boots into the gelding's flanks and clambered up the hill. Hale followed as best he could. Like the horse, he sometimes slipped backward in the mud. Once he fell flat on his belly. Rising, it occurred to him that he was alone for the first time with the white man, the other slaves half a mile off, the other boss with them. Dispassionately he wondered what the handsome man had in mind. He began to wonder if violence would be necessary somewhat sooner than he had thought.

The boss waited at the top of the levee, his horse's nostrils flaring wide from the effort of the climb. "Hurry up!" he called, looking down.

"Yes, boss."

Covered head to foot with mud, Hale reached the top in spite of his chains. The boss nodded toward the outside of the levee and said, "Get down there." Walking to the other side Hale remembered what old Simon had said. No one ever came back from beyond the levee. It was where the bosses took slaves for whom they had no further use. He reached the far edge and looked down in the relentless rain to see the swamp had risen ten feet higher since his feverish arrival to this place. The floodwater was now more than half-way up the outside of the levee and climbing. Hale looked back across the fields at the distant rows of slaves steadily chopping cotton. This water was already far above their heads, and they did not know. Millions, no, billions of gallons of it, rising every moment, inching toward the top, where it would break through and rush down and no man, woman, or child would survive. So the vision had been true, at least. That horrible scene, his final word from God, was now almost upon them.

With that realization, something broke inside Hale Poser. Roaring with alien fury he charged the white man. Despite the chains, he reached the rider's side before the handsome man could react. He clawed at his leg with both hands, intent on dragging him down from his horse to lay him on the angry soil where he could stomp him with his bare feet and mix him with the hell he had created. But as he had suspected, he was inept at violence. The white man's oilskin slicker defied his grip, and the horse shied away from his sudden charge, rearing up to strike the air with its front hoofs, driving Hale back toward the outside edge of the levee, where he slipped and fell and slid on his belly down the slope, pursued by a cascade of mud and rainwater. He clutched wildly at the passing underbrush, flipping end over end and thinking—too late—of holding his breath as he sluiced toward the rising blackness of the swamp, where no light could ever follow. He hit feet first, and in the final instant tried to gulp in air but swallowed oozing earth instead as the chains at his ankles dragged him down and he tore at the embankment with widespread fingers.

Something loose and thin touched his flailing hand, then fell away. Desperate, he reached for it again. Blinded as he was by the water and the mud surging above him, it might have been a rope, a root, or for all he knew, maybe even a snake. He did not care but gripped and pulled with all his might, and up he went, filled with joy. He would live! Hallelujah! He would live!

His head rose up above the surface of the deluge, and he coughed up mud and sucked at the air widemouthed, like a grounded fish. Still clinging to the lifeline, he opened his eyes to see it was the thin end of the handsome one's whip, and full of wonder that such an evil man would save him, he closed his eyes again and all was sudden blackness.

Hale Poser came to consciousness belly down across the gelding's back, his hanging arms swaying with each rolling step of the horse, his head a rubber balloon about to burst, a box of angry scorpions, a sap-filled log crackling in the fire. He moaned, and the horse's motion stopped. The handsome man's well-made boots stepped into his downcast field of vision. Unseen hands grasped his shoulders, dragged him from the animal without warning and dropped him upon the muddy path, where he lay in a liquid heap as if he had been robbed of bones.

"Get up," said the handsome one. "You can walk."

Using the gelding's left hind leg for support, Hale fought his way to his feet. He blinked and looked ahead. Before them ran a narrow path. To the left, just inches below the top of the path, lay a limitless expanse of water, swirling around the uppermost branches of isolated treetops and extending out as far as he could see. Thousands of birds occupied the treetops, clothing them with constantly fluttering patches of white and black and pink. On the right, another path ran parallel to this one, no more than fifty feet away. Beyond this other path another ocean extended to the horizon. And between the twin paths—or levees, for such they were—was a swollen canal, its surface many feet below the floods on either side. He had seen such well-worn paths beside canals and bayous and rivers before, beaten into the earth by countless steps of mules and horses towing barges. Often the towpaths lay just beside the water, but sometimes they ran along the tops of levees exactly in this way. Clearly this canal was bordered by these levees for some distance, since the waterway below was flooded, but had not yet fully sought the level of the adjacent risen swamp. Lifting his eyes to look ahead, Hale saw the engorged canal aiming straight and true toward a building in the distance.

"Where we at, boss?" he asked.

"Shut up," came the answer as the handsome one mounted the horse.

Hale stumbled and almost fell at first, but soon his usual short-stepping rhythm settled in and he was able to proceed apace with the gelding's measured progress. The path was alive with animals desperate to escape the flood. More than once the gelding shied at the sudden motion of a nutria, beaver, raccoon, or possum as it burst from brushy cover upon their approach. Only the alligators did not bother to move, coldly taking Hale's measure as he passed. He ignored them, watching the mud at his feet instead for copperheads, coral snakes, and water moccasins. Now and then he lifted his eyes toward the structure up ahead. As they drew closer he made out wooden pilings standing in a row parallel to the side of a long, low building made of cypress and roofed with sheets of rusty steel. It had no windows or any other openings, except for a single pair of massive wooden doors facing the pilings. The floodwaters lapped against the building's wall, no doubt flooding the interior. A few of the pilings alongside the building showed signs of rough abuse and were encircled by thick ropes. As Hale and the handsome man drew closer he began to understand. This was a warehouse, and these pilings marked the edge of a submerged wharf. But look at the size of them! Surely oceangoing ships docked here.

Arriving at the section of levee immediately alongside the building, the slave driver spurred his gelding down the slope and coaxed it into the water. Hale remained at the top, watching until the white man turned and barked, "Come on, boy!" With tiny steps Hale descended the short incline. He paused at the water's edge, but one cold look from the overseer was enough to drive him down into the floodwater up to his waist; then the bottom leveled out and his feet found the submerged wooden planking of the wharf. The rain punched countless tiny circles in the muddy water all around them as the handsome man clucked his tongue to keep the nervous gelding moving, leading Hale along the flooded wharf, wading around the end of the building, and turning to proceed along its far side. Passing pilings on their right and the tall wall on their left, they felt their way forward for almost one hundred yards, reaching the far end of the warehouse at last. There, lashed between a pair of smaller pilings floated a handsome yacht about forty-five feet in length, with a sparkling white house running forward from amidships and a short signal mast with colors flying, and a raised box on the ample stern deck, which seemed to enclose an inboard engine. The overseer rode his horse right up alongside, swung sideways in his saddle and clambered over the low bulwark of the vessel, his well-made boots never touching the water. From aboard the boat he leaned back over the side to retrieve his whip and draw his rifle from its scabbard.

"Get the tack off my horse," he said, without sparing a

glance at Hale, "and pitch it in here."

Wading through slow-moving water up to his waist, Hale approached the nervous animal. He bent with his face an inch above the surface to reach under the horse's belly and release the saddle's buckles. The gelding rolled its eyes and laid its ears back flat as Hale gripped the saddle. "There, boy," said Hale, trying to soothe the beast. But as his left hand grasped the horn the horse shifted sideways, stepping too far in its fright and slipping off the unseen edge of the wharf. For a moment the animal's head plunged below the surface. Immediately it was up again, twice as frightened as before. On board the boat the white man cursed as Hale reached to grab the bridle.

"Let him be!" growled the man. "He'll settle in a minute."

The gelding made to swim at first but then found its footing on the underwater wharf. The instant it could stand again, the animal took off, bounding through the water as if trying to leap clear again and again until it reached the levee, where it charged up to the top and galloped back the way they had come without a moment's pause. Through it all, the white man rained a steady stream of curses upon Hale and the horse and the universe at large, continuing his tirade until the gelding was completely out of sight. For Hale, the overseer's ensuing silence was far more disturbing than his curses. He stood completely still beside the boat, waiting for the blows that would surely come, waiting for yet another lesson in violence from this most excellent instructor.

Strangely he was not assaulted. Instead, the handsome man said, "Bring that saddle and get on board."

Hale waded across the wharf to collect the floating saddle, which had slipped off of the terrified animal's back. He soon returned it to the boat. Pitching the saddle over the bulwark, he grasped the rail with both hands to pull himself aboard, yet without the full use of his legs he only managed to get halfway in, with head and chest hanging down inside and chained ankles outside, dangling in the water. To his great surprise, the white man stepped beside him, gripped his trousers with both hands, and pulled him the rest of the way into the boat.

"Sit over there," he said, pointing to a corner in the stern. Hale crawled to the place and settled in with his legs extended out along the deck and his back against the transom. It was a comfortable position, and the warm rain beat a pleasing rhythm on the deck, and he felt a strange wave of satisfaction as if he could remain just so for the rest of time if it was allowed. Longing to close his eyes and sleep, he watched from under heavy lids as the overseer entered the forward house, leaving Hale alone out on the stern deck, where he closed his eyes again, and slept, and dreamed once more of violence.

18

Although the deck rolled twenty degrees in each direction, Hale Poser might have slept for hours if not for the crying. He opened his eyes to find that he had settled to his side in the steady rain upon the deck. He had no wish to move, but the crying became worrisome, for as his mind cleared he recognized it was a baby's wail. With great effort he rose up to his knees and set one foot on the deck, pushed, and stood with his hands clutching at the railing. Only when both feet were underneath him did he notice his ankles were unfettered.

Standing on the rolling deck, ignoring the open ocean to the starboard of the vessel and the unbroken mangroves on the shifting port horizon, Hale stared at the empty space between his feet. Disbelief rose within him. It was as if he had lost some essential part of his body rather than the foreign bands of iron. Slowly, he lifted his right leg, and then he stomped it down. He repeated this with his left leg. Soon he was striding to and fro across the deck with exaggerated steps and laughing out loud as he reveled in the sweet distance he could place between his feet.

At last the baby's wails pierced his pleasure, drawing his

attention toward the vessel's forward house. Moving hand over hand along the starboard side rail, he approached a side deck door. There, he peered through a windowpane. Inside the pilothouse stood the handsome man, legs spaced wide apart and hands upon a wooden wheel. Even through the optical distortions of the streaming rain against the glass it was obvious the overseer had sailing experience, for he timed the turning of the wheel perfectly to meet each wave a little differently, depending on its height and shape. Occasionally a steep one came along, threatening to crest. These the white man took at an angle, thereby using the wave's geometry to reduce the incline of the vessel's keel as they traversed, much as a footpath angles across a hill to make the walking easier. But their course was apparently perpendicular to the direction of the waves' approach, because whenever possible the slave driver took the seas fine upon the bow.

It occurred to Hale that the overseer did not know he was awake and standing there. Perhaps he could use the advantage of surprise to enter the pilothouse and cross the sole before the handsome man knew he was coming. Then he could bash out the monster's brains. The reverend from New Orleans stood in the rain and gathering darkness, peering into the lamp-lit cabin and wondering if such a thing were feasible, wondering how it would be to do it, engrossed with the possibility of it, until the baby raised its voice again and the overseer turned and their eyes met through the glass and Hale Poser shrank from the window, terrified.

"Get in here!" shouted the slave driver, disdainfully showing Hale his back as he returned his attention to the seas ahead. The baby wailed more loudly. Hale opened the door and entered the dry cabin timidly, knowing he had missed his chance, sickened at the relief he felt, hating his cowardice.

"Yes, boss?"

"Shut that thing up."

Hale found the child lying in a crude basket upon a red velvet settee, still wrapped in its infirmary blanket and filling the air with a fearful wail. Hale Poser marveled that such a sound could come from one so small. Shouting to be heard above the rain and pounding waves he asked, "Boss? What you going to do with her?"

"Throw it in the ocean if you don't shut it up!"

With fear a shackle on him just as strong as iron had been, Hale sat beside the basket, lifted up the child, and held her to his soaking chest. The night passed as he sat that way, staring out through the windows. "Shush," he said from time to time, rocking little Hannah Lamont within the cradle of his arms. "Shush now."

The sun rose somewhere up beyond the clouds. They reached a wide opening in the mangroves on the left. They entered, leaving the Gulf of Mexico behind. Soon the Mississippi River passed beneath their keel, and a deep green wall of trees rose on the other side of two hundred yards of putty gray water, barely visible through the rain. The river rippled and swirled with kaleidoscopic hints of power, lumbering back against them toward the Gulf. A black log drifted slowly by, perhaps thirty feet long, half submerged and very close. Hale thought of rushing out before the handsome man could stop him, of leaping to the log and paddling to safety. But what would be the point? He could never make the shore across the current. He would simply drift to a slow death in the ocean just a few miles off their stern. Better to ride here toward an uncertain future. Besides, he knew such desperate measures were beyond him. He had lost more than miracles. He had lost his backbone. And of course there was the child to think about. As he rocked and gently shushed her, Hale wondered why the white man had rescued him from drowning, and helped him board the boat, and removed his chains while he slept, and let him come inside the cabin where he could be completely dry for the first time in perhaps two weeks. He knew whatever reason lay behind these things, it did not bode well for him or for little Hannah Lamont. From force of long-standing habit it crossed his mind to pray, but immediately he pushed the thought from his mind. I might be a faithless coward, thought Hale Poser, but at least I am no hypocrite.

19

Knee-deep in the water, Marah dumped more mud upon the growing pile. She shook the sludge from the buckets as best she could, scooped out the rest with her fingers and retook her place in the line of women and children, each of them also carrying a pair of leather buckets. She waded through the field of standing water until she reached the place where the men filled her buckets with more of the mud they had carved from the levee's base, which she then hauled back through the rising water in the never-ending circular line of women and children, all of whom likewise dumped their burdens on the growing mound and turned around to do it all again, and again, and again. Just as she could not remember anything like this unending rain, she could not recall the bosses ever telling them to do this kind of work before. But almost in the same instant the handsome one had taken Moses over to the other side, the gray-eyed one, sitting up there on his horse and watching with his rifle in the crook of his arm, had said, "Dig here." So that was what they did, carving away the bottom of the hill one shovelful at a time. No one asked him why because when the boss man set you to a chore you did not ask him why; and because there was no need to ask, for food and shelter were the reasons why, and another day alive, and of course you also did it so they would not whip you or take you up and over to the other side like her poor Moses, which was even worse. You did not ask him why, and mostly did not waste time with speculation, but ever since they took her Moses, old Marah had been wondering more than usual about things, even if she kept her wondering to herself.

For instance, walking back and forth in her place in line, she wondered about the animals coming over the hill by the hundreds, so many they had stopped killing them for food, and now just chopped the snakes and left the other ones alone. And she wondered about the rain. Moses said it would not stop, and up to now it had not. In all her seasons, it had never rained this way before. And she remembered Moses warning them about tall water on the other side, saying it would break through the hill and pour into the fields and everyone would die beneath it. Some of the other old ones laughed at that. It was something they had not seen before, so it would never happen. But they had never seen the like of all this rain either, or been put to digging out the levee this way, so how could they say new things never happened?

It was unclear in her mind: did Moses really say the water would break the levees down? He told them all the levee would come down; she remembered that. But did he tell them why or how? She could not recall. Maybe this digging was what he meant. Maybe all this digging was not to let the rising water out, as some of them believed. What if there really was tall water standing out there, and all this digging broke the levee down and let that water in? After all, her Moses had been right about the rain. For the first time it occurred to her—if he was right about the rain, and maybe right about the levee, what about that Jesus world he told them all about? Was he right about that, too?

She had been too angry to consider the possibility before. All this time she had longed for vengeance, not some blue-eyed reminder of the past who talked about a god of every color. She had set him free, hoping he would come back like his namesake, setting plagues upon the bosses. Although his miracles astounded her, she had not been surprised. Miracles were what she sent him out to learn. But she had never dreamed her Moses boy would come back talking freedom on the inside instead of freedom from the bosses. And now he had gone and left them without any kind of freedom whatsoever.

What if he was right about the flood? He fed them boar to save the milk goat for the baby, stilled the storm, picked Simon's cotton, gave up his shoes, and although none of that was what she had expected or desired, it did hold true with his words. Was the Jesus world a place of kindness like that? She had always feared the Angry One above the clouds. She had heard he tore down towers and sent down floods and swallowed people up inside the earth. She remembered all of that, had seen it in the evil other place just as she had seen the white man hanging on a tree and the baby in the basket, and seeing all those things she had given Moses to the Angry One with hope that he would give her back just one delicious thing: a rain of fire upon the bosses, or boils, or some such fearful miracle. But the Angry One had fooled her, and now here come her Moses working different kinds of miracles, talking about freedom on the inside. She should have known the lightning thrower would not give her what she wanted. He did not care about her or the others in this place. He had never cared.

As Marah waded through the field, looking up at the levee she had feared and taken comfort from for so long, suddenly she thought there might be worse things than going to the other side, far worse things even than her bad time in that evil other place. Oh, how she ached for her boy Moses! Oh, how hard it was to have him again after all these years, to come so close to telling him everything, only to lose him to the other side again. They said a body would die over on the other side, but she knew a spirit could die right here where she stood, and thinking that, she wondered if a death out there could be harder than this kind of living. The answer seemed so obvious that the only question left was why it had taken her so long. So Marah resolved to go after Moses. If his Jesus world was out there filled with every color that there is, she would not wait here for the proper kind of miracle. She would go and get her own.

When Teddy Beauregard called him on the wireless with the news, Deputy Wallace Pogue collected the Winchester and hurried over to Tibbits's wharf to wait on Papa's yacht. At first he considered rounding up a couple of the fellows to lend a hand, but it did not pay to cause undue excitement, especially when a Negro was involved. So he sent a boy to let Rosa know about the baby, and left it at that. But of course the Winchester was a dead giveaway. Captain Waterhouse saw the rifle as the deputy hurried past Delacroix's Dry Goods. In his cups as usual, the pilot hollered after him, asking why he was armed, and that attracted the attention of all the usual loiterers. In spite of the rain, the boys followed Wallace all the way out to Tibbits's transient pier. Old Reverend Vogt was there, fat and flushed from the walk over, and that hothead Julius Gray, and a couple of the oystermen, all of them pestering Wallace Pogue with questions, as if they had nothing better to do with the river rising every minute. Three kids raced up and down the dock, burning off excess energy with a game of tag while they too waited to see what would happen. Even Jean Tibbits—who could usually be counted on to mind his own business—even Tibbits stood at a distance, watching quietly. Of course, Tibbits had the other wireless in town, so had probably overheard what Teddy said.

The yacht came steaming around the point. The vessel never failed to amaze Wallace Pogue, with its gleaming brass rails and portholes, its smoothly varnished house and crisp weather canvas. The only blemish on the pristine hull was the dingy brown place where the river water painted a mustache at the bow. The yacht approached fast, long and low and more like a torpedo than a proper boat, turning midriver and slicing across like there was no current at all. Wallace Pogue figured there was enough engine in that thing to power three shrimpers, and it probably burned more fuel in a single day than one of Tibbits's boats burned in a week out on the Gulf.

Now Rosa Lamont arrived at the dock, hiding from the rain beneath a small oilskin tarp wrapped around her shoulders and over her head like a huge scarf.

"Y'all step back and let Rosa through," called Deputy Pogue.

The arrival of the colored woman drew murmurs of surprise and speculation from some of the white folks, yet they all did what Wallace asked, respectful of Rosa's grief. When she reached Wallace Pogue's side, the two of them stood silently, staring out at the approaching boat. The rain fell straight and steady, dripping off the narrow brim of Wallace Pogue's fedora. He held the Winchester with the muzzle down to keep water out of the barrel. If he had it to do over again, he would have brought his Colt revolver instead, and hid it under his raincoat, and walked a little slower coming over so as to avoid attracting all this attention. Crowds begot crowds. There were at least a dozen men standing at his back now, with more on their way. They ought to be thinking about leaving town before the river got too high. They ought to be loading the boats instead of giving him worries about what they might do if Teddy Beauregard told that story again, right here at the dock. Well, of course there was no "might do" to it. They *would* do, and they would do it right quick. And if he wasn't out there in the swamp somewhere, still looking for his baby after all these weeks, James Lamont would probably take the lead. At the thought of that, Wallace Pogue shook his head. One colored boy lynching another . . . That would be a switch.

As usual the yacht came in too fast, proudly throwing up a bow wave until it was well within the turning basin. With the river up this high, the wake rolled right over the finger piers. Then just as the yacht seemed about to ram the dock its engine roared in reverse and stopped the boat almost dead in the water as it spun around and drifted in sideways, slow as you please. Now Teddy was at the bow tossing a line to the boys, then running aft in those pretty boots of his to toss another line, then back amidships for the spring line, and the boat sat calmly at rest before the nearby shrimp and oyster boats had stopped bobbing in its wake. A low murmur of admiration rose from the gathering crowd. There was a mean streak and an inordinate sense of superiority about Teddy Beauregard that Wallace Pogue had never much liked, but mercy, you had to admit the man could run that boat. Even the fishermen and pilots seemed impressed. Then all thought of Beauregard's seamanship vanished as he emerged from the side door of the pilothouse holding little Hannah Lamont.

"My baby!" screamed Rosa, and Wallace had to hold her back, for she had stepped blindly toward the boat, unmindful of the gap between the gunnel and the dock.

His face set in his usual superior expression, Teddy bent

to pass the child into her mother's arms. Rosa took Hannah
to her breast, huddling over to protect her from the rain,
pulling back the infirmary blanket and touching her daughter's cheek, when a raindrop hit Hannah's chin and she
screwed up her face and let out a powerful wail, and everybody except Teddy Beauregard laughed, white and Negro
alike.

"Rosa, why don't you take her on home?" said Wallace,
smiling.

"Yes sir," whispered Rosa, and the crowd parted again as
she moved away, weeping, with her slender arms tight
around her child.

"Hey, Ted! Where'd y'all find her?" called someone on
the dock.

Teddy opened his mouth to speak, but Wallace interrupted. "Tell you what, fellas, let's get out of the rain. How's
about y'all head over to Delacroix's? We'll be along directly
to tell y'all about it. Won't we, Teddy?"

Wiping water from his face, Beauregard said, "All right."

"How come you totin' that rifle, Wallace?" called Captain Waterhouse, slurring his words.

"I'll explain it over at Delacroix's," said Deputy Pogue.

"What's wrong with here?"

"It's raining, in case you didn't notice, Captain. I want
to get under cover before my outside gets as wet as your
inside."

Everybody chuckled, but Waterhouse would not back
down. "There's somethin' goin' on, Wallace. We got a right
to know why you're totin' that rifle."

"Captain," said the deputy, "you know how floods bring
out the moccasins and copperheads. I figured—"

Someone in the back shouted, "Look! Ted's got a colored boy in there!"

Wallace Pogue turned to see a black face staring out

through a pilothouse window. The face pulled back into the dark interior, though not before Wallace recognized him with a sudden flush of anger. He had trusted that man, shown him case notes, encouraged him to keep looking for the Lamont kid, and yet all along he was the one who did it.

"What you doin' with a nigger on board, Ted?" demanded Waterhouse.

Beauregard looked at Wallace Pogue as if expecting him to answer, while Wallace, still struggling to get his anger under control, said nothing.

"He's the one took James and Rosa's baby, ain't he?" shouted Waterhouse. "Get him out here!"

Someone else yelled, "Yeah! Let's see him!"

The small crowd pressed closer to the boat.

Roused by their movement, Wallace Pogue raised his rifle to quarter arms and faced the men. "Back off!" he barked. "Y'all just back away."

"Get him out here!" insisted the drunken Waterhouse, and two of his companions edged forward.

Pogue cocked a round into the chamber and swung the rifle toward them at hip level. "Get back, or so help me, I'll gutshoot the both of y'all." The rifle and the violence of his words stopped the men, their hands unconsciously moving to cover their stomachs. But they did not back away. Wallace Pogue inwardly cursed the fear that made the Winchester tremble slightly in his grip. This was no time to display weakness. "I'm not going to warn y'all again," he growled, doing his best to sound like he meant business. "Get off this dock right now. Go over to Delacroix's, and I'll come by and tell y'all the whole story just as soon as I can."

Reverend Vogt spoke for the first time. "Come on, fellas. We shouldn't be acting this way. Let Wallace do his job."

"Shut up, Silas," snapped Waterhouse. "We got a right to know what happened here."

Vogt blinked at Waterhouse. "But I—"

"Shut up I said! Unless you want to join the deputy there. Maybe the two of y'all end up in the river with the nigger."

Several men shouted "Yeah!" and "I'm with you, Captain!" Vogt and a couple of the others backed away, but the rest of the crowd pressed forward another step until those in front were less than two paces from the muzzle of Wallace Pogue's rifle. He raised the Winchester to his shoulder and took aim at Captain Waterhouse's head. "You'll be the first," he said. "I swear you will."

"Get him, men!" shouted Waterhouse, fearless in his cups.

"*Waterhouse!*"

The name was bellowed from somewhere off to the side. Most of them looked that way, but Wallace kept his eyes on the crowd.

"*Waterhouse!*"

This time Wallace recognized the voice and turned. Just beyond the crowd, Jean Tibbits stood on an upended oil barrel looking down at them with his hands on his hips.

"What is it, Jean?" asked the drunken pilot.

"You wanna keep using my docks for you pilot boat, you?"

"Why, I—"

"And you, Bill Wiggins! You wanna keep you shrimper here, you? Or maybe find a slip somewheres else?"

The fisherman said, "Ain't no other dock this close to the pass, Jean. You know that."

"I do. An' I tellin' every one you wanna use my docks, you turn around and get off of them, an' do it now, you!"

Waterhouse turned red. "You can't—"

"I can't?" Jean Tibbits reached behind his back and pulled a huge revolver from his belt. "You know I can,

Captain. An' you know me long enough to know I will." He stood with the revolver aimed at no one in particular. "Ain't gonna be no lynching here today, no. Now y'all get off my dock."

With the Negro safe for the moment in Wallace Pogue's small office, the deputy sat heavily behind his desk. "I'm obliged, Jean."

Standing by the locked door, Jean Tibbits nodded.

Deputy Wallace Pogue shifted his gaze to Beauregard and said, "All right, Teddy. How's about you tell me what happened."

"Why sure, *Wally*," replied Beauregard, stressing the childish name and smiling just a little in that irritating way he had. "Like I told you on the wireless, I was taking the boat up to Tidewater to put her on the hard for the flood, you know, and I spotted this nigger in a pirogue. I was worried about him, with the water rising an' all, so I looked him over with the glass and saw he had a kid with him, and that got me curious, you know, what with the news from here an' all, so I thought why not check him out? And sure enough, there was that little picaninny wrapped up in a blanket, like you saw." Beauregard leaned back in his chair, examining his knuckles. "Well . . . me and the nigger had a little disagreement at first, but I managed to convince him to see things my way, and here we are."

Wallace Pogue looked closely at Papa DeGroot's right-hand man, whom he considered too handsome by half. "That's your whole story?"

"What else should I say, Wally?"

Turning to the Negro who stood handcuffed beside his desk, Deputy Pogue asked, "Is that the way it was?"

The stranger said nothing.

"Come on now. I need an answer. What were you doing with that baby?"

When the colored man remained silent, Beauregard spoke up. "Check his ankles, Wally. He's been in the joint, for sure."

Eyeing the stranger carefully, Wallace Pogue said, "Lift up your trousers."

The Negro gripped the ragged fabric at his knees and lifted, revealing thick calluses at his ankles. Wallace noticed that the scars looked fresh.

"Where'd you get them at?" asked the deputy.

"From leg irons, Wally," said Beauregard.

"Yeah, Teddy. I know that. I'm just wondering where."

"Why, anyone can see the nigger must of broke out from a chain gang." Beauregard flashed his perfectly white teeth. "Say . . . maybe I'll get a reward."

Turning back to the stranger, Wallace Pogue said, "That right?"

Still he did not speak.

"You know," said Wallace Pogue, "I trusted you. Seems like the least you could do is answer a few questions." He waited, but the silent Negro would not even raise his eyes up off the floor. "All right," said Wallace with a sigh. "Maybe a little time out back will get you talking."

Grasping the Negro by the shoulder, he led him through the communicating door between the front office and the cell in back of the small building. It took less than a minute to lock the iron gate behind his prisoner and return up front.

Beauregard was on his feet. "I need to get up to Tidewater."

"All right," said Deputy Pogue. "When you coming back?"

At the door Beauregard paused to look back. "Why?"

"If this water keeps rising, we're gonna need every boat we can get."

"Depends on Papa, Wally. It's his boat."

The handsome man pulled the collar of his slicker up around his neck, hunched his shoulders and stepped out into the driving rain. He did not bother to close the door behind him. As Wallace crossed the office to shut the door against the rain, Jean Tibbits said, "You know he lying, right?"

"Uh-huh," said Wallace. "But I'd appreciate hearing why you think so."

"The way that colored fella walk."

"Little tiny steps."

"Yeah, mon."

"Like he's still in the habit of wearing shackles."

Jean Tibbits nodded. "I don't think he move that way before, no?"

"No," said Deputy Pogue, staring out through the rain at Theodore Beauregard's departing back. "He did not."

||M||arah's old knees ached as she climbed the levee. It did not occur to her to dwell upon the pain. Pain was life, and bad as it was, she had not yet reached the place where she would complain about living. So instead she blessed the clouds for veiling the moon. It took a long time to reach the top, and she feared nothing more than being seen in the moonlight before she could get to the other side. But when at last she stood to look beyond the earthen walls, the outside world as she remembered it was gone. Gazing across the flooded wasteland, she allowed herself to dwell on memories almost fifty seasons old. They had taken her from here in a strange wagon moving on the water, a long ride to a magic place with pure white tree trunks lifting up a roof so high the birds could fly below it, and walls so solid the rain could not get through. Inside were many bright colors, and strange windows that showed her own face back at her, like looking in a sideways puddle that never trickled down the walls, and woven fabric on the ground as if the earth itself wore clothes, and something in her cup like glass that made her drinking water oh so deliciously cold.

She remembered all those terrible nights with the white man, and then her precious baby, and the growing of her Moses, and the day she sent him to the Angry One, and the white man's terrible anger, and riding back a knowing woman in both her body and her grieving soul, and seeing something of the outside world along the way and thinking, My Moses is out there somewhere. My Moses is just fine. In the seasons since then, she had held her memory of that outside world at bay, fearing it, avoiding it, doing her best to beat it back because it came with so much heartache, until after all this time she wondered what part of her memory was real and what imagined. But nothing in her past, real or imagined, could have prepared her for the sight of endless water that lay before her now.

She was no longer a young woman. She had no floating wagon. She did not know which way to go. She had never learned to swim, of course, and she was leaving everything and everyone that she had known for almost seventy plantings. But she had to keep on going, for this ocean all around her world where none had been before was proof her Moses had been right.

Marah stepped into the flood, following her precious baby out into the Jesus world this time.

Hale Poser told himself the white deputy would not believe him. Nobody would. He told himself this was why he had been silent when they asked him to explain. Lying there in the cell, savoring the luxury of idleness and listening to the hollow sound of raindrops beating staccato on the metal roof, he even tried to tell himself that none of it had been real. He had gone off looking for the baby, gotten lost in the swamp, and become delirious for days and days. He had suffered awful nightmares and delusions, yet somehow found the child anyway, and that handsome white man happened on him in his pirogue like he said, so that now here he was, a prisoner by mistake. No slave plantation could exist in 1927 alongside wireless radios, electric lights, and aeroplanes. Like candlesticks and carriages, slavery was a thing of the past, a fading nightmare for the oldest generation, an embarrassment for the young. But no matter how he tried, Hale Poser could not deny his callused forearm or the new-formed scars upon his ankles. Real or imagined, slavery had become his personal nightmare.

A key turned in the heavy lock on the door between the hall outside his cell and the little room up front. Expecting the deputy to enter, Hale stood up from his bunk and put his hands behind his back and his eyes down on the floor, and waited as submissively as possible for whatever the lawman might say or do. But the voice that greeted him was gravelly and unfamiliar. Glancing up, he saw Papa DeGroot enter, the kindly old man who had funded the Negro infirmary and once shook Hale's hand with casual familiarity, as if he were not colored.

"Deputy Pogue, could I trouble you to bring along a chair?" asked the old man.

The deputy, who stood behind Papa DeGroot, returned to the front room, got a chair and brought it back.

"Place it here, if you would, Deputy," said the old man, pointing with his cane at the floor outside the cell. "And there is no need to stay. Reverend Poser and I prefer to speak alone. Do we not, Reverend?"

At the respectful intonation of the words *Reverend Poser*, Hale's eyes welled up with tears. They overflowed and ran freely down his cheeks. He did not know why he cried, and could not find a way to stop. He made no move to wipe his eyes, for that might draw attention. He simply stood and watched the floor.

"You sure you want me to leave you alone?" asked the deputy.

"Yes, Deputy. I believe that would be best."

"All right then, Papa. But I'll be right outside if you need me. Just holler."

"Holler? Ah, yes, indeed. I will surely . . . holler."

With great difficulty the old man lowered himself into the chair as the deputy retired. He stood his cane up straight between his legs and crossed his mottled hands upon it and inclined his head to peer up through the flat iron straps of the cage. "For goodness' sake, sit down, Reverend Poser," he said. "It is too difficult to look at you this way."

Hale settled upon the cot. Through the iron cage Papa DeGroot stared hard at Hale's tear-streaked face, as if memorizing his features. Slowly the old man's own expression of detachment changed to appear more and more overtly interested, even fascinated. He leaned forward in his chair. The two men sat that way for several minutes, one dejected, one eager, both of them motionless. At last Hale wiped his eyes. This gesture broke the strange inertia that had settled on them, for in an instant Papa DeGroot's face became an impassive mask again and his obese upper body relaxed and he leaned back. "I suppose you have been wondering how it came to this." When the prisoner said nothing, he continued. "I wish to tell you a very old secret, known by very few. I wish to reveal it to you, in particular. Perhaps I will even tell you why I wish to do this." The man's age-spotted hands shifted on his cane as he bent forward to get a better view of Hale Poser's face between the bars. Staring for a moment, he said, "Shall I tell you why? I wonder . . ."

Propping his cane against his right thigh, Papa DeGroot removed a leather cigar case from the inner pocket of his white linen jacket. He selected a large cigar and carefully clipped the end with a tiny pair of scissors. Withdrawing a wooden match from a vest pocket, he struck it on the arm of his chair and lit the cigar, twisting it round and round in the match's flame and sucking on it until it burned with a steady glow and filled the air around his head with smoke. "Where to begin?" he said, shaking out the match. "At the beginning, I suppose, although it is a long story.

"I am of Dutch descent, as you probably guessed from my name. My great-grandfather came to Louisiana in 1835. He lost his first wife to pneumonia and married again, and wanted to start a new life in America. So he sold his holdings in Holland and came here with his bride and my grand-father and my grandfather's wife and children. They trav-eled up the Mississippi as far as Vicksburg, searching for good land to start a cotton plantation. They soon found that the best property had already been taken by the Spanish, French, and British who had come before. My family had no political contacts here, you see, and so no way to press the government for land. All they had was money.

"At first I suppose it must have looked as if they would have to settle elsewhere. I believe South America was dis-cussed. But then my grandfather had a brilliant idea. Plaquemines Parish was huge and largely unoccupied because of the swamps and regular floods we have here on the delta. My family was Dutch, after all, descendants of a people who had stolen an entire nation from the sea. Could they not steal a few thousand acres from the swamp in the same way?

"For next to nothing my great-grandfather bought a huge parcel of swampland here on the west bank of the Mis-sissippi. His holdings extended north from two miles south of Pilotville to a line almost halfway up to Tidewater, and all the way west to the Gulf of Mexico—hundreds of square miles of mostly flooded land. I have no doubt his neighbors to the north thought it was amusing. An ignorant foreigner buying worthless swampland. But they soon learned differently." The old man nodded in a cloud of cigar smoke. "Oh, yes. They learned.

"In 1836, our first slaves were purchased in New Orleans and put to work on the levees. Our plan was to begin at the river's edge, reclaiming land from there westward by building a system of levees and drainage canals during the winter and funding the expansion with summer crops. Each year a few more acres were added. Each year a few more slaves were purchased. Each year a few more barges piled to overflowing with DeGroot cotton were towed north to the New Orleans Exchange, and those who had once laughed were forced to compete against a new family on the river with ever growing resources. My great-grandfather died in 1853, at the age of sixty-eight. I am unusually old for a DeGroot, you see. My father did not see fifty. Perhaps it was the war that killed him. He could not bear failure. It broke his heart, I suspect. But I digress. Let me see. . . .

"I was born in 1845. I had three brothers, all of them older. Life was sweet back then. I remember taking breakfast on the verandah and listening as my father and grandfather discussed the business of the day to come. Seed to be ordered, labor to distribute among the fields, that kind of thing. It always fascinated me, the family business. Perhaps that is why I was chosen to remain at home when the others went to war. Or perhaps it was my age, although many another teenaged boy marched out beneath the stars and bars."

Papa DeGroot sighed heavily, then knocked an inch of ash from the end of his cigar onto the jailhouse floor.

"It was 1861, the first year of the war, and I was the only DeGroot man left here. My father was a major in the army and my brothers all lieutenants. We had political connections by then, you see. We were the wealthiest family in Louisiana, so rank as officers went without question. Everyone was having a marvelous time killing Yankees away up north somewhere, and I was left with the women to mind the crops. During that first year, we saw no Federals here, but in spite of my tender age I was not a fool. The Mississippi was the lifeblood of the Confederacy. I knew the Federals would come when they were able, and they would come in force. I also knew they would commandeer everything along the river that would be of use to them, and destroy the rest.

"Anticipating this, I set half of our niggers to demolishing the levees on the fields along the river. We would return that land to the swamp, leaving no sign that it had ever existed. With the easternmost fields beneath the swamp again, it was my earnest hope that the Yankees would pass by without giving thought to the absence of trees along our side of the river. At the same time, I charged the rest of my slaves with digging a new canal from the edge of our westernmost fields clear across to the Gulf. I believe you saw this canal, Reverend Poser. Was it not impressive? It was a significant undertaking, you know, to dig a ditch twelve feet wide and four feet deep and almost ten miles long, but we owned a steam shovel and almost thirteen hundred niggers back then, not counting the females and children, and that is a lot of manpower. We went a year without planting, but I managed to get the canal across in only fifteen months."

DeGroot paused, staring at Hale as if expecting praise. Rain beat steadily upon the sheet metal above the cell. When Hale remained silent, the old man grunted and continued.

"As it happened, just one month before the first Federal gunboats arrived, there was a massive flood. The clearings along the riverbank where our fields had formerly been became natural collecting grounds for the debris that washed downstream. Thousands of uprooted trees piled up there, forming a continuous barricade along the shore. By the time the Federals arrived, nothing could be seen from their riverboats to hint of our existence.

"There was still the distribution problem. I had to plant in order to survive, but where could the product be sold? Naturally the New Orleans Cotton Exchange was out of the question. So I sailed to Vera Cruz and struck a deal with a concern over there. Jorge Vargas and Sons sent two clippers in the autumn of 1863, and we loaded them with cotton at our new wharves on the Gulf coast, far from the usual shipping lanes and a hundred miles away from the Federal blockade at the mouth of the Mississippi. The product was grown in a number of fields including the one where you have recently been occupied, then floated through the swamp to the coast along our new canal. We ginned it right there on the wharves, which were built a quarter mile inland behind a rather confusing mangrove swamp. Only those who knew exactly where to sail could hope to find those wharves. And although our volume was diminished by the loss of land along the river, I took pride in being the sole remaining producer on the lower Mississippi. During the next three years, I grew and sold tons of cotton right under the noses of the Yankees. They never suspected a thing."

Again Papa DeGroot paused. "Are you not impressed?" he asked.

The prisoner merely nodded.

"We lost the war of course. Only my father and one brother survived. The country was in such disarray, it took them ten months to find their way back, and for my part, I had only just learned of the South's defeat when they arrived. The isolation that allowed us to continue growing cotton also made it difficult to stay in touch with outside events, you see. When it came, news of defeat was devastating. I was still in the throes of depression when my brother Peter and my father came poling through the swamp in a humble pirogue, searching for some sign of their home. Peter was amazed to find us still in production. He was eager to learn the details, but my father was a broken man who took little interest in anything. My mother had died while they were away. Peter had never married. Nor had I. So it was just we three, and the niggers, alone on an island of our making, far from the changing world.

"Peter assumed the niggers would have to be set free. He expressed grave concern that they were still enslaved so long after the war had ended. When I explained that I had only just learned of the outside situation, he warned me that the carpetbaggers up in New Orleans would fail to give that fact consideration and might well impose heavy penalties upon us, perhaps even place us in prison for kidnapping."

DeGroot snorted and rolled his half-smoked cigar between his fingers. "Kidnapping!" he said. "Imagine that! Naturally, I would have none of it. I reminded my brother that the slaves were our property, purchased at a dear price, or bred and reared at great expense. But Peter insisted we were in a pretty fix. If we released them, word would surely get back to the Yankees up in New Orleans and our freedom would be forfeited. Of course, neither of us could bring ourselves to kill them, for they were a precious resource. So, after several days of difficult contemplation, we agreed to take the one remaining course of action open to us.

"By then it had been over five years since DeGroot cotton had been shipped to the New Orleans Exchange. In those long years everything had changed. None of the rightful authorities remained in power; the carpetbaggers had seized their offices. Few of our peers were still in business. In fact, few planters remained on their ancestral land. Most of the venders who once sold us seed and implements had gone bankrupt. Who remained in the outside world to whisper into Yankee ears about a lost plantation down in Plaquemines? I convinced my brother we could remain in business. Had I not proven that already by producing three crops right under the Yankees' noses in the middle of a war? So we continued operations as if nothing had changed. The Mexicans kept coming year after year. The language barrier guarded against communication between them and the niggers on our docks, so the slaves learned nothing of their so-called emancipation, and the Mexicans did not suspect that our dockworkers were still slaves. No other contact between the niggers and the outside world was allowed. But then, it never had been.

"Father died shortly after the war. Peter was kicked in the head by a mule in 1871 and expired within twelve hours. That left only me to reap the profits. And they have been substantial." DeGroot moved his hand, and cigar smoke trailed behind the gesture like incense in the hands of a rogue priest. He said, "I was the absolute master of my world in the most literal sense. Now and then I visited Vera Cruz to maintain my business relationship with the Vargas family. They have been fine partners through the years. Perfect gentlemen. It would never occur to them to ask questions about my source of labor, or any other private aspect of my business. More than once I called on Galveston when traveling to or fro. I almost married a lovely young lady there in the 1880s, but it seemed too large a risk. Telling her my secret would place my fate irreversibly in her hands. How could I be certain she would understand? And by then I was too well accustomed to controlling my own destiny. So I lied. If she lives, I suppose she still believes I operated a shipping concern in Savannah. But I very much doubt if she still lives." The old man sighed. "I am somewhat surprised that I still live, for that matter. The only thing worse than old age is death. Nevertheless, you must not feel pity for me, my boy. For although I could not take a bride from among my own people, there was a woman in my life."

Lifting his head, he inhaled deeply from the cigar and seemed to peer above Hale Poser's head into the past. "She was quite beautiful. About twenty years younger than I, with smooth skin, a handsome figure, and surprisingly delicate features for a colored girl. Really, quite beautiful in her way. It is strange, but lately I find myself remembering her smile, and her delightful habit of humming that curious tune."

After taking one more puff on the slowly burning cigar, Papa DeGroot closed his eyes, pursed his liver-colored lips and exhaled, and along with a thin blue stream of smoke came a low whistle. The notes sounded strong and true, and as they softly filled the air, Hale Poser lifted his gaze from the floor in astonishment, for here was a tune as familiar to him as his own heartbeat. Caught up in a kind of reverie, the old man gently waved his hand, marking time to an ancient melody from another continent, and to his horror Hale realized he might not have failed in everything after all.

His bizarre kidnapping and bondage had obscured the quest that began with a manila paper folder, soft and mildewed from New Orleans humidity, its faded pages bearing the terse, clerically phrased story of a boy of three or thereabouts, brought north from down beyond the end of everything, to be raised with other orphans in a peeling twelve-room mansion. It was many days since Hale had spared a moment's thought for his own history, but the melody this monstrous man produced—a melody Hale had heretofore considered his alone—resurrected his desire for a mother's touch, or a father's, or even for the sight of a name on a tombstone, together with the cold comfort that the name was also his.

Papa DeGroot paused to stare pensively at the cigar he rolled between his fingers. Watching him, Hale Poser whispered, "What happened to her?"

The old man shifted his rheumy eyes to Hale, saying, "Why, Reverend Poser, at last you speak." He returned his gaze to his cigar and continued, "Unfortunately, the dear girl was plagued with superstition, as I find you coloreds tend to be. One day I caught her looking at the pictures in our family Bible. Normally I would have whipped a nigger for looking in a book, but I was weak and broke my own rule. I told her the stories that matched the pictures. It became a nightly ritual; she would sit and listen like a child as I read bedtime stories. She was especially interested in the baby Moses. She had me tell that story over and over, until she had memorized every detail. She was pregnant by this time, you see, and I thought her interest was connected with the baby, especially after the child was born and she named it Moses." The old man sighed. "She seemed to be happy for two or three more years. I was very foolish not to see what she had in mind until the day her boy went missing. I searched everywhere on her behalf to no avail. I was deeply worried for her, afraid that grief might drive her to some desperate act. But then one afternoon I caught her humming her favorite song—the one I was whistling just now— and, well, to me this seemed inconsistent with the actions of a grieving mother. I questioned her quite forcefully. She confessed to setting the boy adrift in the swamp in an old pirogue, abandoning him to his fate like the baby Moses in the Nile."

The old man laughed bitterly. "She did more than confess. She bragged of it. Even in my anger I marveled at her courage. Still, it was too much of course. I could not have her sending my sons off to oblivion, so I turned her back into the fields. It was to be a temporary punishment, you see. She would be reminded of that difficult life and gladly recommit herself to me. But after the first month, when I offered to return her to my home, she was most unenthusiastic. No privilege thereafter could convert her; no threat could make her mine. Heaven help me, I confess I even begged, yet her indifference was impregnable."

Like Hale Poser, the old man turned his sky-blue eyes to the floor, his voice a whisper now. "I outwitted an army, my boy. I conquered nature. In a way you could say that I have frozen time itself. I am a man to be reckoned with. But nothing in my power could bend your mother to my will after she had set you free."

21

Hale Poser sat silently with Papa DeGroot, thinking of a wrinkled face, callused hands, warm brown eyes. A fantasy become a memory. Marah. His mother.

The old man sighed and shifted in his chair as if to go.

"Please," said Hale, "I have so many questions."

The old man settled back. "Of course."

Hale did not know where to begin. He said nothing else at first, and Papa DeGroot did not seem to mind but waited patiently outside the cell. Finally Hale asked, "Why did you tell me this?"

"Now and then," said the old man, "I do wonder if I have made the right decisions. It has been a lonely life. Money no longer holds the same appeal. Power now seems unimportant. In the last few years I have often thought advancing age would be less unsatisfactory if one had someone ..." He searched Hale Poser's face. "You look very much like her, you know. Remarkably like her. Except for your eyes, of course. Your eyes are mine."

Hale said, "You let me out because I am your son?" He hated himself for hoping it was true, but hoping nonetheless.

"That is one reason, perhaps."

Frustrated by the equivocation, Hale asked, "Why else would you do it?"

The old man shifted his attention to the cigar in his hand. "James Lamont is still searching for his child. Did you know that? No. Of course you did not. How could you? But it is true that he has been out in the swamp for weeks. He comes back only for fuel and food and water and then returns immediately. It appears he will not give up."

Hale said, "No father would stop looking for his child."

Hale Poser's father said, "You are naive."

When Hale did not respond, the old man continued. "Theodore Beauregard reported that James Lamont's vessel came very close to the plantation recently. If he continued searching, he would find the levees eventually, and then of course we would have to kill him."

Remembering the sound of the diesel engine that had so disturbed the overseers, Hale believed him. "If you would kill Mr. Lamont," he said, "why didn't you kill me?"

"As I said, you look very much like her." Papa took a deep drag on his cigar and shrugged. "Perhaps I also am naive, but only in regard to Marah. I will never allow the plantation to be discovered. I would destroy anyone else who stumbled upon it. If necessary, I would even destroy the plantation. But of course in this case it was far easier to stop the search by simply returning the child to its parents."

"That explains why you brought out Hannah. But why me?" asked Hale, torn between revulsion for this man's atrocities and a stubborn refusal to admit that the father of his dreams had no redeeming virtues.

"I could not simply have the child appear after all this time. There had to be an explanation."

"You want them to think I kidnapped her?" Hale felt a rush of fear and sorrow. "They'll hang me."

Papa took a final puff from the cigar, dropped it to the floor and ground it with his heel. "All you have to do is tell them about the plantation."

Confused, Hale frowned. "You just said you would kill to keep that secret."

"Nevertheless, you must tell them everything. Describe the plantation, your daily life there, the food you ate and the work you did. Tell them about your mother and me. Tell them everything."

"What good will that do?"

"No one will believe you, of course. In fact, the more details you reveal, the more convinced they will become of your insanity."

Sighing, Hale sat back against the flat iron bars of his cell. "They'll commit me."

"I shall see to it."

Visions of a young boy in an orphanage flashed through Hale Poser's mind. "I won't live in an asylum. I'd rather hang."

"Dear boy, I no more desire to see you in an asylum than I wish to see you hang. I never desired any of this. In fact, I have been your protector for these last few weeks. Mr. Beauregard planned to kill you as he has others who discovered our secret. Only I sustained your life."

It was the closest Papa DeGroot had come to admitting that he cared what happened to his son, yet now that Hale heard the words, they were couched in lies. "You made a slave of me!"

Papa's response was calm. "You were warned to stop your search for the Lamont child. I told you to leave it to the sheriff. You ignored my advice and found the plantation. The results were unavoidable. You brought them on yourself."

"No," said Hale, shaking his head. "No. No."

Papa leaned forward, speaking quickly. "You must understand I never wished you harm. On the contrary, since the moment when I saw her in you, when I realized who you were . . ." Hale Poser looked up, hoping to hear his father say he did not want his son to suffer, but apparently desire was too naked in his face, for Papa DeGroot paused, collecting himself. After a moment he continued with less emotion. "I had been hoping you would stay here indefinitely. I had hoped that you and I might get to know each other. And I am now offering you a way out of this situation. Assuming of course that we can reach some kind of understanding, I will see that the judge sentences you to treatment at the infirmary here in Pilotville. And in due time, I will see you are set free."

As the old man's plan became clear, Hale marveled at its efficiency. The search would stop immediately when James Lamont received word of Hannah's return. Cries for justice would be silenced by his capture. And if he tried to defend himself by telling the truth, his own credibility would be forever lost, he would never be able to save the others at the plantation, and he would be committed to a locked room at the infirmary instead of hung, allowing this twisted old man to maintain his delusions of benevolence toward a long-lost son. Just one question remained.

"Why did you take the Lamonts' baby?"

As with everything else, Papa DeGroot was ready with his answer. "Genetics, my boy."

"What?"

"Genetics. A fascinating branch of science that deals with the characteristics we inherit from our ancestors. Genetics is what made me white and you colored." He paused, toying with the handle of his cane. "Of course, based on that definition, I suppose you have little use for such science."

"God made me what I am for a reason."

"Ah, a fatalist. I wonder if I would be so comfortable with my lot in life were I of your race."

"I didn't say I was comfortable." Hale leaned forward to look at Papa's face. "What does this have to do with taking the baby?"

Papa DeGroot did not answer immediately. Instead, he sat stroking the cane as if at a loss for words. When he finally spoke, Hale thought he was avoiding the question. "We never dreamed our labor supply would be cut off. If we had, perhaps we would have invested in more breed stock. But when the war befell us, there were less than 150 females on the plantation capable of bearing children. During the difficult time when the levees had to be destroyed and the new canal was dug, it was often necessary to place the women in the ditches with the men. That year alone we lost 119 breeding-aged females to snakebite, malaria, dysentery and such. Soon we were down to only eight. By 1885, all of our original stock was gone. Of course they were replaced by their own daughters. Unfortunately, there was no one to breed with the new generation, except for the cousins and brothers of the girls. Then, by the turn of the century, that generation had largely passed the age of productivity and their children began to reproduce. This is where the harsh realities of science would have entered in, you see. The offspring of cousins and siblings is one thing, but the sons and daughters of brothers and sisters . . . Well, as a student of genetics, I knew the results would be less than satisfactory: cleft palates, curvature of the spine, mental retardation, and other unfortunate deformities.

"Long before that happened it became apparent that I would need a new source of genetic stock. The problem was finding them. In the early years we simply took the new blood we needed from among the coloreds who had been so unwisely freed. From an abundance of caution we were careful to take our stock from among many different communities so there would be no discernible pattern. Not that a pattern would have necessarily caused difficulties. No one listened to complaints from coloreds during those early years. But as time went on, it became more problematic. Although one can still acquire slaves in certain countries, it is an arduous and expensive process, and it seemed such a waste with so many niggers living so close by. Sadly, one cannot go about abducting niggers off the street anymore. Even here in Louisiana that is frowned upon.

"The solution walked in my door one afternoon. The pastor of a church in Tidewater came to see me at my town home, begging for money, as you ministers always do. He brought along a medical doctor who had come from New Orleans to speak to a few influential citizens about the shortage of health facilities available for the Negro race in the South. I did not take him seriously, of course, until he mentioned the vast number of illegitimate children your kind produces. He said your offspring often require medical care, which is unavailable in most areas. The infant mortality rate was apparently quite high. When I heard that, the opportunity was obvious. The doctor made a most impassioned plea, followed by a few words from the minister. They expected me to contribute a few hundred dollars, I suppose, and I believe they were quite taken by surprise when I offered to fund an entire clinic. I made just two stipulations: first, it must be at the old Methodist mission building here in Pilotville, where there was no access by land and I could better control the surrounding population; and second, I must be allowed to handpick the doctor who would run the clinic."

"Dr. Jackson," said Hale, visualizing the thin white man with an alcoholic's swollen nose.

"Of course. He and I have served the Plaquemines Negro community side by side for thirty-one years, as I believe I mentioned when we first met."

"You started the infirmary in order to get babies. To get new blood."

"We had been acquiring new stock for many years, but the infirmary made it much easier."

"But why take babies?"

"When the inbreeding problem became apparent, I first thought of taking adult slaves, but in the long run newborn babies were a better choice. They could reveal nothing of the outside world to the other slaves. And there is the matter of mental conditioning. A child raised in the fields knows nothing else, and therefore sees no reason to rebel. Most adults raised in freedom would strive to regain it."

Hale Poser thought of Qana and the others who had scoffed at his promise of a better world beyond the levees, and he knew this evil man was right. They had not believed him because they had no idea what freedom really was. And hard on the heels of this, another realization filled his heart with shame. Why should they have believed him? He had played the selfless Great Deliverer, bestowing miraculous gifts from on high. Feasts of boar and silenced storms and many rows of cotton picked as in an instant—he had offered these and more. But the cost he had required was more than they could pay. He demanded they believe a man too high-and-mighty in his own estimation to bother with the simplest gift of all. He had strived to be their great deliverer, but he had not stooped to be their brother.

Searching his face, the old man said, "Are you well?"

"Yes," lied Hale.

"You look troubled."

Annoyed at this ability to sense his distress, Hale Poser spoke too loudly. "You're talking about taking babies from their parents and turning them into slaves!"

Mistaking Hale's meaning, the old man tried to reason with him. "I have just explained why babies are a better solution for my needs. There is also the basic expedience of the thing. It is nothing to transport a baby to a waiting boat, while an adult, even unconscious, can be a very inconvenient burden. And adults have established connections with society and would therefore be more widely missed. In addition to families, adults would have employers, co-workers, friends. They would owe money to people who would earnestly desire to collect the debt. They would leave other matters behind that might inconvenience some enough to cause them to search quite diligently."

"No one would search harder than a parent for a baby," said Hale.

"Ah, there is that naiveté again. A most endearing trait. I do agree, parental instinct is curiously strong in some, as James Lamont has shown. But we tried to choose the children of those least likely to cause a fuss. Prostitutes. Drunkards. Mostly, though, we told the parents their children were deformed and died soon after delivery. Some of them asked to see their babies anyway, but we managed to convince them that the sight would be too horrible to bear."

"No one tried to tell the Lamonts that Hannah died in childbirth."

"Yes, well, you caused a bit of trouble there, didn't you?"

"Me?"

"Certainly. Jackson gave the Lamont woman a substance to bring on stomach pain, then diagnosed it as a breech, or something of that kind. We were prepared to remove the baby after the delivery and explain it in the usual way. Then you came along. I understand you remained by the woman's side until she gave birth, and nothing could be done to make you leave her without raising suspicion."

Hale Poser's shame deepened at the implications. "Are you saying there was never really a problem with how that baby lay?"

"Of course not."

"So when I touched Rosa, it wasn't . . ."

"Wasn't what, my boy?" Through the black iron cage, Papa DeGroot watched him curiously.

The Reverend Hale Poser drew a callused palm across his face, stretching his cheeks out of shape as his thoughts filled with the cries of a birthing mother with his hands hot upon her belly. He remembered the sudden syncopation of voices in two churches, and a resurrected blackbird. Could it all have been coincidence? One by one the details of his miracles flowed across his mind and for the first time he considered other explanations. Persimmons, allowed to grow to maturity so near to town simply because everyone had stopped looking. A boar, naturally seeking high ground. A thunderstorm, ceased by chance at the moment he raised his arms. Confusion in the rainy darkness about which rows he had picked for Simon and which had been picked before . . . everything, all of it, might have had nothing whatsoever to do with him. He sat silently, lost in the ramifications until at last Papa DeGroot broke the silence.

"I will leave you now. When they come for interviews, I do hope you will remember my suggestion. Tell them everything, dear boy, exactly as it happened." Pressing against his cane, Papa DeGroot rose to his feet unsteadily. He stood a moment, staring in at Hale as though memorizing his features, or recollecting something already memorized half a century before. "Are there still niggers speaking patois in New Orleans? Is that how you learned it?"

"What?" asked Hale distractedly.

"I was wondering how you come to know the language. I thought patois was quite dead, except for certain regions in Georgia and the Carolinas."

"I don't understand."

"I am asking who taught you the language of my slaves."

"But they speak English."

"Indeed? Then Marah must have taught them, although that has always been forbidden." Hale saw a hint of amusement in his face, perhaps even admiration. "Did she also teach you their language?"

"Nobody taught me anything like that."

"Truly? Then it is remarkable, indeed. You were only three years old when she set you afloat in that pirogue. I would have thought you might remember a word or two, but to return after all these years and speak their particular patois so fluently, as if you never left—"

"But I *don't* speak patois!"

"Don't be ridiculous."

"I tell you I don't know it!"

"Do you take me for a fool?" Papa DeGroot cocked his head to look at him curiously. "My dear boy, do you really expect me to believe you do not know we have been speaking it all along? Why . . . we are speaking it now."

||J ames Lamont reflected for perhaps the hundredth time on the unsearchable ways of God. Like the Good Book said, who can understand them? Day after day he had steered *La Vie Joyeuse* around the edges of the swamp, wishing he could travel deeper in to search for Hannah just beyond that stand of tupelo, or around behind those mangroves, but the six-foot draft of Mr. Tibbits's trawler had forced him to stay outside in the channels. More than once, he ran aground and had to winch himself free. Then came the flood, and the waters rising every hour, and the realization he could go almost anyplace he desired in the southern half of Plaquemines Parish. Thanking God, he drove the trawler up coulees just inches deep at any other time, and straight across broad flats usually so shallow you could wade right through mile after mile of water lilies and hyacinth. At first he was ecstatic with this freedom of mobility and filled with renewed hope that he would find his baby girl. At first he was certain God had sent the flood for that very reason. But then he began to wonder about Rosa and the kids. If the water was this high down here, how were things up in Pilotville? And that got him to thinking about how God does

things, giving and taking away. The same child that had threatened Rosa with a sideways birth and caused them so much worry, bringing joy instead with her miraculous delivery . . . only to break their hearts after all. The same flood that made it possible for him to search for Hannah might also harm the rest of his family. He had spent the last few weeks wishing he could go deeper in the swamp, and when he got his wish, all he could think about was getting back to Pilotville to make sure Rosa and the children were safe. Health and sickness, joy and sorrow, peace and trouble . . . Why didn't God ever give a simple blessing?

He had gone far into the swamp before worries about Rosa grew too strong to subdue, and the flood he had first seen as an opportunity destroyed his hope instead. Standing in the pilothouse, callused hand upon the wheel, James Lamont no longer fantasized about finding his baby adrift in some insane trapper's pirogue or lying in a crib at a Cajun hermit's camp. Whoever took his child had hidden her too well, or else gone north to escape the flood, or else drowned somewhere out here with his baby girl. That last possibility, once he finally allowed it, seemed most likely. And once he allowed it, James Lamont knew he had been alone too long, eating sardines and peaches straight from the can, sleeping two or three hours at most, bearded, wild, filthy in spite of the rain, and holding conversations with himself as if he were two people. James began to wonder if he had lost his mind. Once, he thought he had heard angels singing. Well, truth be told there was no *thought* about it. He had heard them singing, plain enough. He had killed the diesel to be sure. But after the voices had stopped right in the middle, he knew they were not real, for a choir of angels would not fall silent all of a sudden that way; they would taper off and put a finished end to things. So he knew his mind had slipped a little, and he had cranked the engine back to life and turned the wheel to starboard and slowly looped around the way he'd come, deciding then and there to find the way back home.

All he had to do was to steam back to the east and sooner or later he would find the river. Trouble was, which way was east? During a moment of frustration early in the search he had thrown a childish fit, cursing at the top of his lungs and storming through the pilothouse, flinging things left and right with enraged abandon. A crescent wrench had made an end to the glass lens on the compass, and from that day on his only means of orientation had been the daily hints of dawn and dusk. All the rest of the day, the uniform grayness of the cloudy sky betrayed no trace of the sun's position, and of course the moon and stars had not appeared for weeks. Other than the waters themselves, he saw nothing but treetops, and they all looked alike. For all he knew, he might be steering in huge circles.

Then he found the old woman sleeping in a tree.

Although all hope of finding Hannah had long since died, still he scanned the passing vegetation out of habit, and just after dawn, as he steamed alongside a stand of cypress treetops, he saw her sitting on a broad limb just a few inches above the flood. With her back against the tree trunk and her eyes closed, she looked peaceful, as if she were the happiest person in the world. He called to her, and she started and almost fell into the water, then turned toward the trawler with terror written plain across her face. He smiled to reassure her, though smiles did not come easy anymore, and waved and asked if he could help. She said nothing in reply but looked around wildly as though searching for an escape route.

Bringing *La Vie Joyeuse* up right smartly to the tree with the old woman's perch amidships, he tied off to branches fore and aft. She was rigid in his arms as he lifted her aboard. She wore a simple garment made of roughly woven cloth, like a sack with holes for head and arms. The stitching was crude, the material a homespun yellowish brown. She was darker than James, but he could tell from the lighter places underneath her arms that hers was a deep blackness born of many days in the sun. Her hair hung long and ropy as if she had not washed or combed it for quite a while. Years maybe. He asked a lot of questions. What's your name? Where are you from? How did you come to be sleeping in that tree? He told her something of himself. I am James Lamont. I am searching for my child who was taken from her bed. I am lost but hope to find my way back home directly. No matter what he asked or told, she would not speak to him except to say "Yes, boss" in reply. He asked her why she called him "boss." She simply stared at him. It was as if she did not speak his language. Eventually he decided she was deaf. She was a very old woman, after all.

He offered her a can of peaches, which she examined with great skepticism. He withdrew a slice from the can and ate it, then offered her the can again, and this time she consumed its entire contents with enthusiasm. Clearly she was starving. As he opened up another can of peaches, it occurred to James Lamont that he had saved her life.

Lose a child; save an old woman.

Why didn't God ever give a simple blessing?

River water trickled through the cypress walls of Hale Poser's cell to creep across the floor. He lifted his bare feet onto the bunk and called for help. Coward that he was, his calls soon turned to screams. No one came. Watching helplessly as the water slowly rose, he tried to beat his panic back with thoughts of Marah.

He thought about her eyes: the gentle way they had gazed at him that first time in the shack, when he had awakened wracked with pain and she had been there, tenderly moistening his cracked lips, holding a callused palm against his forehead. As Hale thought of her, grief replaced his fear of the rising water. He had been a motherless son among motherless sons for all his life, aching with so much desire that he would abandon the orphanage merely because of the word *Pilotville* written on a yellowed piece of paper, would desert a hundred children to go looking for a last name, even if it must be read upon a tombstone. But when at last he found his mother, he had been too full of himself to recognize his oldest dream come true. He had been so certain he was God's prophet, sent out into the wilderness to save her and the others. Now he suspected God could have used her to save him, if only his pride had allowed it. Oh, how he longed to return to her . . . but that would take a miracle.

Laughing bitterly, Hale Poser shook his head. A miracle? Would he never learn? It was miracles that led him to this hell on earth. He had no further use for them. But in defiance of this thought came yet another miracle, a vision rising up before him, a view into himself. He saw a man and woman in a garden, naked and not knowing, not ashamed. He saw a beautiful man passing through a crowd, a woman healed by the touch of his robe when his back was turned. He saw another man, ignorant of his own faith, a tool of perhaps more usefulness than most, precisely because of his ignorance. He saw that man get educated, get credentials, get religion. He saw himself seeing his own nakedness. He was ashamed.

When he set his foot upon the floor again—it must have been two or three hours later, although the darkness was now total and of course he had no clock—the water stood up to his ankles. He was much more calm this time as he shouted for help, but his voice could not compete with the ceaseless rattle of the rain upon the roof and the distant calls of Pilotville residents. He supposed they were preparing to evacuate. He wondered if they would remember him in their haste, or if they would leave him here to drown. After shouting for a very long time, he sat back on the bunk to wait.

He thought about that other answered prayer: Papa DeGroot. Papa. Father. A man who had said to him, *"My dear boy . . ."* The thrill of it offended Hale, yet he could not stop himself from savoring those words.

"My dear boy . . . Why, we are speaking it now."

Then Hale remembered his reply.

"But I don't speak patois."

Remembering, he wondered . . . to be naked and not know. To heal when your back is turned.

". . . we are speaking it now."

And remembering, he felt he had come at last to the precipice of an overwhelming vision. It was there, just before him, if only he would not try so hard to see.

23

H ale reckoned dawn was near when he heard someone moving in the outer office. By now the water was almost up to the top of the bunk. "Help!" he shouted. "Help!" There was no reply, but after several minutes the door opened and Deputy Wallace Pogue entered the tiny cellblock wearing waders and a dark raincoat and carrying a kerosene lamp, keys, a set of handcuffs, and leg shackles.

"Put these on," said the deputy, passing the restraints into the cell.

It took Hale a minute or two. "Hurry up," said the deputy. When Hale was done, the deputy held the lamp close to the bars of the cell and said, "Come over here." Lowering the lamp a little, the lawman first checked Hale Poser's handcuffs. Lowering the lamp a little further he said, "Lift your foot." Hale raised one leg high enough for the deputy to see the iron band around his ankle, just below the surface. "Now the other one." Hale lifted his foot to show that one, too. Satisfied, the deputy slipped a key into the gate and opened it.

"Step out."

Hands clasped together at waist height like a monk, Hale Poser shuffled out through calf-high water, the shackles familiar on his ankles. At the deputy's instruction he led the way through the front office door and on outside.

Hale Poser paused on the threshold to take in the eerie scene, lit as it was by the golden glow of many kerosene lamps hanging from pilings along the boardwalk. He had suffered violence at the slave drivers' hands and learned he would never be a match for them. But compared to the devastation happening here, even those most violent of men were but amateurs. Where once the stilted town of Pilotville had hovered high above the swamp like a collection of tree houses among the cypress and tupelo branches, now water flowed freely around the structures and across the boardwalks and through any doors left open, and on the swollen current traveled logs and limbs and every kind of man-made debris. One house had tilted sideways and lay half underwater. Several others had also settled on their pilings and looked ready to float away at any moment. Someone had strung hemp ropes between some of the trees and pilings. Those few residents still trying to move along the flooded boardwalks used these lines as handholds. Others drifted through the village in pirogues, holding lamps up high, dodging the drifting flotsam, their shock obvious in the slackness of their faces. It appeared to Hale that he and the deputy and the few stragglers he could see would be the last ones out. A massive tree emerged slowly from the surrounding darkness. Enormous leafy branches followed by semi-sunken trunk followed by wild tangle of muddy roots, it drifted silently up against a section of boardwalk, where its inertia slowly drove the pilings over, and as the kerosene lamps dipped into the flood to fizzle out one by one, the tree broke loose to continue southward toward the Gulf. A peculiar hush hung above the ruination of Pilotville, as if nature so scorned the works of man she would not deign to comment on their downfall. All Hale Poser heard was rain, always rain, slapping at the flowing water and tapping on his skull.

"Get moving," said the deputy.

Could his mother be alive in this? Hale's hopes faltered. If the water was so high here along the river, it was surely near the top of the levees. Memories of the vision he had seen returned to haunt him: soil bursting under great pressure, water pouring in so rapidly it arced through open air, and bodies, lifeless bodies, drifting slowly in the aftermath.

"Move it!" barked the deputy again. "We got no time to stand and stare."

Praying silently for Marah, Hale turned right toward the river, where he assumed they would board a boat, but the deputy said, "Not that way," and grabbed his upper arm to guide him in the opposite direction. Hale did not ask where they were going. Just as the shackles felt familiar, he had developed the habit of doing as he was told. He moved inland. A few feet from the jail they stepped into the current. The unexpected force of it drove him sideways, and he might have lost his footing if not for the deputy's firm grip upon his arm. Together the men reached one of the hemp lifelines. Hale grasped the line with both hands and slid along it as he shuffled down the boardwalk. The water was now up to his thighs. Twice they had to avoid large debris drifting through the village—another tree and a small section of somebody's roof. As they approached the other side of town they reached the last lantern. Beyond it yawned a gaping blackness. Hale stopped, afraid to continue. The deputy struggled past him to hold the kerosene lamp higher and illuminate the way. From then on, the deputy led and Hale followed as they progressed slowly to the outskirts of the village. The drumming of the rain upon the water's surface underlay everything, constant as their heartbeats and almost as unnoticed. With each passing minute the water rose, inching up their bodies until it reached their waists. The current felt like a living being, straining to knock them from their feet. Only constant vigilance allowed them to advance, step by carefully placed step, clutching the lifeline and leaning into the flow.

Hale saw a glowing ethereal shape in the distant blackness. As he inched closer, the amorphous specter slowly took on form, ragged edges becoming sharp, the sense of motion caused by the dancing rain decreasing, until at last it coalesced into a steady row of flickering yellow rectangles hovering over the water, and he knew they must be windows. The beckoning sanctuary of the Pilotville Negro Infirmary so absorbed Hale Poser's attention that he did not see an uprooted palmetto coming downstream until it struck him in the shoulder.

Instantly he lost his grip on the lifeline and fell below the surface. Unlike before, when he had nearly drowned beside the levee and the handsome man had saved him, Hale now felt no panic. Instead, an odd composure settled on him. Tumbling underwater, he touched the wooden planks sliding by and knew he must stop his downstream motion or he would go over the far side of the boardwalk and his chains would drag him down forever. Here was the very worst kind of violence—slow, methodical, irresistible— yet he merely thought it sad that his fingers found no purchase as he slipped toward his doom. He thought no more of miracles, or of matching violence with violence. Instead he waited patiently as this eerie calmness stretched the seconds into minutes, and in that timeless flow it occurred to Hale that this very moment might be the vision he had seen while standing in the cotton field. This thought gave him hope. It meant Marah and the others might survive. Oh

God, he thought. I submit to this, I truly do. Please let it be me instead of them. Take me, Lord. Please take me instead. He felt the risen Mississippi's warm embrace upon his flesh, drawing him down. He heard odd creaks and groans within the water, as if the ghosts of those who had been this way before were out there somewhere, calling. He saw nothing but blackness. All was lost at last; he had finally reached the precipice of the vision, and he would look. In those stretched-out seconds he saw fresh explanations for everything, as if a secret door had been unlocked inside his mind, only to reveal another, and another, all of them opening onto richly appointed rooms he never dreamed existed. Strangely, once he looked inside, he realized he had always known those rooms were there but feared their very richness. He marveled that such minor apprehensions ever held him back. There was nothing like impending death to put one's fears in order. Now he allowed himself to reenter a peculiar serenity he had lived in for all his life without knowing it was possible, for in it was the answer to the riddle at the gates of heaven. To be naked and not know. To heal when your back is turned.

Yes.

"We are speaking it now."

All of this occurred to Hale Poser in the eternal instant that he offered his own life in place of Marah, Simon, Qana, and the others—forsaking violence, forsaking miracles, forsaking himself—and then his back hit something solid, which held him steady long enough to get his footing on the boardwalk and push up to the surface. He coughed and stood and gulped in air and clung to the only piling above the water for twenty feet in either direction.

"You all right?" called the deputy across the flood between them.

Speechless with elation, Hale Poser nodded in the lantern light.

"Stay there!" said the deputy. "I'll come get you."

The deputy crab-walked across the boardwalk, feet spread wide, buffeted at every step by the unrelenting current. When he reached Hale's side, he set the lantern on top of the piling and said, "I never should have put them things on you. Let me see your hands."

Hale did not release his grip upon the piling.

"I've got you," said the deputy.

Once he felt the lawman's hand grasp his arm, Hale lifted up his wrists, and with his other hand the deputy unlocked the manacles.

"I don't think I can get your shackles off," said the deputy.

"It's all right."

"I'm very sorry."

"Everything's all right."

"Think you can get back across?"

Without answering, Hale leaned into the current and set out toward the lifeline on the other side. The deputy held the lantern high as each of them steadied the other, fighting their way upstream inch by inch until they regained their former positions beside the lifeline. The deputy retook the lead, and with Hale following closely they resumed their journey.

At last they stood waist-deep on the flooded boardwalk opposite the infirmary. The lower floor of the infirmary lay completely underwater, as the flood passed freely through the windows of the second floor. The lights they had seen earlier all came from the third floor. After battling so desperately to reach that vantage point, it appeared there was no hope of crossing the final fifty feet that separated them from safety. A strong current parted around the building to form menacing swirls and back eddies. Even if his ankles had been free, Hale knew he had no hope of swimming through the angry waters.

"Jean!" shouted the deputy, waving the lantern from side to side. "Jean!"

Hale saw a man in silhouette at one of the windows.

"That you, Wallace?" shouted the man.

"I got Poser with me, but we can't get across!"

"What you bring him here for, you?"

"You gonna come get us, or you gonna let us drown while you ask stupid questions?"

"Keep you teeth in, mon. I be there directly."

The black silhouette disappeared, and minutes later a small motorboat appeared around the downstream side of the building. The outboard motor threw up a thick blue cloud of smoke as Jean Tibbits puttered slowly toward the stranded men, angling his little boat across the current. When Tibbits reached the water above the boardwalk he threw the deputy a rope, which the deputy quickly wrapped around the lifeline. Jean Tibbits smiled and lovingly patted the top of the outboard motor. "I tell you she good for something besides scaring off de catfish, no?"

"I don't trust them things," grumbled the deputy, gripping the gunwale.

"You don't trust nothin' but horses and silver money, you."

"Could we talk about this inside?"

"Why you disagreeable?" asked Tibbits. "I just makin' conversation."

"It's been a little rough, you know? I want to get inside."

"I still don't see why you brought him, Wallace. They gonna be trouble."

"Where else could we go? The boats all left. You know that."

"I sayin' they gonna be trouble, is all."

"Just help me get him in."

Because of Hale Poser's deformed hip and the chains on his ankles, he could not step into the boat. It took both of the white men to drag him over the gunwale. When Tibbits saw the shackles, his cheerfulness evaporated.

"You coulda got him drowned, Wallace."

Untying the rope around the lifeline, Deputy Pogue said, "How was I supposed to know it was gonna rise so fast?"

Tibbits merely grunted and directed his attention to the outboard motor's tiller. Soon they were off, sliding across the current toward the infirmary. With the deputy and Hale Poser clinging to the gunwales, Jean Tibbits guided the little craft along the side of the building, steering upstream several dozen feet beyond the corner before turning. His reason for this maneuver became apparent when the current gripped the boat as it angled broadside around the end of the infirmary, driving them rapidly back downstream toward the infirmary wall. Tibbits throttled up and propelled the boat across the flow as quickly as possible. Hale watched as the second floor wall of the old building came rushing toward them. Just when it seemed they would be thrown against the infirmary the boat made it round the far corner. He had not been afraid.

On the other side of the building now, they moved quickly downstream. About midway down the facade, Tibbits steered toward the gabled roof above the flooded ground-floor entrance. Jean Tibbits drove the bow of his little craft onto the shingled slope as if it were a beach. Deputy Pogue leapt from the boat to the roof with the bowline in his hand. Standing near the peak, he held the bow steady as Tibbits killed the motor and helped Hale out of the boat. Together the three men edged across the incline toward a window overlooking the roof. Halfway there, Hale Poser's shackles tripped him. He went sliding on his bottom toward the water. Tibbits responded quickly, grabbing Hale's shirt and tugging him back up toward the ridge.

"Wallace," said Tibbits, breathing heavily from the effort, "I can't believe you put them things on him, you."

"Lay off, will ya? You act like I was trying to sink him."

"Well, this a bad way to help him float."

"Who went clear across town in this mess to get him out of jail? Answer me that."

"Just take them things off his legs, no?"

"I will not. He's okay now, and besides, he's a prisoner, Jean. I will not let him get away, flood or no flood."

Jean Tibbits said no more, shaking his head instead and careful to keep one hand firmly on Hale's arm for support. Reaching the wall, Tibbits and the deputy helped the prisoner crawl through a window into a third-floor storage room. Although Hale Poser knew the room well as the place where he had once kept his cleaning supplies and dirty linens, his short life as the Pilotville Negro Infirmary's janitor now seemed part of someone else's memory. He felt as though everything before his ordeal in the fields was mere fantasy, and the only true thing left was his newfound peculiar peace.

"Come on, fellas," said Jean Tibbits. "We get some coffee."

Dripping wet, the deputy and Hale followed Tibbits out of the room and down the hall to the third door on the right—a children's ward, if Hale remembered properly— where a flickering yellow light fell out onto the floor. They entered the long and narrow room where they found beds against both walls, divided by bedside tables, upright lockers, and thin white curtains strung on wires. Apparently the patients had been evacuated, for healthy people sat on the floor and on the beds or stood in small groups watching through the windows as the flood destroyed much of the small town they had built. Some of them had sheets or blankets wrapped round their shoulders. Few spoke. Many seemed to be in shock. A sense of tragedy hovered in the room, as if they had come upon a wake or a deathbed scene. Kerosene lanterns burned on many of the bedside tables, and on a cabinet beside the hallway door someone had found a way to brew a pot of coffee. Jean Tibbits grabbed two white ceramic mugs and thrust them into the hands of the deputy and Hale. "You fellas probably need a little pick-me-up," he said, turning to lift the coffeepot from its stand.

As Tibbits filled their mugs, a barefoot white woman in a damp cotton dress came to stand beside the deputy. Wrapping his free hand around her waist, he pulled her close and kissed the top of her head. "Told you I'd be all right," he said. Saying nothing, the woman laid her cheek against Wallace Pogue's chest and stared with open animosity at Hale Poser.

Reverend Vogt and Brother Julius detached themselves from a small group huddled by a nearby window. The pastors of Pilotville's two churches approached with grim faces. One tall, fat, sloppy, and white, and the other short, thin, dapper, and black, the only similarity between them was their solemn expressions. Silas Vogt said, "Wallace, what is that man doing here?"

"There's no place else to put him," said the deputy, pulling away from his wife.

"Doesn't matter," said Brother Julius, "this isn't right." He glanced across the room at Dorothy Truett.

Reverend Vogt nodded solemnly. "We can't have a child molester here, Deputy. We got children in this room."

Hale Poser said nothing.

The deputy said, "Right now he's just a suspect, Reverend. We don't know he's a child molester."

"What else could he be?" asked Brother Julius. "Him out there with the baby all that time? James and Rosa got no ransom money, so we know it wasn't that."

As the two men's voices rose, several people nearby glanced their way with frowns, and in spite of Hale Poser's peaceful frame of mind, he thought it might be wise to run. But that was impossible with his ankles chained again.

"Brother Julius," whispered the deputy, "you need to keep your voice down. There's a few white folks here would lynch this fella if it crossed their mind he done that."

Ignoring this, Julius said, "Did you know Rosa Lamont is here with her children and her little baby?" The pastor pointed to the far end of the room. "She's sitting right over there, scared to death James isn't gonna come back alive! He wouldn't even be out there in this mess if this . . . this . . . *suspect* hadn't taken their little girl!"

Hale turned his eyes to Rosa Lamont, who sat upon a bed cradling her baby in her arms. It was good to see the child in her mother's arms. He thought again of Marah. He wished he could remember what it had been like—lying in her arms that way. Looking around the room Hale also saw Dorothy Truett, watching him. She quickly dropped her eyes. White and black alike, every face in the room revealed revulsion at his presence. He felt sorry to be the cause of so much ill will. He tried to explain, to make them feel better. "I only tried to save the baby," he said.

"If that's true," said Reverend Vogt, "how come you've been hiding her in the swamp all this time?"

"Yeah!" shouted someone across the room. "How come you didn't bring her back?"

"I couldn't," said Hale.

"*Wouldn't* is more like it!"

"I wanted to bring her sooner," said Hale. "I wanted to bring them all back. But they wouldn't come, and the boss had me chained the whole time, and besides, I wasn't sure where we were, and—"

Someone said, "What's he talking about?"

Another voice called, "Get him out of here!"

Deputy Pogue stepped to the prisoner's side and gripped his forearm. "Ain't goin' nowhere," said the lawman. "Not while he's my prisoner."

Meanwhile, Jean Tibbits stared at Hale Poser thoughtfully. Leaning close to the deputy, he spoke quietly, "You hear what he just say?"

"Yeah?"

"You remember how he walk yesterday, yes?"

The deputy glanced at Tibbits. Then he turned to stare at Hale. "What was that you said about being chained?" he asked.

Hale Poser said, "You won't believe me."

"Try me."

Hale opened his mouth to speak when someone shouted, "We could give him a trial right here!"

"Shut up, you!" yelled Jean Tibbits. "Let de fella have his say!"

Hale Poser caught Rosa Lamont's eye. "Do you believe what they're saying?"

With a sad expression the woman looked away, and Hale Poser knew he had no allies in that place. He had survived illness and hunger and thirst and whips and chains and grinding bondage; he had survived wicked slave masters and a mob of drunken racists, only to find himself beset by Christian people of both colors who were willing—no, eager—to believe the worst of him. With this realization came a full understanding of the cruel trap Papa DeGroot had laid in bringing him back to Pilotville. His only hope to survive was in telling them the truth and by so doing convince them of his madness. And yet telling the truth would surely doom the slaves who might still live behind the levees, for just as no one had believed him there, no one would believe him here, and these people would look no further than his madness for an explanation to the crimes his father had inflicted upon James and Rosa and little Hannah Lamont and all those other parents and children for so long. Perhaps with lies he could deceive them into looking for the levees, tell them something that would make them think he had confederates or other victims still out there to be found. But lies, deceit, and false miracles had caused too much pain already. So Hale Poser told the truth. Beginning at the beginning, with a yellowed file discovered in the attic of a peeling mansion on a red-brick street in New Orleans. He told them everything. Everything but his own heritage. His deepest blessings and curses would be best kept to himself.

24

Ever since they brought that so-called reverend in from the swamp yesterday, Dorothy Truett had been furious at the way he had fooled her into thinking he was some kind of miracle worker. Obviously, he was the very opposite of that: an evil, evil man. She could think of little else. Even as the water crept into her house, even as she ran around collecting her most precious things to save them from the flood, thoughts of how he had tricked her set her teeth on edge. Yet now, as he told his story, she felt herself drawn in by the drama of it all, and when he finished she could only stare at him speechlessly, wondering if it could possibly be true.

Julius Gray's laughter broke the spell. "I do declare," he said. "That is by far the finest lie I ever did hear."

Dorothy knew it was important that no one guess how close she had just come to believing this man. Joining the attack, she said, "I think it's scandalous, standing here and talking this way about Papa." Many others agreed in angry tones. Everyone in that room owed something to Papa DeGroot, especially the Negroes.

Joining in, Brother Julius said, "Why would Papa have

men watching these people with whips and rifles?"

"They're *slaves!*" exclaimed the prisoner, that so-called reverend. "Don't you understand? They're no different from our grandparents, except they were never freed! They've been out there in those fields all along!"

Lifting her chin high, Dorothy said, "If that were true, I think we would have known."

"Of course we would have known," said Reverend Vogt, turning toward the prisoner. "And even if these slaves are really there—which of course they are not—you say the reason they won't come out is because we don't all go to the same *church*?"

This set Julius Gray to laughing once again, so Dorothy smiled along with him, although she had to force it.

"No!" said the so-called reverend. "I mean it's not the way you make it sound. They said they'd come out if I could promise a place where colored folks and white folks get along, but . . . I couldn't lie to them."

"Lie to them?" said Reverend Vogt. "But we *do* all get along! And I for one am very proud of that!"

Shaking his head, the stranger said, "You folks here are decent people, near as I can tell, but come Sunday morning y'all go off in different directions. In the things that matter most you still can't get together."

"Well, that's just silly," said Dorothy. "We could get together any Sunday we wanted to."

Brother Julius looked at Dorothy and said, "Sister, I wouldn't go that far."

"Maybe you wouldn't, Julius," said Dorothy, glancing sideways at Reverend Vogt and the deputy, "but I'd be comfortable as can be over at the white church. In fact, I even think of going there sometimes, except it's a longer walk from my house, you know."

"Sister Truett, it's not your place to go there," said Brother Julius.

"Oh, she'd be welcome, Brother," assured Reverend Vogt. "You, too, of course."

"That's not what I mean."

The white pastor frowned. "I don't understand."

"With all due respect, Reverend, the Negro Christian is not responsible for our current separation, so it would not be proper for the Negro Christian to take the first step toward correcting it."

Oh God, thought Dorothy, when will you teach this fool it's best to go along?

Sure enough, she saw the blood rush to Reverend Vogt's face. "Are you saying my congregation has done something wrong?"

"*We* did not enslave *you*."

"I have nothing to apologize for! I wasn't even born until 1877!"

"That's not the point. You have to—"

"It certainly *is* the point!" interrupted the white pastor. "You act like it's our fault we don't worship together, but everyone knows the only reason is all that wild dancing and singing you people do."

"What's wrong with dancing and singing?" Dorothy saw Brother Julius's chest swell up like a gamecock's. "David leapt for joy before the Lord! And the psalmist says to make a joyful noise before him!"

"Maybe we should calm down a little," said Reverend Vogt, showing Brother Julius his palms. "I'm just saying we have different ways, and they wouldn't blend together very well. I'm not saying there's anything wrong with that."

"That's right," said the deputy. "The Lord don't care where we all worship, so long as we all do."

Then the so-called reverend took Dorothy Truett

completely by surprise. At first she had feared some of them might pitch him out into the flood. Now they were all so busy arguing among themselves, she thought he might be safe. But either he was too dumb to see his opportunity (which she did not believe for a minute) or he was up to something she did not understand, because although she would have been as quiet as a mouse in *his* position, the so-called reverend straightened up and said, " 'Now the God of patience and consolation grant you to be likeminded one toward another according to Christ Jesus, that ye may with one mind and one mouth glorify God—' "

"Don't you quote the Scriptures to *us!*" interrupted Brother Julius, turning on him.

"If you had a better education," added Reverend Vogt in a patronizing tone, "you'd know that verse simply means we should all agree on basic doctrine."

"Exactly!" boomed Brother Julius, narrowing his eyes.

But the so-called reverend did not seem to care about the warnings in their voices. He said, "What about the verse that says, 'Holy Father, keep through thine own name those whom thou hast given me, that they may be one, as we are'?"

"We *are* one!" insisted Reverend Vogt. "Whether we worship together or not has nothing to do with that. Isn't that right, Brother?" When Brother Julius remained silent, the white reverend turned to him and said, "Julius?"

"There can be no doubt that Negro and white believers are divided," said Brother Julius in the booming voice he usually reserved for the pulpit. "Still, it is no fault of ours."

The look on Reverend Vogt's face scared Dorothy just a little. "That's an outrage!"

"Fellas, fellas," interjected the deputy. "I don't understand half of what the Good Book says, but it seems like God has better things to worry about than the color of the people in his pews."

"Yes," said Dorothy. "Couldn't we talk about something else?"

But the so-called reverend would not let it go. He said, "Tell that to those slaves. Tell *them* color doesn't matter."

"I'm not saying it don't matter to *us*. I'm saying it don't matter to God!" said the deputy.

"But if it doesn't matter to him, why should it matter to us?"

"Why, because . . . because . . . Aw, you got me all turned around."

Dorothy saw the prisoner clasp his hands together and shake them like a beggar. "Please! All I'm asking is for some of you—some Negroes and some whites—to come back out with me. I think I can find that place again. And it might not be too late. We could take some trawlers or pilot boats. With the water so high, we could float right through the swamp. If we did that, if we went there all together, they might believe enough to come here where it's safe. But we have to go together, Negroes and whites. To show them there's a better place. Oh please, won't y'all go back with me?"

Mr. Tibbits said, "All my trawlers left out for New Orleans already, filled to de gunnels with them that lost they houses first. De pilot boats, too. Why you think we all here, mon?"

The deputy threw up both his hands. "For crying out loud, Jean. Will you listen to yourself? Explainin' things like there really are a bunch of slaves who won't come out because we ain't cozy with the coloreds on Sundays."

"Maybe he lyin'," said Mr. Tibbits. "But he walking like he got shackles on when he come off de boat. I wish someone tell me why he do that."

"He's probably a convict, just like Teddy said," replied the deputy. "And I blame myself. I should of known it. At first I thought he was a flimflam man, with all that miracle talk and all. I should of trusted my instincts."

"Whatever kind of man he is," said Brother Julius, "the fact remains that we don't want him here."

There was a general round of loudly assenting voices. Dorothy joined in.

"All right, all right!" snapped the deputy. "Where am I supposed to take him? Should I just throw him out the window and let him drown?"

"Don't be ridiculous, Wallace," said the Reverend Silas Vogt. "Just put him in another room somewhere . . . anyplace, so long as he isn't here among us decent people." And Dorothy Truett felt a swell of pride, because when Reverend Vogt said "decent people," he was looking right at her.

With the prisoner safely locked up in a closet down the hall and everyone calmed down, Wallace Pogue could not stop thinking about that story. Slaves and a lost plantation. He had been a lawman for all of his adult life. He had heard a lot of lies. He knew them when he heard them. And of course this was a lie. But there was something . . .

No. Don't be ridiculous. He glanced around as if afraid someone might guess how close he had just come to believing all that nonsense. Everywhere people slept on beds or chairs or curled up in little nests of blankets on the floor. One or two still wept quietly for their disappearing homes, or for fear that missing loved ones might be hurt. Here and there a lantern burned, though most had been extinguished to save the kerosene. The two preachers had retired to different corners long ago, surrounded by a few of the most faithful. Each of them had talked into the night and then finally fallen asleep. Over there Jean Tibbits snored loudly. Closer by, Rosa Lamont and her children lay entangled on two beds pushed together, faces angelic in their sleep. Dorothy Truett slept sitting up against the wall across the way, a pillow propped behind her head and a thin line of drool running across her chin. Wallace smiled. She would be petrified if she knew about the drool. But at least she could sleep. As he sprawled in the wooden chair beside his slumbering wife's bed, dreams eluded Wallace Pogue. Instead, the prisoner's story replayed itself again and again in his mind.

He slid two fingers into his shirt pocket and removed a crumpled pack of Lucky Strikes. Shaking one out, he slipped it between his lips and fumbled for a match. Of course the man was crazy. Or at least his story sure was crazy. It turned everything around. Papa wasn't a philanthropist; he was a monstrous parasite. Pilotville wasn't a sanctuary from racism; it was a breeding ground for human cattle. The infirmary wasn't a healing place; it was a gateway into hell on earth. And the Lord's house wasn't filled with love; it was divided by apathy and mistrust. The story was an upside-down vision of the world—where good was evil, safety was danger, and benevolence was hate.

But say it was all true, just for the sake of argument.

Wallace lit the cigarette.

Usually when they lied, it was easy to pick the lies apart. The best lies were simple, and stayed as close to the truth as possible. But this story was a whopper. Anything but simple. Rather than holding closely to the truth, the prisoner denied almost everything about the way Wallace saw his world. So it was an unusual lie, at the very least. Yet if you were crazy enough to accept just one thing about it, you had to admit the story hung together. Say, for example, that Papa DeGroot was that kind of man. Wallace had known

Papa for many years. He had seen Papa among Negroes, shaking their hands, holding their children, lending them money and helping them in a thousand different ways. One thing Wallace Pogue had never seen, however, was Papa laughing with them, or crying with them, or showing any kind of emotion whatsoever. Wallace had always felt a kind of distance around Papa, as if the old man lived behind a wall of glass. And the old man wasn't just that way around colored people. As far as Wallace could tell, Papa held whites at a distance, too. When Jenny got beat up that time, Papa came by with flowers and said all the right things. They had appreciated the visit, but after he was gone, Jenny had turned to Wallace and said, "That man makes me nervous." Her words had seemed ungrateful at the time. He had said so, and they had fought about it. Now, glancing at his wife curled up beside him with her face so much like a child's, Wallace felt a twinge of shame. For truth be told, Papa DeGroot made him nervous, too.

So say that part of what the prisoner said was true. The remarkable thing about his crazy story was, if you said that, if you allowed that Papa was a monster in disguise, then everything else made a kind of twisted sense. In fact, it explained some things that had bothered Wallace Pogue for many years now. Was there even the slightest possibility? wondered the lawman.

No.

Of course not.

Exhaling a long stream of blue smoke, Wallace stared off into nothing.

Papa DeGroot was a fine man, one of the best, who spared no expense for the sake of the poor and was always ready to lend a helping hand to the Negroes of Pilotville. It took a lot of guts to take the stand he did in this day and age. There was no Klan in Pilotville, and those who ought to know said Papa was the reason. There had never been a lynching thereabouts in the entire time Wallace had been a deputy. And you didn't see a WHITES ONLY sign anywhere in Pilotville. Whites and Negroes lived side by side, worked side by side, and played side by side. Wallace had always felt proud of the fact that the races got along so well in his adopted hometown, doing everything together.

Well, almost everything.

The prisoner was right about Sunday mornings. But for some reason, that had never bothered Wallace much. He didn't mind fishing with his colored friends, or eating barbeque with them. He didn't mind attending their weddings and funerals, or telling jokes and lies with them over at Delacroix's. But when it came to church, he and Jenny always went to the white one without a second thought.

Now along comes this fellow, a very evil man for all Wallace knew, asking questions. Why did they have two churches in such a tiny town? Why did all the whites go to one, and all the coloreds to the other? Yes, it was remarkable in this day and age for the races to work and play and laugh and mourn together as they all did. So didn't that make it all the more remarkable that they worshiped apart?

Taking another deep drag on his cigarette, Wallace had to admit they were interesting questions. The really fascinating thing was the way those questions had made so many people mad. And they had been mad. You could see it in the way they got all defensive, with Silas saying the two churches was because of the way the coloreds sing and dance (which, he had to admit, did make Wallace a little bit uncomfortable), and Dorothy first denying it altogether, then saying she didn't want to walk that far (as if the white church were miles away instead of just around the corner), and Julius blaming it all on whites (he always was a hothead). Every single one of them got all heated up about it, while Wallace didn't understand what all the fuss was about. It wasn't as if the Poser fellow came right out and accused them of being a bunch of bigots, after all. More like he just thought they'd done a fair job of work, but then left the very last part undone. Maybe so, although Wallace was pretty sure God didn't care if everyone went to church together, so long as they went to church. And if there really were slaves out there somewhere, people trapped behind levees so high they couldn't see beyond them to the outside world, well, surely they had better reasons for staying where they were than the trivial one this prisoner come up with. Imagine someone saying he would not do the one thing that would set him free just because the white folk and the coloreds didn't get together on Sunday mornings.

Nope. That dog won't hunt.

But it was still pretty interesting how it made them all so mad.

Wallace took a final drag on the cigarette and stood to find a place to put it out. As he walked past a window, something outside caught his eye. Pausing, he leaned closer to try to make it out through the ripples of rainwater running down outside the glass. A light, weaving through the trees and moving slowly toward them where no light should be. Two lights. No, three. One white and high, one red, and . . . there, yes, the other one was green. Wallace Pogue pushed his nose against the glass, staring hard until the cigarette burned his fingers. Wincing, he dropped the butt to the floor and ground it out beneath his boot. Then he looked outside again, his right hand settling on the revolver at his hip.

||James Lamont steered the trawler right across Pilotville, doing his best to remember the layout of the town below the surface. With most of the surviving buildings more than halfway submerged, it was obvious he had plenty of water under his keel, but it wouldn't do to run up against one of the cypress boardwalk pilings. How strange it was, to be cruising through town in an oceangoing boat, training his searchlight back and forth across the water, watching out for flotsam as the metal roofs of his neighbors' houses slipped slowly by to port and starboard.

Mercy, look at that. Ralph and Louise's brand-new place, leaning up against a stand of trees, yonder. Used to be a hundred yards to the east. But over there, Bill Walker's little shack still proud and straight in spite of all this mess. The old woman stood beside him, staring wide-eyed at the circular glimpses of metal roofs and cistern tanks provided by the searchlight beam. She had brought him luck. From the moment he took her aboard, it was as if another hand had guided his upon the wheel. After all that running round in circles, he never wavered, but steered directly to the river.

James Lamont had known before they got here it would

be very bad. He did not even pause to try to find the docks, which were surely under twelve or fifteen feet of water. He looped around the edge of town instead, around behind the roof of the Acme Shrimp and Oyster packing plant, staying clear of most of the other buildings and boardwalks and setting out toward the one place where survivors might be gathered, if any still remained.

Strange as it was to see his town from the deck of *La Vie Joyeuse* with everything flooded to the eaves, the total lack of any human being was the strangest thing of all. He had not expected that. He had assumed there would be others here, floating around in boats or sitting in the rain upon their roofs, waiting for help. He had expected to find rescue work to do. But apparently the pilots and his fellow fishermen had already finished that job, for the entire town seemed to be evacuated. He trained the searchlight on each roof that he passed, seeing nothing, not even a dog, as beside him the old woman stared into the darkness. "We almost there," said James, but she stood silently beside him like he was not there. Ever since she came aboard it had been that way, with him talking and her pretending she did not understand. It bothered him that she would not speak. After all, he had saved her life. He was curious about a few things, such as who she was and how she came to be out in the middle of the swamp. After so much time searching for his baby all alone, it would be good just to speak to someone, so it was frustrating to have her acting like he wasn't even here. Just a little conversation—it seemed a small thing to ask, a common courtesy.

"Don't see why you won't talk to me, ma'am. I ain't a bad fella, you know. I'm a family man, and an honest fisherman. I'm a deacon at my church. But I been out here a long time all alone. Couldn't we just talk a little? I surely would appreciate it."

She turned toward him, her eyes showing what looked to be fear. "Yes, boss" was all she said.

He gave up on her entirely and concentrated on steering the boat, and on swinging the searchlight to and fro as he scoped out a clear path to the infirmary. Soon enough he saw the dim flicker of lanterns through the trees. With bittersweet emotions he steered a couple points to port and aimed straight for them and, after a few more minutes, saw it was indeed the building he sought. There in a window was a man's silhouette. Part of him prayed that Rosa and the children were high and safe up on the third floor, for he did not trust their welfare to any other captain in this flood, and preferred to take them out himself. But another part of him prayed he would not find his family there, because that would mean the moment was upon them when they must admit their baby girl was gone forever. As he drew near, he wondered for the hundredth time how to put things to his wife. "I guess we got to let our baby go" was the best he could do, and it wasn't nearly good enough. It was such a simple thing to turn the bow of *La Vie Joyeuse* into the current and walk her over to the wall, but if his Rosa waited there, he was steering into misery.

The man in the window turned out to be Deputy Pogue, and now Mr. Tibbits stood in another window, both of them ready to man the lines. In this current it would have been a help to have the old woman go to the bow and throw a rope to Mr. Tibbits. But at the sight of the men in the windows, she backed into the aft corner of the house, where she cowered with the same look of terror he had seen upon her face when he first found her. James Lamont tried to smile again, to let her know that all was well, only he could not bring himself to raise the corners of his mouth and bare his teeth. Everything in him was against it, for all was far from well. So he focused his attention on docking alongside the third floor of the Pilotville Negro Infirmary and he let the strange old woman be.

Once the vessel nudged the bricks, James threw the wheel over all the way to port and left the engine in gear at idle speed. That way she would press against the building just a bit, holding herself steady while he ran out into the rain to toss the lines. It was a strange feeling, tying up to the infirmary with dock lines running in through third-floor windows, but soon enough they were secured as though it were a proper dock, with Mr. Tibbits and Deputy Pogue both shouting questions from the windows. What took him so long? Where had he been? What did he see out there? Was the rest of town still standing? He tried to answer quick as he could, knowing it did not pay to ignore the questions of a lawman or your boss. When he could wait no longer, he said, "Is my family here?"

Mr. Tibbits smiled. "They here," he said. "They *all* here."

James thought it strange the way he said that, because of course they were not all there. One of them was forever lost. Then he caught the merry look in Mr. Tibbits's eye, and he turned to Deputy Pogue and saw something there as well, and all of a sudden he knew, he just knew, and without an instant's thought he dove headfirst through the open window, hit the floor on hands and knees, rose up and looked around, and there, over there beside that bed, there they all were, every single one.

With all the crying and hugging and praising Jesus going on, it took a little while for James Lamont to get around to asking how his baby had been found.

Wallace let Dorothy Truett tell the story, since she seemed so eager to get involved. He listened as she told how Teddy Beauregard claimed he'd found the Poser man and

the baby, and how "that so-called reverend" said he'd been
a captive at a slave plantation of all things, but how nobody
believed that, of course. Wallace Pogue took a deep breath
when she started in to telling James the man who took his
baby was locked up in a closet down the hall.

This is the tricky part, thought Wallace. If I was him, I'd
want to kill that fella, sure enough. So he watched James
Lamont very closely, ready to come down hard on any sign
that he might try to take the law into his own hands. To
Wallace Pogue's surprise, the baby's father seemed calm,
almost thoughtful at hearing the news.

Suddenly the fisherman hit his forehead with his palm.
"Can't believe I forgot!" he said, striding toward the window. "I got an old woman out there. Found her stuck up in
a tree."

As James crawled out through the window, Wallace
asked, "How come she didn't come in with you?"

"She real scared, Mr. Pogue."

Everybody moved to the windows, waiting for James to
reappear from inside the trawler's cabin with the old
woman. It seemed to take longer than it should, and Wallace became suspicious. What if he's got a gun in there?
What if he comes out with a shotgun and demands to see
the prisoner? The lawman's hand found its way to the hol-
stered pistol at his hip. He thought about telling everyone
to stand back from the windows. Then came the muffled
sound of a raised voice from the trawler, then a woman's
scream, and a moment later James emerged again, empty-
handed. Wallace let out a heavy breath, unaware he had
been holding it for all that time.

"She won't come," said James.

"Why not?" asked Wallace.

"I don't know. She don't say nothin' to me except 'Yes,
boss.'"

"Why would she say that?"

Dorothy Truett said, "She's probably just frightened of climbing in the window, poor thing. Who wouldn't be?"

"Well," said James Lamont, a little doubtfully, "she pretty old . . ."

"Oh, for goodness' sake," said Dorothy. "Let me out there." Hiking up her skirt, the nurse threw one sturdy leg over the sill, and then the other, and soon she stood upon the trawler's deck. James moved aside to give her entry to the cabin door, where Dorothy disappeared inside. The men waited. This time no loud voices could be heard, and no screams. After just a little while, Dorothy reappeared. "Give her room," she said, and James stepped forward, leaving a clear deck to the window closest to the cabin. Dorothy ducked inside the boat again but only for a second, and when she came back out the old woman was with her, clinging to her arm.

In the darkness Wallace could not be sure of what he saw, but when James and Dorothy helped the woman through the window and she stood fully in the lamplight of the infirmary he could scarcely believe his eyes. The home-spun shift she wore, the long ropy hair, the horny bottoms of her feet—which had obviously not seen shoes in many years, if ever—her deeply cracked and callused hands. Everything about the woman spoke of a long life of hardship and hard labor. Stepping closer, he said, "Who are you?"

The old woman cowered back.

"It's all right," said Wallace. "You're safe here. Will you tell us your name?"

She said, "Yes, boss," and nothing more.

"What's the matter with her?" asked the Reverend Silas Vogt.

"I don't know," said Wallace.

"You're scaring her!" said Dorothy, wrapping a protective arm around the old woman's shoulder.

"I'm just standing here," said Wallace.

"Well, give me a minute. I'll find out who she is for you."

Dorothy Truett guided the old woman toward the far end of the long room, whispering to her all the way. Although Wallace tried to hear, he could not make out what the nurse said. He did notice that the old woman did not answer Dorothy. Then, as the women passed the bed where the Lamont children had been sleeping, the old woman pulled away from Dorothy to approach a small picture hanging on the wall. Reaching up with her gnarled hand, she touched it and said, "Jesus?"

"Sure," said Dorothy Truett, nodding.

It was as if a floodgate had been opened. The old woman turned back toward Dorothy and began to chatter rapidly. Waving her hands in the air at the picture, her voice rose louder and louder until she was fairly shouting, the unintelligible words coming fast, waking the few still sleeping in the infirmary ward and echoing out beyond that room to travel through the entire building.

"Marah!" came a voice from far away. "Marah!"

The old woman fell silent. "Moses?" she whispered. And suddenly her face burned with joy, and she shouted "Moses! Moses!" and she pushed past Dorothy Truett and ran out through the hallway door.

Despite his sinking hope, despite floods and death and betrayal, the strange tranquility remained so that only one desire had consumed Hale Poser's heart: thy will be done. He longed to speak the words but did not dare just yet. There was a time when he had meant them so sincerely that he rarely felt the need to give them voice. Then came

Pilotville, and confusion about who was doing what, and the phrase became a kind of compromise, a disguise for discontent and doubt. There was a blessed time when he had not worked miracles, if miracles were something far outside the norm, exceptions to the rules, wholly unexpected. Before Pilotville, he had *expected* to find persimmons when he asked for them, and resurrected blackbirds, and believers' voices folded in together as if one. Before Pilotville, he had known no miracles, just the constant ways God showed his love, which were not miracles at all, for they were with him every day, invisible because they were so much in evidence. Then someone spoke that word *miracle*, and it entered his foolish head to ask for what he already had, and miracles had seemed to come, and in his heart of hearts he saw them as an outgrowth of his faith, which was of course the very death of miracles, because he had found the surest way to lose a miracle is to try to hold it in your hand.

Sighing, Hale Poser bowed his head. His knowledge of this paradox had come too late. Too late for Marah, too late for Simon, too late for High, and Low, and even Qana, who, brute that he was, had been the only one with sense enough to ask the question properly.

"Are the niggers out there really free?"

Now that Hale remembered miracles were everywhere, and therefore nowhere, he saw his self-deception. Knowing the truth of a thousand affronts endured by every American Negro, knowing that his race was not truly free, not even in the Jesus world, he had answered Qana's question with silence because that truth would not get the thing done properly, and in his pride he would not offer them a lie. He had remained silent, as if telling that particular truth or that particular lie had been the only options. But now, with Qana's question ringing in his memory and the paradox of miracles standing plain before him, Hale Poser saw the full dimensions of his error. Just as he had placed himself between the Lord and miracles, he had placed himself between the Lord and Qana. That huge man and all the others had no need for the almighty god of miracles, no need for Marah's Angry One, high up in the clouds, roaring with thunder and eager to cast down lightning. Qana and the others knew that god too well, had lived with his image every second of every day for all their lives. That god ruled the bosses, sitting high up in their saddles with whips coiled at their sides. And heaven forgive him, that god had ruled the Reverend Hale Poser, late of New Orleans, Louisiana, healer of pregnant women, procurer of meat, silencer of storms, and too puffed up with fine theology to answer Qana's simple question simply. The slaves had seen enough of this kind of all-powerful multicolored god. What they needed was a God of sweat and calluses, a God of tears and sorrows, a God of muddy feet and hard labor who knew exactly what it was to live in chains of bondage, a God who was just one color—theirs.

Hale Poser, temporarily insane with the miraculous, had forgotten who his Savior was. If only he could go back to tell them! But of course he had no right to ask for that, and even if he had, free or slave, alive or dead, in the bosom of his mother or orphaned once again, it would have been the wrong request. There was just one miracle he needed now, one thing he could ask for to be certain all would end up as it should. So Hale Poser prayed for that one thing. Fully prepared again at last to accept whatever blessing he might receive, even if that blessing came in somber robes of grief, he whispered the words, "Thy will be done."

In the instant that he said it, a heavenly voice came to him.

We are speaking it now.

A voice so laden with emotion it must surely come from

paradise, speaking Jesus' name, praising Jesus . . . no, begging him.

We are speaking it now.

And gradually, as Hale descended from his reverie, he began to understand the voice was praising Jesus here on earth, in his ears and in his heart, and he heard familiar rhythms in it, and he knew the voice—it was the one in all the earth he most deeply longed to hear—and he shouted out her name.

"Marah! Marah!"

The voice stopped instantly, as if someone had gagged her. Indeed the abrupt silence half convinced Hale Poser that her voice had been a dream, but then came "Moses!" shouted loud and clear, and "Moses!" again, much louder, and she was outside in the hall calling for him, and he was calling back, and both of them were laughing. Then the door swung open, and the deputy was there, and she, his mother, pushed past the man and entered, standing before him, finally free, a miracle, and he, her son, stood before her with hands and feet in irons . . . and the joy upon his mother's face slowly vanished like a sunset.

"Oh, Moses," she whispered as she touched the bonds on his wrists, "you said we would be free. . . ."

Curiosity plain upon their faces, Deputy Pogue, Nurse Truett, Brother Julius and Reverend Vogt crowded close outside to watch Hale laugh and cup the old woman's cheeks in both his hands. "I *am* free," he said.

She seized his manacled wrists and gently pushed them away. "Don't talk foolishness."

"But—"

She pressed a finger to his lips. "I am your mother. I birthed you and suckled you and learned you your first words. Please don't make me listen while my boy acts the fool."

Hale Poser trembled as he spoke the word past her finger, "Momma."

"Oh, Moses, Moses . . ." She embraced him. "You was always special. From the earliest day I seen it. Everybody did. Even the ol' Master knew that you was different. It's why I named you like I did."

"I am Moses."

"Yes." She pushed back. "You the baby in the basket. I set you free, Moses. I sent you in a pirogue to the Angry One and all this time I know you gonna come back holding miracles in your fist. Blood in the water. Flies. Frogs. Terrible sores on all the white men. I knew you gonna come with death in your hand for their children, just like they put ours to walking death in the fields. But you don't work no miracles like that. You come back from the Angry One talking all this foolish talk. Oh, he a cruel one to do this to me! After all the waiting, the Angry One send you back talking foolish talk like this."

She broke into sobs. Although his chains would not allow him to embrace her, Hale stepped close and touched her arm. "God isn't cruel. He loves you."

"Loves me? How can that be? You seen what he done! I an old woman, Moses. I lived my life without you. I give you up for nothing."

"But God does love you. And, Momma—" Hale stooped to place his face close to hers—"you asked me what color he is, remember? And I said he's every color that there is?"

Wiping her nose, Hale's mother nodded.

"I was wrong to say that. It isn't true. God loves you so much he came down from heaven just to tell you so. And he didn't come all high-and-mighty like he could have. Not with thunder and lightning and power." Pausing, Hale Poser bent still further, seeking her eyes. "Listen to me now, and I'll tell you a miracle, the biggest one I know. Are you listening?"

Eyes down to avoid him, she nodded.

Hale Poser said, "God came down a nigger."

She was staring at him now, her eyes awash but steady. When she spoke, it was a whisper. "The Angry One come down like that?"

"Yes, Momma. He came just like us, chains and all. Everything they do to us he let them do to him, to prove he really loves us. He did it to show us how to be free no matter what they do."

Still whispering, she said, "Why didn't you tell us?"

Hale looked beyond her to the hallway, through the open door, searching the faces of the black and white believers standing there together, yet apart. "For a little while," he said, "I forgot."

"You *forgot*?" She screamed it at him and her eyes flashed, and he thought she would slap him. Apparently the deputy thought so too, because he charged in, laying hands on Marah. The old woman begged, "Moses! Moses! Don't let him take me!"

"Momma!" cried Hale. To the deputy, he said, "Please, sir! It's all right! Please let her go!"

The deputy released her, and she ran to wrap him in her arms again, kissing his cheeks and begging, "Forgive me, Moses! I didn't mean it. Please forgive me!"

"What's going on here?" asked the deputy.

"You've been right there listening," said Hale, chained in his mother's embrace. "You know as much as I do."

"I don't know nothing of the kind. How am I supposed to know, with you two speaking all that gibberish?"

"Gibberish? What gibberish?"

Wallace Pogue looked back at the others. "Anybody understand these two?" They all shook their heads.

"Momma," said Hale, calming Marah. "Momma, tell him you're all right. Speak slowly so he'll understand."

Hale's mother looked up strangely. "How can he understand me, Moses? You know I don't talk the white man's way."

Hale Poser felt the earth shift just a little, for although he had learned the paradox of miracles, here was one last mystery revealed.

We are speaking it now.

He remembered that terrible night when he had found three small logs and placed them crossways in a puddle on the ground. One for the Father. One for the Son. One for the Holy Ghost. He remembered asking God for one more miracle, tripping on the paradox and rising up with bitterness, sure his prayer had gone unanswered. But now Hale Poser understood his miracles were constant, even when he made an idol of them. He remembered the handsome overseer, looking at him curiously and saying, *"You understand her, don't you, boy?"* And his father, with that same look of curiosity, saying, *"My dear boy . . . we are speaking it now."*

We are speaking it now.

Despite the chains, Hale drew his mother close and spoke the words a mother longs to hear, and heard the words a son desires, and in that precious moment he felt bathed in love completely, for this was language he had not learned and yet had spoken all along. Finally he understood that every single moment of his time with her had been a miracle, invisible because it was so much in evidence.

26

Back in the infirmary ward, with the prisoner safely locked inside the closet down the hall and the old woman huddled below the portrait of Jesus, obviously terrified of every white person in the room in spite of Nurse Truett's constant reassurances, Wallace Pogue took Jean Tibbits quietly aside. "Jean," he whispered, "was that some kind of Cajun they were talking?"

Jean Tibbits shook his head. "I hear me some français, but that not Cajun, no."

"Could you understand them?"

"Not me, no."

Brother Julius Gray approached. "I have heard it before."

"What is it?"

"A kind of patois. Part English, part French, and part African." The preacher stared hard at the old woman. "My grandparents grew up speaking it—in the days when they were slaves."

A fantastic thought came to Wallace as he, too, stared at the old woman. From the first she had allowed only Dorothy and James to touch her, and backed away from Julius Gray and the other Negroes present, backed away from Wallace and his wife, Jenny, and from Jean and Silas and all the other white folks. The fantastic thought came to him, and as if in confirmation Jean Tibbits drew close and softly said, "Look at the inside of her arms." Then Wallace saw the calluses there. He had seen that very thing before. Those marks along her inner wrists and forearms could only come from passing a thousand handfuls of cotton back into a tow sack, brushing up against the bag again and again until the bleeding stopped and exactly that kind of scar was formed. And as surely as he saw it, Wallace knew there would be others.

"Dorothy," he said as calmly as he could, "would you do me a favor?"

"Yes sir. If I can."

"Take her back behind that curtain and lift that thing she's wearing, and have a look at her back. Take a lamp with you."

At first she seemed puzzled, then understanding dawned and a hint of horror crossed her face, and he thought she might ruin everything with hysterics, stirring up the old woman all over again, but the nurse controlled herself and with calm whispers guided the old woman back behind the screen. They all waited for a little while, and when Dorothy came out, the look upon her face was one part fear and one part rage, and Deputy Wallace Pogue knew that, in spite of all the arguments to the contrary, everything that poor man in the closet down the hall had said was true.

Reaching for his keys, he strode toward the corridor. His hand shook a little as he fit the key in the closet door lock, thinking about what it must have been like, living all those weeks a slave in shackles only to be placed in irons again when he returned. How could he apologize enough for that? Somehow, "I was only doing my job" did not seem adequate. But self-recrimination proved unnecessary, for when he turned the key and opened the door, the handcuffs and the shackles lay open on the floor and the rain poured in the window, and Wallace Pogue did not need to look outside to know that Jean Tibbits had lost his precious little motorboat, at least for a while.

When the shackles clicked and opened and fell away from Hale Poser's flesh, all he thought to do was to sit and praise the Lord. But this had not been done for his sake only, so when a voice—or something in his mind—whispered *Go and free them,* he rose up and stepped out onto the roof and settled into Mr. Tibbits's boat (which he knew somehow would be returned) and pulled the rope to start the engine and backed away without knowing how to do it and steered straight into the swamp, never veering right or left but moving as in a dream, unconscious of himself or of the way he moved, and focused just on going. Then came one last temptation: thoughts of Marah in his arms, and he longed to return to her, to be close to her, to hold her close again and call her "Mother," and hear her call him "Son," and stay with her forever. Yet he had precious work to do— to go and free them—so he praised God for her freedom, another miracle he did not work, and sped on into the swamp, his heart on fire with grief and joy together because the temptation was so great. But she had named him *Moses,* had sent him to his Father in a pirogue, and it was so horribly wonderful that he began to think this might truly be a dream and he was still locked up in the infirmary, or maybe in the Pilotville jail, or maybe he was sleeping in his little room back at the peeling mansion in New Orleans with a hundred children in his care, and he had never really found that yellowed paper in the attic or abandoned all those orphans to search for a mother he had just found and left behind again. Whether real or not, somehow Hale Poser knew exactly where to go, and go he did at a very high rate of speed, the little boat not squatting down in the water like a pirogue but instead rising up on top, merrily bouncing across the surface like a skipping stone. Dreamlike, he wondered how he missed the trees out in the darkness as he skated by again and again without so much as the brush of a leaf against his cheek. The motor roared in his ears and he delighted in it, trailing the sound behind as he charged along, knowing he must go and free them, knowing he had precious work to do, and dreaming, dreaming, dreaming of the Lord.

Time might have passed. Something might have told him he should stop. Still not understanding how he knew what he should do and giving it no thought, Hale Poser turned off the motor. Momentum carried him forward until the little boat slipped into the upper branches of an ancient cypress tree. He tied the bowline to the tree and dove head-first into the water. Swimming blindly in the darkness, his fingers soon touched mud. He stood and waded up the levee, like his namesake climbing Sinai. Hearing their voices on the other side, he called out in a language he had never learned, telling them the wonderful truth. He stood atop the levee shouting down about the Jesus who is more than the red of sunsets, more than the green of fields, more than the blue of the sky, and much, much more than the white of the bosses. Come up, he shouted. Come up and find a God who is more than every color that there is, because he is willing to be less. Jesus is black as the mud beneath our feet, black as the mud he made us from, a nigger that they beat and spat upon, just like you and me.

But they would not believe, and kept on digging at the levee as Qana shook his giant fist and bellowed up in anger, shouting Who are you to stand up there so high-and-mighty, talking 'bout a God like us? You ain't down here! You don't know! And understanding both halves of his vision at last, Hale Poser forsook the idolatry of miracles and finally went down to them, down there to the bottom, right down there with Jesus and the other niggers, and Hale reached up to touch his brother Qana's angry face and the earth gave way beneath his unshackled feet and the flood behind him ripped away the levee and a massive wave charged in to swallow those who toiled beneath it, spinning them together in the roiling deluge just as he had once foreseen, and as he tumbled round and round below the surface, trapped by the fury of the falling waters, lungs burning for air and knowing he was dying, Hale Poser finished working the one long miracle of his life, for God had told him *Go and free them,* and in his dying he did not curse his failure but wondered who it was that he had surely freed.

||**A** flock of starlings exploded from a mangrove stand, and a great blue heron erupted in protest, squawking mightily as it stretched ungainly wings to flop into the air with all the clumsiness of a baby's first steps. Nearby a nutria slipped beneath the water's surface, leaving barely a ripple in its wake as one by one a row of turtles fell like dominos from the log where they were sunning, the last creatures to react when the cause of the commotion came into view: a row of pirogues drifting silently into the liquid clearing. Each little boat bore one man standing in the stern and a low pile of provisions strapped in at the bow. Each man held a wooden pole to propel his craft across the swamp. One by one the pirogues came, until all four had emerged through the opening in the brush. Three of the men wore sweat-stained khaki uniforms; one did not. A Lucky Strike dangled from one man's lips as he stood looking up. "I'll be dogged," said Deputy Wallace Pogue. It had taken them three months to get started and three more weeks of looking, but they must be getting close now, for high in the ancient cypress tree above his head a little motorboat dangled from a rope, slowly twisting round and round like a hanging man.

From the state of Missouri all the way down to southern Louisiana the water had receded, rebuilding had commenced, and the great flood of 1927 had already begun to pass into history. But the men and women who survived the deluge together in the Pilotville Negro Infirmary did not think of what had happened as over and done with, and they would not rest until the truth was fully known. At first those in authority in southern Louisiana had assumed no one would believe their fantastic story, which was why they were allowed to tell it freely. Indeed, skepticism and disbelief were the kindest reactions among the populations of New Orleans and Baton Rouge. Most white people had grown weary of the specter of slavery and therefore scorned anything that might bring it back before the public eye. Others vehemently denied the story, for less than a week after it stopped raining, Papa DeGroot had been found dead of natural causes in his plush New Orleans apartment, and his many friends, dependants, and beneficiaries expressed unanimous outrage that anyone—especially any white person—would cast such dark aspersions on the great philanthropist's shining reputation. Dignitaries such as Leander Perez and gubernatorial candidate Huey Long attended Papa's funeral and spoke from the pulpit there against what the press had begun to call the "Pilotville Account." But even these important men could not convince the northern public to ignore the old woman whom James Lamont had found, the woman who spoke in a dying language known only to the few elderly Negroes still surviving from the days of slavery. Through them it had been learned her name was Marah, and she affirmed all that the vanished orphanage chaplain had said. Still most of the white people of the South laughed it off.

Then the others appeared.

They came in from the wilderness, some of them com-

pletely naked, some clothed in homespun rags, yet all of
them speaking the same dying language. A Cajun fisherman
found the first one deep in the swamp. The next two
showed up on their own, filled with terror, but driven to
Pilotville by starvation. Then another was found, and
another, until almost twenty ragged, scarred, and fearful
Negroes who did not speak a word of English had been
gathered together in Pilotville. Marah's joy on seeing them
had been irrepressible, and no one doubted they had all
come from the same place, for the jubilant cries and unintelligible chatter when they first met was something to
behold. But their joy soon sank into sorrow, because, as the
old ex-slaves explained it, these new ones claimed they had
left behind a hundred others or more, dead beneath the
waters of the flood.

It had been impossible to keep things quiet after that.
One muckraking New York paper had published a human-
interest story headlined *Last Slaves Out of Bondage*, which was
then picked up by other papers until mounting pressure at
the national level finally caused the sheriff of Plaquemines
Parish to agree to detail three men to search the swamp. He
did this, secure in the knowledge that three men had virtually no chance of finding anything in the thousands of hect-
ares of virtually impenetrable wilderness around the mouth
of the Mississippi River. It was a measure of the interest with
which the "Pilotville Account" had been received that the
sheriff also agreed to allow a reporter to join the search
party, although he insisted on only one reporter, a man
whom the sheriff handpicked from the staff of the *Times-
Picayune* with the expectation the venerable New Orleans
newspaper would respect the local situation, no matter what
was found.

And so, as Pilotville and the rest of the world along the
southern Mississippi rebuilt itself, Wallace Pogue and three

others had searched for Hale Poser and a lost plantation. From the start the other deputies had belittled their mission. In spite of the unlikely group of Negroes assembled back in Pilotville, this was clearly a fool's errand undertaken for publicity, or rather to offset publicity, and they were only in that miserable location because of a bunch of meddlesome Yankees with nothing better to do than to stir up trouble down in Dixie. The reporter, while less vocally opposed to the search, still tended to agree that it was hopeless. Only Wallace Pogue felt enthusiasm for their task, but then, only Wallace Pogue had met the Reverend Hale Poser.

Now, as the other three stood in their pirogues staring up in disbelief at Jean Tibbits's hanging motorboat, Wallace Pogue broke the silence, saying simply, "Fan out, boys."

Ten minutes later the reporter's voice rang out. "Over here!" he shouted, and the others poled their pirogues quickly toward him. The local interest man from the *Times-Picayune* had already left his boat and now stood at the foot of a massive wall of soil extending in each direction until it ran out of sight beyond the heavy cover of tupelos, cypress, and mangroves. Wallace knew it was the levee, exactly as Hale Poser had described it. But just above the reporter was something Poser never mentioned: a gap in the upper half of the wall, more than fifty feet wide. Understanding what it meant, Wallace felt a tightness in his narrow chest as he poled his pirogue close and set foot on the hill. The reporter had gone on ahead of them, standing with his back to the outside world when Wallace joined him in the bottom of the breach, with the top part of the levee walls still above them to the left and right.

Below the men lay a giant lake, rectangular in shape and at least half a mile long and wide. The water lapped right up to the break in the levee where they stood, a full ten feet higher than the level of the surrounding swamp. Wallace realized at once that this could only be the field Hale Poser had described, submerged now beneath waters that had poured through this gap in the embankment, only to be trapped inside by the portion of the levee that remained below the breach when the rest of the flood receded. To get a better vantage point, he crossed the gap and climbed up to the top of the unbroken levee beside it. From here he saw something lying down along the shore about a hundred feet away. He set out walking along the top of the levee until he was immediately above the object, then descended the inside slope to the water's edge, where he knelt and lifted up a high-top brown leather shoe with a hole cut in its side and white laces.

28

Dorothy Truett did not need Deputy Pogue to tell her what lay out in the swamp. From the moment Brother Julius had explained about the language Marah used, Dorothy had understood. The appearance of the others from the swamp over the next few weeks merely confirmed her belief; the actual discovery of the slave plantation only served to drive her deeper into sorrow. She took no satisfaction in learning that Papa DeGroot was dead, his reputation now in ruins, or that Dr. Jackson was a fugitive, as were Theodore Beauregard and the others Papa had used to run his plantation. No amount of praying made it better, nor did anything that anyone could say about the merciful forgiveness of the Lord. Everything she had said, everything she had done, came down on her like a tombstone when she realized Reverend Poser had not lied, for that meant she had helped to build a suffering place of bondage and misery, and when the Lord had offered her a chance to change it, to join with white believers and go and give those poor lost people a good reason to come out, she had blithely denied that such a thing was even necessary.

If that had been her only sin, it would be much easier to

face. But Dorothy Truett knew her guilt began long before Hale Poser ever told them of the slaves. It began years and years ago, when she decided the way to get along with white people was to pretend that everything was fine. It began when she turned her back upon the walls right there among them, in Pilotville, not just those out in the swamp. For a few Negroes and whites standing together at the top of a levee would not have changed the fact that the people of Pilotville did *not* look at the heart and ignore the skin. They might have stood together on a levee, but they did not stand together where it mattered most. That had been her way of retreating from responsibility all along—standing falsely, denying the walls as if denials made them go away. Now she saw those walls for what they were: erected between God's people *by* God's people, who of all people should be rid of walls. But it was too little too late, for although Hale Poser's life and death had forced her to face her self-delusion squarely, the walls were still there, exactly where they always had been, and no amount of looking at them made them go away.

In the end, only one thing had changed. Dorothy herself no longer had a wall to hide behind.

She had tried to tell herself a black woman in south Louisiana had no chance to make a difference—no chance whatsoever—but while that was true in the outside world, here in Pilotville she knew the Lord had offered her a precious exception, and she had ignored the offering. How ironic, then, that habit drove her to seek comfort in her church. Yet for a month of Sundays now, Brother Julius had reveled in the fact that their church was roofed and walled while the other church remained a work in progress. Oh, he never said those words out loud, never actually made the comparison, but Dorothy knew Julius too well, and she knew every time he stood behind that pulpit with his chest out like a rooster and said "*We* have sacrificed" and "*We* have given God the glory," what he meant in his heart of hearts was We did this without *them*.

Then, last Sunday, heaven help her, she had realized she could learn to hate him.

Would she really add that sin to all the rest?

Better to stay away. She did not deserve to be in the house of God, even without such thoughts. It was better to do something constructive. It was all that she had left. So this Sunday morning, for the first time in as long as she could remember, Dorothy Truett made a conscious decision not to go to the house of the Lord. She went to the infirmary instead. Although the colored people in her town had rebuilt the church before turning their attention to their homes, they had not shown the infirmary similar respect. Who could blame them? All had memories of slavery, or of their parents' or grandparents' stories, and many had lost children, brothers, sisters, grandchildren to the atrocity in the swamp, so no one wanted anything to do with Papa DeGroot's gateway to the last slave plantation in America. The Pilotville Negro Infirmary was a place corrupted forever.

Yet it was all she had.

Dorothy had devoted herself to work, never marrying, never bearing children, because she knew the need was great. Few who had her training offered care to Negroes, especially in the South, and fewer nurses still were colored themselves. Yes, she had worked with Dr. Jackson and accepted Papa's money, and yes, she had taken sinful pride in being respected by her neighbors and by whites, but although those evil men had corrupted everything she stood for, the work still needed doing, and there was no one else.

So this morning she donned a pair of denim trousers

and wrapped her hair in a bandanna and set out for the
infirmary with a shovel in her hand, thinking if prayer and
preaching could not drive away her guilt, maybe hard work
would.

The Reverend Silas Vogt spoke of his thankfulness for
their new church building, for the sacrifices of the congregation and generosity of the strangers who had contributed
to its construction. As the reverend preached, Wallace
Pogue felt his wife squeeze his hand, but while Jenny's simple sign of affection would have lifted his spirits under other
circumstances, and while most everybody else inside the
brand-new church seemed full to overflowing with thankfulness, Wallace Pogue took no comfort whatsoever. He had
just heard shouts of "Amen" and "Tell it" coming through
the trees outside their walls, and he knew over on the other
side of Pilotville another congregation was also feeling
thankful for a church building that had also been rebuilt
almost exactly as it was before. Everything was exactly as it
was before, which was exactly why he felt so low.

He leaned close to Jenny's ear and whispered, "I got to
go outside."

She shot him a worried look.

"Don't worry," he whispered. "I just need some air."

Wallace sensed the Reverend Silas Vogt's suspicious eyes
upon his back as he walked up the aisle. They had spoken
privately of his concerns, and Silas had explained that his
position was unchanged, so they had agreed to disagree.
The Reverend Silas Vogt still insisted they went to separate
churches mainly because of differences in the way they worshiped. He had said white people would be uncomfortable
over there, and Negroes would not fit in here among us.
Wallace believed this to be true—and knew most of his black
and white neighbors in Pilotville were not racists—but after

seeing those massive levees, he no longer believed the reasons were what mattered.

Wallace Pogue experienced relief when the front doors of his church had closed behind him and he stood outside at last. He was not supposed to feel that way, but there it was: relief to be away from the house of God.

Lighting a cigarette, he began to walk. Over there was a spot upon the boardwalk, invisible to everyone but him, where Hale Poser had been standing on the day they met. He walked directly to it, stood right where that man had been, and tried to remember what it had been like on that other Sunday morning, months ago. As he thought about it, an idea occurred to him. He flipped the cigarette away and shut his eyes and reached one hand toward the new church, the other toward the voices coming through the trees, and he closed his fists and tried to pull them all together, and yes, wasn't that something pulling back against him, and didn't the voices seem to blend and flow together? No, it was only his imagination, for in the end he was nothing but a foolish man, thinking miracles could save him.

Embarrassed, Wallace Pogue continued down the boardwalk. Who was he to stand here praying like he had a right to ask for anything? He had missed his moment to ask for help. He could have said, "Now, wait a minute. Maybe we should listen to this fellow." That old pagan Jean Tibbits had believed Hale Poser for a minute, and he—Lord help him—he had talked Jean out of it. *"God has better things to worry about than the color of the people in his pews."* He would never forget his words, and he would never forgive himself for them. For who could say but in that moment, maybe all those poor people had still been alive behind that levee, and if he had not been so blind—or stubborn, which was worse—they might have found a way to go and show them there was a place where colored folks could feel safe with white folks, because the love of God was in them all.

But of course the love of God was *not* in them all, and that had begun to bother him almost as much as all the bodies they had found out in that evil lake. So here he was, a poor imitation of Hale Poser, asking the Lord to come down and work a miracle, to change them all. He had started out pretending God didn't care, and ended up hoping God would fix it all. Some might say it was a step in the right direction, but he wondered if he was just going from bad to worse. What was God supposed to do? What specifically should Wallace pray for? Dear Lord, please give us white folks a little more rhythm and settle the Negroes down a little, so we can all agree on what to sing? Wallace laughed out loud. That would be Silas Vogt's prayer, he supposed, but if the Reverend Hale Poser had taught him anything, it was that God expected a whole lot more than that. Wallace Pogue just wished he knew exactly what.

Ever since the waters went back down, Marah had been living with the pretty young woman who had helped her that first night. At first she had trusted the young woman's kindness, but then old Simon and High and Low and the others came to this strange place, and in her kindness this woman took some of them in, too. And the more of them who came, the more she saw that the young woman was unhappy, and Marah began to see her kindness as a trap to keep them from the Jesus world, for it was not right to sit around all day while others did your work. It was the worst kind of way to live, the bosses' kind of way. More and more, as she felt herself being drawn along a path she did not wish to tread, Marah longed to do her part. She had discussed it with Simon, High and Low, and all of them agreed: though this woman spoke the boss man's language, she acted like she was their slave. Fixing their food, washing their clothes, tending to their every need. No, it was wrong to let yourself get used to having someone else do for you, wrong to do no work yourself, yet every time Marah or the others tried to join the woman's labors they were motioned away and forced to sit and watch, which seemed to make the young woman feel better, so at least that was something. But this was not what her boy promised—a place where there were no slaves, because everyone did for everyone else—and although at first Marah tried to stand aside and let the woman do all the work, she would do that no more. Since the Angry One really had come down here the way her Moses said, it could not be right to let another person ease her way through life. What kind of person would she be, to sit around doing nothing when the lightning thrower came down like a slave to set her free like that? She had to thank him somehow, and all she had to offer back was labor.

So this morning, when Marah awoke and saw the pretty young woman walking away with a shovel, she quickly rose and took a hoe from the shed out back and followed. Here was work she knew how to do.

When Dorothy reached the ground-floor doors, she almost turned back. Since the flood receded she had been unwilling to revisit the scene of her most shameful moments, so the extent of the devastation at the Pilotville Negro Infirmary took her by surprise. Hardened mud stood three feet deep within the entry hall, where the ground-floor walls had blocked the cleansing currents and allowed the sediment to pile in drifts along the walls and up the corners. Everything was stained a dirty brown: walls, curtains, doors, furniture, even the few pieces of unbroken window glass remaining. Desks lay overturned. Mildew, moss, and small ferns grew on the upholstery, and animals had carved homes into the mire along the halls. She had come here hoping for deliverance, but her depression only deepened. It was as if the evil lying under the foundations of this place had slithered up to smear its mark upon her world more openly.

With that final thought, Dorothy went to work. While she knew it was beyond her power to make any kind of difference that would matter, she would not leave this evil here unchallenged. She would do her best and leave the rest to Providence.

She decided to begin at the front doors because she had no bucket or wheelbarrow to carry away the mess, and from the front doors she could simply pitch each shovelful out into the yard. At first the work felt foreign. She was an educated woman after all, unaccustomed to such labor. But a rhythm settled in, she began to make some progress, and to her surprise the steady repetition had a calming effect, stilling her mind and relaxing her nerves. For the first time in many weeks, her thoughts drifted away from guilt and settled into peaceful places. She began to hum in time to the rhythm of her shovel, and with her own humming in her ears and her eyes down on the soil, she did not notice Marah until the old woman slammed a hoe into the ground beside her.

Startled, she straightened up as Marah carved at the mud with the energy of a woman half her age, making much quicker progress than Dorothy's pitiful efforts. "No, no," said Dorothy, shaking her head and waving her free hand. It was just the latest in a long series of such scenes, with Marah trying to help and Dorothy trying to make her realize she would never accept anything from the old woman. Indeed, Dorothy was determined to wait on her hand and foot until the woman's dying day.

"No, Marah," she repeated, smiling bleakly. "Please."

But Marah would not stop. She set her chin with a

resolve Dorothy had not seen before. The old woman attacked the dried mud with such aggression it seemed obvious there was something more behind it than a mere desire to help. Dorothy watched the casually efficient way Marah wielded the hoe, moving more earth in less time than most young men could have done. And then old Simon arrived, also with a hoe, and High, and Low, and all of them together tore into the job with a ferocity she did not understand at all.

Dorothy Truett tried to imagine how she would feel in their situation. After a lifetime slaving in the fields, what would make them want to work like this? As she stood and watched, she decided that, no matter what the reason, she should let them have their way. For if she had lived at the beck and call of evil men for all her years, wasn't independence the one thing she would want above all else?

So Dorothy bent to work again, and the two women dug the soil away side-by-side at the entrance of the infirmary for most of an hour while the men worked a little farther in, and they made such easy progress that she could not forget this was how these people had spent their lives, and because she could not forget she felt unworthy to labor here beside them. Just as the company of others at her church no longer gave her comfort, now the company of these poor souls reminded her of what they had endured because of her hypocrisy. So there was no place of refuge for her, not even here where she had always felt she was of use. Realizing that, suddenly it took all her strength to hold back tears, yet she was bound and determined not to let them flow, for what right had she to tears, surrounded as she was by such as them?

"Miss Truett, how come you ain't in church?"

Turning, she shielded her eyes to look up at the boardwalk. With the sun behind his back, all she could see was a silhouette, but she knew that voice. "Hello, Deputy Pogue."

"Does Brother Julius know you're playing hooky?"

She felt the guilt surge higher. "I . . . I suppose so."

"Don't sound so worried. I'm skipping out myself."

"I see."

Dorothy dropped her hand from above her eyes and looked down, away from the sun. The deputy remained where he was, unmoving. It was an awkward moment. She felt there was something she should say, but could not imagine what it might be. They stood without speaking as a cardinal chirped gaily off in the bushes somewhere and Marah's hoe thudded into the soil again and again.

Finally the deputy said, "That's a mess of work you got to do."

Nodding toward Marah and the others, Dorothy said, "I've got help."

"You surely do," he said. "But I guess you could use some more."

"It would be nice to have Reverend Poser around again." She did not know what made her say it.

"Yes . . . that would be nice." Another awkward pause followed, and although she felt uncomfortable, strangely, Dorothy did not want him to go. Then the deputy asked, "So, could y'all use a hand?"

Shocked, Dorothy said the first thing that came to mind. "Oh, no sir! We'll be fine. But I thank you." The deputy said nothing. Embarrassed, she rushed to fill the silence. "I do thank you."

"That's all right. I just thought . . . Well, I'll be going."

"Much obliged, Deputy Pogue."

"I didn't do anything."

It was a strange thing to say, and as he turned to go she wondered if he was talking about here and now, or another time and place. *"I didn't do anything."* It was the whispered accusation she could not escape, the one charge against which there was no defense. And suddenly she felt sure it was the same for him, exactly the same as it was for her, and before she could think better of her foolishness, she called out, "Deputy!"

He stopped and looked back at her.

"We could use some help. . . . That is, if you don't mind."

"Ma'am, I guess it would be a pleasure."

Without hesitating, the deputy removed his coat and tie and rolled his sleeves up to the elbows and with some gentle persuasion convinced old Marah she could rest awhile, and took her hoe and joined in beside Dorothy. Before long she forgot herself in her work and began to hum a familiar hymn. To her surprise the deputy started to sing along, soft and low, as if embarrassed by his voice. But she thought it a good voice, and slowly the strangeness of working beside the white man melted away and the two of them grew bolder, lifting up their voices loud and pure, together.

Jean Tibbits walked along the boardwalk all alone as he often did on Sunday mornings. He enjoyed the solitude while most everyone else was in Pilotville's two churches. The sounds of the surrounding swamp and the muted singing of hymns in the background sometimes seemed to blend together and inspire a feeling he would never admit to anyone. This Sunday as he walked along the fringes of the little town he thought about that strange fellow he had first seen coming through the river mist. He remembered the persimmons. He wished he had asked the fellow a few questions that morning, instead of letting him walk off. He wished he had asked his questions later on, when the fellow came back with a nickel for the dockage. He wished he had asked while they had him in the jail, or that last night when the fellow disappeared. He wondered why he had never asked and, after thinking on that for a while, decided the reason might have something to do with why he would not admit to having this feeling when the sounds of the swamp mixed in with the distant Sunday singing.

But asked or not, the questions had been slowly rising ever since he spied that fellow reaching out as if he had a line on both of Pilotville's churches, drawing them together. The blended voices that morning had given him this same feeling—which he did not understand and could not name—and he had been strangely called outside himself just as he was right now, except when that fellow pulled those voices together there had been a sense he could be part of it, but now he knew there was no chance of that.

Still, it had been beautiful to see and hear.

Jean Tibbits frowned and cocked his head. Wasn't the singing this morning coming from a new direction? He went looking, and ended up on the boardwalk staring down at Wallace and Dorothy, who did not spend much time together under normal circumstances but were working like the dickens down there cleaning up the old infirmary and singing hymns in harmony. You would think they had been practicing to sing that way for all of their lives.

They did not see him standing up above, and he did nothing to signify his presence. Thirty minutes passed as he listened to their voices, and he felt that strange feeling getting stronger, until he began to think it might be good to talk to them about it, to see if they could feel it, too. But then the churches both let out at once and some of the people who had also heard the singing came over to investigate. Even though they stood right beside him looking down, he felt distant from them, as if his reverie had placed him where he could see but not be seen. He listened as some of them muttered about desecrating the Sabbath, shook their heads and walked away, and his momentary instinct to say something about this feeling went away with them. But to Jean's surprise, a few of the others, both whites and coloreds, came back again with their work clothes on and hoes and shovels in their hands, and they went down the steps and joined in the labor and joined in the singing, and before that afternoon was done the entrance to the Pilotville Negro Infirmary was cleared of all debris.

Once, James Lamont looked up at the boardwalk and asked him to join in, but Jean preferred to watch and listen from up here. It was not that he was lazy—everyone knew that wasn't so—but just that he could see and hear it all from high up on the boardwalk, and Jean Tibbits wanted more than anything to see and hear it all. Because in watching and listening he sensed that feeling coming stronger, the way he felt when the fellow pulled at the churches that one time, and like that time, Jean Tibbits had the strangest sense that he could join them if he liked, and he would blend right in. Thinking about that, Jean gripped the railing harder. Oh, just look and listen! All those folks down there, all of them together. There was something about the way their hoes and shovels kept time with their voices that washed the staleness off the words and gave the hymn an implication he had never understood before, something foreign yet familiar, and at last he recognized this ancient melody from a distant continent, from a perfect place he had once trod upon, then almost forgotten. As his memory returned, Jean Tibbits realized he had asked one question of Hale Poser after all, perhaps the only one that mattered. Watching as the filth upon their hands and feet somehow sanctified the joy upon their faces, he knew that question had been answered just as surely as if Hale Poser were still there to explain; for here below him, mixed up together with all this mess and slobber, was the reason God Almighty laid his Son down in a feed trough.

Athol Dickson

Athol Dickson studied painting, sculpture, and architecture at university, followed by careers as an architect and writer. He is the acclaimed author of three previous novels, including *They Shall See God,* a Christy Award finalist for suspense. Dickson has also written the best-selling autobiographical memoir *The Gospel According to Moses.* He and his wife, Sue, live in Dallas.